# Being Enough

Sara Alexi is the author of the Greek Village Series. She divides her time between England and a small village in Greece.

http://www.saraalexi.com
http://facebook.com/authorsaraalexi

Sara Alexi

# BEING ENOUGH

oneiro

Published by Oneiro Press 2016

Copyright © Sara Alexi 2016

This book is a work of fiction. Names, characters, businesses, organisations, places and events are either the product of the author's imagination or are used fictitiously. Any resemblance to actual persons, living or dead, events or locales is entirely coincidental

ISBN-13: 978-1530308330

ISBN-10: 153030833X

# Chapter 1

At this time of year there is an exquisite sense of anticipation, the thrill of the summer to come. Soon there will be days that are so hot there will be no choice but to be lazy and life will all but come to a standstill. The cool of the winter has quite gone and now the days are deliciously warm, making every hour a pleasure.

Rallou stretches and yawns. Under her bare feet, the terracotta tiles on the veranda of the old stone house are still cool from the night. Later in the season they will be warm to the touch, and, in the height of summer, too hot at midday. The house stands just a little apart from the village, if the cluster of houses that surround her can be considered as such. The hamlet is named *O Topos Sta Synnefa* – The Place in the Clouds – and it is as far from the sea and from any other houses as it is possible to get on the island. The locals refer to it simply as Korifi – the summit.

Rallou screws her eyes up tightly and stretches her hands above her head. Although she has slept well and has had time to reflect, anger still bubbles in her thoughts, her chest, her stomach. There is no doubt about it, she was right to do what she did. Her arms drop limply to her sides and her eyelids open. The land falls away from the house, both to the north and the south. In front of the house the long island stretches a finger into the sea. From one corner of the veranda she can see the Mediterranean in three directions. Its flat surface is freckled with pale-blue islands that float undisturbed as the water burns softly orange and silver in the early dawn.

When she walked away she hadn't planned to come up here. She needs to be at home; there are chores that need her attention. The washing, for one, needs taking off the line, and the dough she left to rise overnight needs baking into fresh, warm loaves. But after what was said she could not have stayed.

Exhaling loudly, hands on hips, she acknowledges that at least she is lucky enough to have such an amazing place to run to, and there is no denying the beauty that surrounds her.

Rallou smooths her hair with both hands, and her fingers interlink on the back of her neck. Her head drops back and her vision is filled with the blue of the sky, a seagull high, high above her, so small that at first she takes it for a plane. Then she drops her head forward and contemplates her own bare feet. Her little toenails need cutting. They grow faster and are thicker than the rest, and more so with each year that passes.

But her nails will have to wait. Right now she will brush her hair and put on her shoes, and spend the day happily helping her baba with the things that need doing. This is not the first argument she has had with Christos. They have been more frequent in recent years and each seems worse than the last. But this one doesn't feel like the others. It feels like it could, in fact, be the last. But if it is, what more could she have done? She has been more than patient. Even if only half of what Harris has implied over the years is right, he is lucky that she has stayed this long.

'Stop it,' she says to herself. Dwelling on who said what to whom is not going to help. She must give herself time to settle, assess.

With a last glance out to sea, Rallou turns and goes back into the dark of the house, and as her eyes adjust she brushes her hair in front of the mirror that is so old the silver has mostly turned to black. The wooden veneered surround has rippled with age and the catgut twine has stretched so she has to bend her legs slightly to see all of her face at once. There was a time when this same mirror was too high for her to use. She brushes down the other side of her face.

The eyes that stare back at her look tired, and there are lines at the corners. Below her chin there is a hint of the jowls to come. But it is not a bad face for a woman of her age. Her hair is still thick and shiny, and the arch of her eyebrows has not dropped. Her mouth still has a pleasant upward curl to it. But yet she sees a sadness – or is it fear? – hidden there. 'You've missed your chance,' the face in the mirror states, but not unkindly. 'Perhaps,' Rallou agrees.

But the chance for what? To travel more widely? To learn new things? To have interesting conversations? What exactly has she missed? What is she yearning for? Or does she just need love?

She waits but no answer comes. Out through the open door, across the sea towards the mainland, a wooden fishing boat putters into view, moving with no great hurry. The fisherman will know every inch of this stretch of water between the island and the mainland, and every knot in his net. If the fishermen, who do nothing but fish and drink coffee, can be content on this island, then why can't she?

Turning from the view, she resolves to distract herself with action.

The patched and darned apron hangs on a hook at the corner of the house, just as it has always done. The ties used to go twice around her when she was a child, but, after three children of her own, all fully grown now, the strings are just long enough to tie a tiny bow. The rock that weighs down the top of the feed barrel has worn smooth and shiny. With a scoop of feed in each pocket of the apron Rallou replaces both the wooden lid and the stone weight and wanders to the coop that stretches away down the hill and around the trunks of a couple of hardy pines. It is not hot enough yet for the cicadas to be calling, but she knows that it will not be many more days before, amongst the pines, their serenades are deafening.

Most of the hens are crowded in anticipation around the chicken wire gate, the frame of which she fashioned during a visit last year, tying and nailing together a branch, two old and split chair legs and a piece of driftwood from the beach below. Or maybe it was the year before?

The sun glistens off the birds' backs: rich reds, shiny whites, warm creams. The cockerel displays a rainbow of petrol colours on its sickles and under its breast feathers, contrasting sharply with the red of its saddle and neck. He is at the front.

The stragglers come running at the sight of the apron, their claws curling into limp balls as they lift from the ground, talons splaying wide again as their claws hit the dust, trying to gain purchase on the compacted soil.

'Has it all gone already?' Rallou asks them, referring to the abundance of green that shoots up in the large enclosure every spring, only to be eaten or trodden by the chickens and browned by the sun before summer has even really arrived.

The birds cluck in unison; a dominant black one pecks a small white one on the head, and the second cockerel is at the back, skinny and lean compared to the hens.

Inside the pen she throws the feed as if she is sowing corn, steadily walking the length of the enclosure to give all the birds a chance to eat their fill. The thin red chicken with the limp is still there, and it hangs back. It has learnt that if it does so it will get a little pile of corn to itself. Rallou is familiar with her baba's capacity for favouritism.

The corn is all gone but the pockets of the apron remain open, sagging with age. They have used this method of taking the corn from the barrel by the house to the chickens for as long as she can remember, and certainly from before she could tie the stings herself. Harris, her older sister by three and a half years, had shiny hair that would brush against her cheek as she bent and impatiently showed Rallou how to tie a knot and a bow. Later, Rallou taught little Evgenia. A sigh escapes her for poor little Evgenia, who lies on the hill under a mound of dirt and dust and pebbles.

Involuntarily she looks to the place. A stone marks the spot.

'Coffee?' her baba calls from the porch, his hand shielding his eyes.

'Just getting the eggs.' Rallou breaks her stare and waves a hand.

The chicken shed, where the hens shelter at night, stands on wooden legs at one end of the enclosure, elevated to waist height to guard against predators. It is so easy to recall, as if it was just last week, the day that Yanni brought his two donkeys lumbering up the dusty track, each laden with wood. She, Harris and their brothers didn't know who he was then and, after he had left, their baba explained that his family also lived up on the ridge, but far away to the east of the island, above the main town.

As it turned out, she and Yanni were the same age, but at the time they had not known this either, and Harris had so shamelessly flirted with stony-faced boy that Rallou, in shock at this behaviour, had felt the need to apologise on her sister's behalf, muttering unclear words as he tidied the ropes.

'Thank you,' she said to Yanni as she drew water from the well for the donkeys and stroked their soft necks, being careful to avoid the even softer muzzles that hid long yellow teeth. 'Sorry. She feels …' But the words floated away on the breeze. She had no idea what Harris felt then; her ways and manners sometimes seemed odd around that time. But Yanni didn't acknowledge that Rallou had even spoken, and once his donkeys had drunk their fill he left the way he had come.

Rallou remembers that, despite her embarrassment, the delivery of the wood provided a welcome distraction from the tedious routine of their lives, and it was followed by a week of excitement in which Baba sawed and nailed the wood, the construction growing all clean and new.

She lifts the lid of the nesting boxes that Baba built on the side of the chicken shed for easy access. The eggs, still warm, are placed carefully into the now empty pockets of the apron and then, walking carefully and slowly, she leaves the chickens to their breakfast and returns to the house. Her baba is bent over, trying to wedge a stone under one leg of the kitchen table to stop it rocking on the uneven floor.

'Have you still not fixed that?' Rallou asks rhetorically. He talked about making a wedge out of a piece of wood for the table at the end of last summer, then again in the winter when they took it indoors. And how many times has she had the same sort of conversation with Christos – things he has promised year after year to mend in the house, but never got around to?

'I may not have fixed the table, but did you notice that I have painted the chicken shed?'

Rallou turns her head quickly to look. It is noticeably whiter than the last time she was up here.

'Oh yes.' She places her hands under the bulging pockets of the apron so the eggs do not knock against each other as she takes the two steps up onto the balcony.

'Do you recall how we used to need every egg the hens could lay?' Her baba is sitting at the little iron table on the veranda, and he waves at a cup of coffee as Rallou hangs the apron, eggs and all, on the doorknob. 'And now I don't know what to do with them all. I have taken to giving some to the Kaloyannis brothers.'

'I thought the boatyard kept them too busy to come up here in the winter?' Rallou takes a sip of coffee and sits on the other chair.

'They come, now and again. Mostly to ready their house for the summer.' He leans back in his own chair, the one with the fancier spindles in the back. The rush seat is worn and has been carefully repaired over the years, his handiwork improving with each mending now that there is no one on the island who cuts and weaves rushes any more. 'Tolis trades them for fish for my supper now and again, and Takis takes them all the way into town when he goes, and sells them to Costas Voulgaris to use in the *kafenio.*'

Costas Voulgaris's *kafenio* is on the water's edge, and Rallou's house is some streets back from there, in amongst the maze of houses that make up Orino town, stretching up the hill from the port and out on either side, around the harbour. There, her world seems small, and her days are filled with tending her home and keeping the big house for the Americans – cleaning windows, washing sheets, sweeping away dust.

'Good boys, Takis and Tolis.' Her baba muses. 'Tolis, Takis, Costas and Yanni. Men now.' He takes a sip of his coffee and watches the return of the small fishing boat. 'Children of their own. Do you remember them when you were at school?'

His eyes moisten, and she presumes he is remembering her, aged seven, standing by her bed in her best dress – her only dress – with her little cardboard suitcase and her hand-me-down teddy. Her baba carried the case as Yanni, leading his donkey, called from the track that he was ready to take her down to Orino town where she was to stay with her eldest brother, some twelve years her senior, and his new wife. She had been so excited in the lead-up to her going but when the time came she did not want to leave.

'You will be fine.' Her baba had pulled her in for a hug and then he bent down and looked her in the eyes but said no more. Reflected in his wide pupils she could see her own terrified face and he pulled her closer and buried her face against his chest until she could hear his heart beat.

That's what she wants now, for her baba to pull her in close, encircle her in his muscular arms and tell her it will be fine. But the arms are withered and his strength is almost gone.

'So, daughter of mine, what is wrong? You cannot think for a moment that I believe this is a social visit. What has happened?'

# Chapter 2

The coffee cup doesn't make it to her lips before her sobs explode and her baba gently takes the drink from her hands and puts his arm across her shoulders.

'Oh, Baba.' She allows herself to wail like a child. He tightens his embrace and pats her far shoulder. Up here, away from her role of citizen, neighbour, mama and wife, it is safe to cry, to be small. She knew he would be deeply concerned at whatever was ailing her. But she is also aware that he has seen much of life: been through a war, lost his wife and one of his daughters, and witnessed the village on the hilltop slowly emptying of its inhabitants until now he is completely alone for too much of the time. There is nothing much that life can throw at him that he has not experienced before, and his grip around her shoulders is sure. She is glad of that, and it allows her wail to become a sob, to become a sniff, to become a wipe across her nose with the back of her hand. Her baba's arm unwinds from around her and they pick up their drinks in unison and look out across the sea, creasing up their eyes against the sun.

A click-clicking signals the presence of a gecko, which runs across the tiles on the balcony, its back wiggling comically; then it pauses at the edge and curls over the side, leaving just the end of its tail showing.

Just thinking about Christos quickens her breath, saddens her. She stops looking at the gecko's tail to resume her gaze out across the sea, where a fishing boat sits stationary near the shore of the mainland opposite. Set a little apart from the other houses of the village that have been built in the shelter of a small dip in the landscape, their house is on a rise and commands amazing views on all sides. The stone house has stood for generations, passed down the family. The veranda was added in her baba's lifetime but her room, on the second floor, was her yiayia's when she was a child, and again before she died, and it was her yiayia's before her. The windows are small, to keep out the sun in the summer and the cold in the winter, and the tiled roof has so weathered with time that its colours merge into the landscape, so that, from a distance, it makes the place look roofless and deserted.

'You are still working for the American family, yes?' her baba asks. He thinks he is changing the subject, but for Rallou there could not be a more pertinent question, a more relevant lead-in to her describing to him exactly what Christos has done now.

But where to start, how to explain?

She could start by telling him that Christos did not come home two nights ago, but then how unusual was that? Often, when hunting for birds or snaring rabbits, he is taken far along the top of the island and cannot comfortably walk back the same day, and besides, the next day he would likely want to be at the same end of the island, so it is sensible for him to camp out some nights, especially now it is warmer. If he heads off west from the town, he often sleeps in his old family home, up here at Korifi, on the edge of the tiny hamlet, just a little way from where Rallou is sitting.

She looks in that general direction but the village is hidden in a shallow dell, at the foot of a steep hill that casts just enough shade to keep the houses cool for an hour longer in the morning. From where she is sitting on the balcony of her baba's house, Rallou can see the terracotta tiles on the tops of some of the houses, but a group of pine trees hides the rest of the dwellings.

Although Christos stays in the house for a night or two when he is hunting, the house has not been lived in properly for years. As with most of the other houses there is no running water or electricity, and the last time Rallou went up to the village she found some of the windows broken and the back door rusted off its hinges. Nowadays it is little better than sleeping under the stars, except that the view would be of peeling plaster rather than the wonders of the heavens. No, she would definitely prefer to sleep outside. But she has not been to see it for four or five years or so, and it will be in a much worse state now. The sun makes everything crumble.

Besides, her baba has said that when Christos is up at Korifi he drops in to say *yeia sou*. So no, she could not start by saying that Christos did not come home two nights ago, because Baba would shrug his shoulders as if to say, 'So what?'

Harris could probably explain it to him. When they were having coffee yesterday it all seemed so much clearer.

'You want sugar?' Harris was poised with her spoon over the *briki*, her floral apron over her below-the-knee floral print skirt.

'Thanks. How is Stephanos?' Rallou asked after her sister's husband as she moved the day's newspaper so she could sit on the wooden chair by the smooth wooden table that took up most of the space in Harris's light, bright kitchen.

Lean-tos are often dark but Harris's kitchen has a transparent, corrugated plastic roof so the sun floods in. The back door is permanently open in the summer to let out the heat, but in the winter, with the oven on and a fire lit, it is the nicest room in her house. Everything in Harris's kitchen has its place. Jars, neatly arranged on a shelf, hold rice and lentils, pasta and flour. The kitchen utensils are stuck to a magnetised strip that is screwed to the wall by the two-ringed gas stove. The tea towel is on a hook, the *tapsia* are stacked in size order on a shelf above. Even the rolls of silver foil and greaseproof paper have their own dowel holders attached to the wall. Harris's husband, Stephanos, is quite the handyman.

'Ah, he is fine, very fine. After he came home from work yesterday he painted the kitchen door at the back here where the sun burns it every summer.' Harris sighed contentedly. 'Has Christos cemented in that back step yet,' she went on to ask, 'before you trip over it?'

'No, he stayed up on the hills last night.' Rallou looked at the newspaper without much interest.

'Again?' Harris stopped making the coffee to turn and stare at her.

'Watch it!' Rallou laughed and pointed to the eruption on the gas ring. Harris lifted the tiny pan off and poured the contents into the waiting cup.

'He is never down from those hills!' There was a smile on Harris's face but also a little touch of pity in her eyes as she spoke.

'It's fine,' Rallou said in his defence. 'He comes home with many rabbits and birds to eat or sell.'

'Ah, you are too good, Rallou. You always have been.' Harris began the coffee-making process again, stirring water and sugar over the heat, and then spooning in the coffee grounds, the dry mountain slowly sinking into the water. Then she waited for the water to boil, coffee-coloured bubbles glistening with sugar rising to the top, and just as it was about to overflow she lifted it off and poured it into her own tiny cup.

'I don't know why you say that, Harris. He is loving and kind and he has always made me laugh.'

She laughed as if to demonstrate, but it was not a genuine laugh. How often over their evening meal, she attempted to reassure herself, did Christos slip his boots off so his foot could find its way to the back of her calf under the table, just to make contact, just to be close?

'I don't think there are many like you that would put up with … Well, you know.' Harris let her sentence trail off, and banged the *briki* into the sink, drowning the conversation out with the water rushing from the tap.

'No, I don't know. What are you talking about?' Rallou's smile faded from her face. What happened to the confident person she became when she left the island for Athens all those years ago? Back then, as if by magic, she suddenly didn't feel uncertain any more. Life became clear, and everything felt transparent. That was when she was off the island. But this was the island and Harris knew so much about so many people, and was in possession of sources of information that seemed to just bypass Rallou.

'You know me,' Harris said, sitting opposite Rallou and slurping noisily at her coffee. 'I am not one to get involved. If you can put up with things the way they are, then fine. What business is it of mine? After all, how long is it now? Twenty years? I just think, if your home is in dispute for that long it could at least be well maintained and comfortable whilst you have it. That's all. But, if you agree with Christos, and another day up in the hills catching a rabbit is a better way for him to spend his time ... Well, like I said, what business is it of mine?'

She had a point. The rabbits he came back with made good eating, but a day's work in town would earn him enough to buy three such meals and still leave time to fix the back step, paint the gate onto the lane and maybe even replace the broken window in the *apothiki*.

So when Christos came home that afternoon she raised the question with him. He came in grinning.

'Eh, Rallou, look what I've brought you.' He sounded so pleased with himself. Not a word about having been away for the night. 'Look, I am the fisherman now and I bring you a fish,' he said, carefully holding his catch under her nose by its tail, avoiding the stinging spine and wiggling it to make it look alive. It was a scorpion fish, a bag of bones, skinny fillets not much good for eating, only good for soup. 'Ah, ah!' Christos was grinning, holding up a warning finger. 'I can hear what you are saying to yourself, Rallou, you do not want to skin and cut it. But there is no need, I will cook you a fish soup, you need do nothing.' He stood tall as he delivered this speech, eager for her response, the sun through the back door lighting up his tanned skin, picking up the silver flecks in his dark hair. A boy in man's clothing.

But Harris's words were in Rallou's ears, and she thought that she and Christos could – no, should – manage better than that. 'And who will be eating that?' she asked. Fish soup was a poor man's dinner.

Christos's smile dropped at these words, and his arm, still holding the fish, hung at his side. 'Anyway, I have cooked *pastichio*. What am I to do with that? Throw it away?' Her words, as intended, squashed him. She internally congratulated herself for having stood up against him. Harris would be proud. But then the sadness in his eyes and the hollow feeling in her chest, her desire to throw her arms around him and kiss him and tell him that she would love fish soup if for no other reason than because he had caught the fish himself, pushed her into an uncertain, confused place.

'Well, maybe we can have the fish tomorrow,' he muttered, his voice fading and his joy gone. But wasn't this what he always did: make her feel sorry for him, by pulling this small boy act?

'We need to talk, Christo,' she said seriously, her eyes to the floor.

'Oh no! Now I am in trouble!' Christos joked, and he held the fish up to look in its glassy eyes. 'Help me, little fish! We must swim away quickly. Rallou wants to be serious and that is not good for a man!'

'It *is* serious, Christo. You are away a day and a night and come back with a single fish. Are you not aware that the pomegranate tree is getting too big and needs trimming? Every time I take the sheets in from the line they catch on the branches as I bring them back indoors. Sometimes it is quite a fight not to tear them. And the broom head is coming away again and I am not sure it will take any more nails before it splits. But apart from all the work in the house that needs doing, you could earn far more than a fish by working in town. Take a building job more often. Paint a foreigner's wall …'

Christos lifted the fish to his ear, pretending to listen. 'The fish says that it wants to drown itself now,' but there was no laughter in his voice.

'She said you would make a joke.'

'Ah.' Christos put the fish down by the sink, a frown growing. 'So you have been talking to your sister again.'

'Well, she is right. We've lived for twenty years not even knowing if our home is really our home.' All the time they had lived there, Christos's cousins had been in a dispute over who owned what percentage of the house. The uncertainty of their tenure disturbed Rallou's peace and there was always the implication that one or another of the cousins felt it would be better to sell the house, or rent it to tourists in the summer, or some other scheme that would require Christos and Rallou to vacate their home. 'I need a home, Christo. One I can call my own, one without plaster missing from the bathroom wall and steps that could kill me. One we care for.'

His shoulders slumped and he put his green canvas bag by the back door. 'Now, that is your sister talking, the old witch.'

'Don't you dare speak about her like that! She raised me.'

'Rallou, sometimes you are a fool. Just because she raised you does not make her good. She has been playing these tricks for years, and each time she draws you in and you believe her. She did it just after we were married, remember? Talking about some girl I had coffee with once or twice. The girl from Corfu – you remember. She built it up into something it never was. And then later, with the children …'

'What about the children?' This immediately put Rallou on the defensive. 'Was I not a good mama to them?'

'You could not have been a better *mitera*!' Christos sighed. But maybe you were too good.' He sounded exhausted now, and sat heavily at the small table by the sink.

'And what is that meant to mean?'

'It is meant to mean,' he replied, his head jerking up to look at her, the whites of his eyes dominant, 'that Harris was up to her tricks there as well. Pushing you to be ever more diligent until there was no room left for me and you.'

'You're jealous of your own children?' she asked, and he just looked down at the tabletop and shook his head sadly.

'You know what, Rallou, being married to one woman is difficult enough, but being married to two …!' He stopped talking to take a breath. 'I did not marry your family, Rallou, and this has gone on long enough. You need to sort it out.' He stood up wearily.

'Leave my family out of this!' she demanded as he made his way across the room to the foot of the stairs. As he passed her, he turned so they were face to face for a second.

'I don't think you know who is good for you, Rallou. If you make the wrong choices, one day you are going to wake up and feel very alone.'

'Is that a threat? Have you any idea what it is like for me when you are off on one of your two-day rambles? The ironmonger knows more about where you are than I do! Come to that so does the baker, the carpenter and the fishermen! They must laugh at me not knowing where you are half the time!' She knew she had lost her temper, but she could not hold herself back.

'At least you have to ask!' he spat back, neither of them making much attempt at restraint now. 'The whole town knows where you are and what you are doing with no one having to ask anyone.'

'And what is that supposed to mean?' This last attack confused her.

'Oh come on, everyone knows how much time you spend at the Americans' house. Your sister makes sure of that!'

'Well, at least I am earning money! At least someone is bringing a wage into the house.' Rallou did not understand the insinuation, at least not at first.

# Chapter 3

But Rallou does not relate any of this to her baba, who takes another sip of coffee. Sweet Baba, he has always done his best to support her. But, as always, his silence seems to ring with unspoken feelings.

At one time she thought his silence was because he did not like Christos. But that did not make much sense because, way back, before they were married, he seemed to love him like a son. It was after their marriage and their move into town that his attitude changed. Later, it got so noticeable that she asked him about it, but he denied any alteration in feeling towards Christos. He said he just felt bad at not being able to provide for her.

'But Baba, I am a married woman with a house in town!' she said at the time. 'I do not expect you to provide for me.' She was absolute in her assertion. Besides, she had never thought to question the custom – and anyway, it wasn't personal. They are just like every other family on the island, if not in Greece, and, as tradition dictates, the family businesses – the goats, the olive trees and the pine sap collection – will be inherited by the boys, and the house will go to the eldest daughter, Harris, on that awful day when Baba dies.

She was only tiny when, at the end of a long conversation that she only half understood, he said, '… which means there is nothing left for you, my sweetness,' he spoke like it was a confidence, his eyes moist and glistening, which was a rare occurrence when he was in his prime: he was such a tough man back then. 'I am sorry, I have let you down,' he added. She can remember that she was sitting by his side so she let her head fall on his familiar shoulder. She cared nothing for pine trees or goats or stones and mortar, aware, even then, that she had the most precious thing of all: his love.

Besides, a lack of dowry has made no difference so far. The ownership of the house in town may be under dispute but the truth is that the cousins' arguments will probably go on for another twenty years, so there's no immediate danger of losing their home. But if Christos, in the meantime, could make just a little effort to maintain it, for it to be more of a home, rather than just a shelter …

She takes a sip of her own coffee and looks in the direction of their olive groves.

The boys have had much of their inheritance already. Piece by piece it has been passed to them as their father's strength has lessened over the years. Vasillis, the eldest, has already inherited the olive groves, which are to the south of the house, and out of sight, over the brow of the hill. With the oil from the trees and his shoe shop in town he now lives well. The second brother, Grigoris, has half the goats, which he pastures lower down, near the town, and he will get the rest when their baba dies. He has built his own place on the foundations of their great-great-great-grandfather's house. Now, if he can build a lovely home why can't Christos? Although it is true that Grigoris's wife came with a dowry that included her own house, which they have rented out all these years, so he can afford to make his home comfortable. The other two brothers have already taken over the pine resin business, which they have 'modernised'. What this really means is that, rather than go up there themselves, they now employ migrant workers to plod through the scratchy pine trees collecting the resin from the tins which, long ago, Baba attached below the gashes he slashed into the trees' trunks to catch the sticky liquid. When they were children it was a shared job, the six of them struggling from tree to tree collecting the amber mess and then lugging it down to the beach to pour it into large containers that were picked up by boat every so often, to be refined into turpentine in a warehouse in Piraeus. Collecting it had felt so important back then.

A boat speeds across from the island to the mainland. It could be either Costas or Yorgos, who as well as working the pine business now operate a taxi boat, and they too are more than comfortable.

So, as is the custom, it will be Harris who will get the house when their baba dies – the big stone mansion atop the spine of the island. A place Harris has not laid eyes on since she left to get married just over thirty years ago.

Rallou studies a tiny boat moored over at the mainland. Harris does invite their baba to go and stay with her in town, though, every year. But most years he says he does not feel up to managing such a journey. The last time he went down he stayed with Rallou and Christos.

Her baba glances at her briefly, perhaps still waiting for her answer.

'Yes, I am still working for the Americans.' She sighs. The thought of Lori and Ted's beautifully presented house lifts her eyebrows. There is so much to do before the family's arrival, and she cannot stay up here too long. And with Greg already there, earlier than expected, she will need to remember to pop in and change his sheets soon.

'I sometimes imagine taking a really long trip to go and discover all there is to see in America,' she muses out loud. It is a throwaway comment.

'Ahh. You have always had such an imagination, Rallou.' He puts down his mug and his fingers reach for hers and intertwine with them. 'Do you remember growing up here?' She nods her head. 'You all grew up with work as the normal focus of the day. You tended the animals, gathered *horta* from the mountains, taking it in turns to look after the beehives and generally doing all that was needed. Not one minute was free time. With all your little hungry mouths to feed everyone's help was needed. And the stove back then was outside, do you remember?' He looks to his left where the bread oven still stands, now with weeds sprouting from cracks in the domed top. 'How much of your day was spent outside gathering firewood to stoke it?' He chuckles a little and Rallou turns her head and looks at him. 'But still you would delight me with your tales and fantasies in the evenings, spinning such stories to keep us all spellbound.' He is not seeing the outside world; instead, his eyes are flicking from side to side as he contemplates the pictures inside his head.

'I put this down to you inheriting my intelligence.' His eyes glint as he says this and his mouth twists into a brief smile. There is a long pause before he goes on.

'And when you were not even ten you went to live with Vasillis in Orino, just after he was married. You remember?'

She was told at the time it was because she needed to go to school, but it also meant that there was one less mouth to feed up in the mountains. How different it seemed. She had a room all to herself. At first it felt so empty but soon she began to relish the space. There were orange and white bougainvillea outside the window and the sun would wake her in the morning. In Vasillis's house in town there was no smell of goats and no dull clonking of the bells around their necks in the morning. But there was the smell of fresh-baked bread from the bakery. It wasn't long before she settled in and began helping her brother's wife with the chores around the house, and with the baby when it came; it was a welcome relief from the hard work that was the reality of daily life up on the mountain.

In the end she only spent two years at school, but in this time she proved herself so apt that by the time she left she could read fluently and write with enthusiasm, if not too much accuracy.

'And then when you came home again, I think Harris felt a little left behind, perhaps?' her baba adds.

The first day home she was so pleased to be back that she visited the goats and the bees and chickens, running around all her old haunts with such excitement. She also showed her baba what she could do, writing words and doing sums, and he praised her and hugged her and ruffled her hair. Harris told Rallou about all the dishes that she had learnt to cook whilst she was away, and took a page from one of Rallou's schoolbooks and used it to light the stove. Rallou tried very hard not to cry, because Harris did not know about books and could not have meant any harm. But those books had seemed so precious at the time, and it was difficult to stop the tears.

'But before Harris, or any of us for that matter, could take a breath you were off again.' He laughed as he said this, looking proud.

It was true. Vasillis sent word that the carpet-makers were offering jobs to able youngsters with good pay. Rallou was sent but Harris had to stay behind to cook and keep house for her father and their three brothers. Rallou suggested at the time that perhaps she shouldn't go because of Harris, but Baba was firm. To be a wage earner at nine years old was a blessing. Harris was twelve, and she had her own role in their lives. As for more education, that was not advisable, he said, as it would only render Rallou unmarriageable.

Rallou lazily throws the cold dregs of her coffee over the edge of the porch and watches the ground suck the moisture into a dark streak that quickly fades. An ant comes to investigate.

'Do you want fresh coffee?' Baba leans his weight forward but she shakes her head; he settles back to talk again.

'But you know, Rallou, even before you went to school, her life was very different from yours.' Baba is trying to help, she knows he is, but it is not clear what point he is trying to make. Rallou reminds herself that he is over seventy now. Talking about Harris is the last thing she feels inclined to do right now; she would rather discuss Christos, figure out what is going on between him and her. She thinks she knows what her baba is about to say.

'In one hour, Rallou' – he is looking at her quite sternly – 'Harris suddenly had not one but two younger sisters. And in the same hour you all lost your own dear mama. Which I know was hard on you too – how could it not have been, you were so small? But for Harris, her world changed even more. She was no longer just the younger sister to her brothers. She had to be the woman of the house, with five men to feed, if you include me, and two little sisters to take care of, and one only a baby. It was very hard on her. And I still feel bad,' he says, shaking his head, 'that I did not help her more, but I felt adrift at the time, Rallou. Losing your mama shattered my world.'

'Baba, I know, I know. Harris was an amazing mama to me and Evgenia.' She crosses herself in her little sister's memory. 'She has always been more than just a sister to me.' She scans his face. He has a new liver spot by his left temple, which will fade into his tan as summer comes. He shifts in his seat, as if he is uncomfortable.

'But maybe she has become too much to you, my *koukla*?' he says.

'How can she be too much to me? She has been by my side, supported me, advised me.' She would like to add, 'I wouldn't know half of what was going on with Christos if it was not for her,' but decides not to.

'Do you think it is possible that, because she acted as a mama to you, maybe, just maybe, you are blind to her faults?'

Her lips part, her mouth dropping open just a fraction, but more noticeable than that is a sudden weight in her chest. Troubles with Christos are uncomfortable and hurtful, but questioning Harris seems to shake the very foundation of her world.

The beauty of the view across the sea, the sun sparkling on the now blue water, is too sharp a contrast to how she feels, so she shuts her eyes.

# Chapter 4

The gecko is back on the balcony, and a second appears and they chase each other, along the tiles and back over the edge again. Once out of sight they call to each other with their noisy clicks.

'So, the Americans, are they here yet?' He asks brightly, blinking, watching her, as he changes the subject. 'No, I'm too early, aren't I? They don't normally come until the end of June, do they?' He plays idly with his empty cup, but the movements are slightly too fast to appear totally casual. 'It is so easy to get confused with the days up here! Sometimes I lose weeks, or gain them.' He laughs now, inviting Rallou to join him.

'It is not only up here, Baba.' She accepts his invitation. 'I have lost months, or gained them. I just never seem to know where we are. The seasons, however, I manage to keep up with.' Now they both chuckle.

'But in answer to your question, their son is here.' Rallou knits her fingers in her lap and stares at them and then fiddles with a bit of skin by her thumbnail. It hurts as she pulls at it so she chews it off.

'Which one? Don't they have more than one?' He is talking now as if the subject of Harris has been forgotten but his words are too clipped. He knows there are three sons.

'The oldest one. Greg. He says he is getting divorced.' The word divorce lingers in her mind. Could that really be where she and Christos are heading? When you have been with someone for twenty-nine years, how do you know if divorce is the thing to do? How does she know if she would be happier? And what would she have left if he were to leave? It is a little bit beyond even her imagination, but it is still a terrifying thought. Then again, how much of a couple are they, as things are? Stephanos gives the impression that nothing is too much effort if it makes Harris happy. He even thinks of things independently, to improve or at the very least maintain their home. Christos, on the other hand, seems so absorbed in his own world, and so completely defeated whenever she suggests that he might do things differently, that he might sort out the house or get a job in town, or, worse still, that he himself might have to change.

'I am sorry to hear that.' Her baba puts his palms flat on the table, spreading out his fingers. The little finger of his right hand is crooked with age and the joint near his nail is a bulbous knot; he no longer has movement there. Rallou takes a moment to recall what she had said to him to prompt this answer. Oh yes, it was in answer to the mention of Greg getting divorced.

There is a yellow flower by the bottom step of the balcony. Its stem has pushed its way through the compacted soil and it has bloomed in the shade of the step.

'Lori and Ted offered me a ticket to America, to visit them there, after the summer.'

'Really?' His voice is animated.

He doesn't add, 'Isn't that exciting,' and nor does he ask if she intends to go. She wonders if it is because that would open up a discussion about whether Christos would go too. He is not one to interfere in other people's relationships.

Having mentioned it, Rallou is not sure she wants to talk about it anyway, as it seems that someone in the town has implied that the offer was made, not by Lori and Ted, but by their middle-aged, married, soon-to-be-divorced son Greg. At church last Sunday someone asked if the offer of the ticket was true, which in itself surprised her as she had told only a couple of people. But she had nothing to hide, and said that, yes, it was true – and she felt not altogether unjustified in harbouring a little smugness. After all, how many housekeepers were so valued by their employers? But the response that came back was some reference to Greg and was accompanied by what might have been interpreted by a less generous person as a sneer, and Rallou would have had no idea what this exchange was really about if Harris had not explained it later.

'Yes, really. But they have offered me the ticket not as their housekeeper – just as their friend.' Lori and Ted are so appreciative, but she does no more for their house than she does for her own. When was the last time Christos appreciated her?

Her baba retracts his hands from the tabletop. He too seems to be staring at the little yellow flower.

'Lori and Ted really seem to need me. I think they are the only ones that do, now that my children are gone.' She laughs to make light of her admission, but her stomach tightens.

'I need you.' He says it so simply it brings a lump to her throat.

'You?' She chuckles a little, the embarrassment cutting it short. 'You, who have lived here by yourself for years and years? You need no one! You are the only person I know who is truly content with his own company.' For some reason she wishes she could cry like she used to as a child but these days the tears are reluctant to come. It would feel like a relief if they did, if she could just sob her heart out again and again.

'Am I?'

Any other day she would accept this invitation to talk about him, reassure herself that he is all right up here all alone, but not today. Today she needs to think about herself.

They continue to sit side by side in silence. The cockerel down in the coop crows, its warbling call trilling on the last note, which extends to become a creaking rasp before, out of breath, the bird falls silent. Another boat appears from the direction of Orino harbour, cutting the water, raising a twist of white foam that ribbons out behind it. The red bodywork and its speed tell Rallou it is a water taxi boat. It could be Costas or Yorgos. She has not seen either of them for a few weeks. It is amazing how, in such a small town, she seems to see people either every day or not at all. The boys, or rather men, with grown-up children of their own now, live behind the hill that separates Orino harbour from the smaller hamlet with its little harbour to the west. She can remember when there were just a few houses there, but over the years more have been built until they form a cluster all the way up the hill to connect with the houses that spill over from the main town. She and Christos live on the eastern edge of the town, where the houses start to thin out and the ground rises steeply. The route that leads up out of town, to the ridge where Yanni lives, passes behind her house, and she often hears his donkeys clopping slowly, softly, back up in the evening, or trotting down at dawn, their hooves sliding on the polished marble steps that give way to a rough track further up the hill. Harris lives just across from Rallou, and from her balcony she can survey Rallou's house and all of the road down to the port, as well as part of the Americans' garden. She also overlooks one of the larger squares, in front of the church, where the bright colours of the geraniums and the shade of a spreading pine tree encourage people to gather and talk. Her house is a perfect vantage point, whether up on the balcony, or by her front door.

Back when Rallou first moved with Christos to live in Orino town, it had seemed like such an achievement. Sophisticated, modern. There was electricity and running water in the houses. The shops were only five minutes away and they delivered for free! It felt so decadent! But now, if she was given the choice she would rather live up here, nearer nature, near her baba, with views that are the best in all of Greece. But the reality is that there is no electricity and no running water. Light is by paraffin, which has to be brought up; bathing occurs in the sea in the summer, or there is the option of cold washes from one of the wells, which may or may not have water at the tail end of summer. In the winter, washing is a long, tedious job involving heating pans of water. It may look idyllic here but it is not very practical.

The second drawback is that without a donkey it takes so long and is so tiring to get to town, so, even if Christos's family house were habitable, he could not get jobs in town, and she certainly could not continue to be housekeeper for Lori and Ted, being so remote.

'Do you see much of the boys?' her baba asks, referring to Costas and Yorgos.

'No. I still visit Eleftheria most weeks.' Eleftheria is Vasillis's wife. 'But even that is becoming less regular now their eldest is married and gone. I saw Grigoris on my way here. He was herding the goats down on the low pastures. I waved to him.'

Perhaps it is best just to accept what she has, stop wishing for more. Harris may be right about the house and all that Christos never seems to get done, but life is short. Maybe it *is* best spent up on the hills rather than cementing steps. But if that is the case perhaps it is even better to spend it seeing the world?

She looks past the chicken enclosure down to the area of pasture that leads to the beehives. Her gaze flicks up over the pines and then down across the sea to the mainland.

How many school trips were the children taken on, to one place or another over on the mainland? Delphi, Epidavros, Myceanae, Corinth, the Acropolis in Athens. Each time she volunteered to go, to help the teachers, packing her bag alongside the children's.

'You are going with them again?' Christos would ask, almost like an accusation, almost every time.

'I have made *domates gemistes* and *imambaildi*, two *tapsia* in the fridge. If you want them hot put them in the oven,' she would reply. She always made sure he did not suffer for these trips, but how she used to delight in them, in a chance to get off the island.

'One day we must make our own trip, yes?' he would ask, but it didn't seem like a real question.

'But you have never been off the island. You have no interest in travelling,' she would reply. The first few times he disputed this. But she said that if he wanted to leave the island he would have done it already, and after a while he made no comment at all.

She misses those excursions. The church organises outings to the Meteora and other monasteries on occasion, and she will sometimes go with all the other women of the town, but it is not as much fun as the school excursions were.

'Come on.' Her baba stands and waits for her to lead. He is walking more slowly than when she last saw him at New Year. His feet shuffle a little as if he is afraid of lifting them too far from the ground.

'Are your shoes all right?' Rallou asks. She forgot to put her shoes on after brushing her hair. Feeling the ground beneath her seems to impress upon her the reality of life, reminding her that her relationship with nature is far more important than any other she has had or will have in her life. She forgets this when she lives in town and all the earth is paved in stone and her feet are permanently bound in leather. The dust between her toes feels very comforting.

'Yes. Why?'

'Nothing.'

The top of the island is all rock and shrubs. Down either side of the hill, but more thickly on the north face, the pine trees grow, and lower still they dwindle to nothing where they meet the coastal path to town. On the south side, further along, they give way to olives, but straight down they continue nearly to the water's edge around secluded beaches.

As they walk on, her baba's stride begins to lengthen, a lazy swing of his legs, no hurry.

Neither of them speaks as they walk, and the events of yesterday return to Rallou's mind. Christos had heard the rumours about her and Greg too. But why hadn't he just dismissed them? Instead, the way he dealt with it came as such a shock.

She had just washed and was ironing Ted's and Lori's sheets and pillowcases again. After eight months folded in a chest they needed to be freshened up. She had also changed Greg's sheets as he had already been there about a week. Lori and Ted would come in June. The two other sons, Scott and Bryce, would not be coming out until August this year.

The ironing board was set up in the kitchen and she could see the pomegranate tree out of the back door, still heavy with fruit that had ripened and then split late last summer, as no one had picked it, the branches reaching out to catch her every time she passed. Every spring she watches the pomegranates swell and blush, and resolves to collect them. When the children were young she would pluck them, get the children to peel them. Then they would borrow a press and squash the juice out, mixing it with large amounts of sugar to make a cordial.

The back door was open so she could keep watch for Christos on his way back down the track from his day's hunting, with Arapitsa trailing behind, sniffing at the ground, the fur around her paws grey and impregnated with dust. She would watch him, just a dot high up, getting bigger and bigger. He would look down from the hairpin turn and wave if he saw her. At least he still did that. But he had not appeared yet.

Taking a glass from beside the sink, she filled it with cold bottled water from the fridge. She drank her fill and pulled a face. She had grown up spoilt, with a childhood of fresh mountaintop well water. Then she filled the glass again, this time for the iron. Hissing and steaming, it took most of the glass.

'Rallou?' Christos called as the front door slammed, and his feet clipped against the floor tiles as he marched the short distance to the kitchen.

'Hello, are you hungry?' she asked. He must have come down the other way, the way he went when he wanted to drop in on the hardware shop. Maybe he needed more wire for his snares.

'To hell with your food!' he barked.

She put the iron down and turned to face him, eyes wide.

'What …?'

'Have you any idea how it makes me look?' he snapped, his hunting bag dumped on the ironing board, on top of her clean white pillowcases.

'Er, Christo.' She lifted it off, and noted it was empty, which was not unusual of late. He snatched the bag from her hand and threw it on the floor, but it wasn't enough, and he grabbed the edge of the neatly ironed cases and pulled them, slapping them against the floor and releasing them into a pile on the tiles, then kicking at them with his boot.

Rallou did nothing but stand and stare. It was out of character and she had no idea what his temper was about. It flashed through her mind that it might be to do with the rumours, but he knew her better than to believe any of that.

The sunlight slicing in at the back door lit up the sheets and highlighted the contrast between the clean cotton and his dirty boot marks. It was nothing a scrub and water and sunlight would not bleach … But to make all that work for her – it was not his way.

'Christo, has something happened? Are you all right?'

'Yes, just fine if I like the whole island looking at me like I am a fool.'

It must be the rumour, there was no other explanation.

'Is this about the rumour–?' she started.

'The rumour that is all over the town, and you stand there without a word of apology.'

'Apology? Me apologise? What exactly am I supposed to apologise for, I have done nothing – and you know it! I am not responsible for what people spend their lazy time talking about, any more than you are.'

'You are responsible for what you do!'

'I have done nothing for which I need to apologise.'

'This is a small island, Rallou – it is all about what people *think* you do! Whether you have flung yourself at your fancy American man's son or not is not the point.' There was ever such a slight pause, as if to suggest he was waiting for a denial, but it wasn't long enough for her to offer one – if, indeed, she thought one was deserved or would help. 'If people think you are having an affair how does that make me look, eh?'

'I would hope you would be more concerned with what that would say about us.'

'The whole town is looking at me as though I am a fool who cannot control his wife. I have to be able to hold my head up. How am I going to do that with people whispering and sniggering?'

'No one decent is going to believe it.'

'Really? That is not what I am hearing all over town. You have no discretion in your work, you keep it from no one that you are nothing but a servant for those Americans. You show no prudence in your comings and goings. How can I maintain my pride when my wife is throwing herself–'

'I don't see you objecting to the money I make!' she interjected.

'Ah, yes, well you would bring that up, wouldn't you. Rub salt into the wound.' He leaned towards her as he spoke, flecks of spittle on his chin, in the corners of his mouth. His eyes were watering. It was his pride that was hurt. She earned far more than he did and hers was the steady wage that they relied on to pay the bills.

'We need the money.'

'We have never needed the money.' Born and raised in Korifi, like her, he grew up working hard.

He was so uninterested in material things that he had never even thought of owning a new pair of trousers until the day they married. Quality of life had always been his priority, and for him that meant being in the hills, just him and Arapitsa, and the rabbits, or grouse, depending on the season. Now the children were gone it made for a lonely life for her.

'You don't need money because we have it!' It was not that she really resented his choices in life, but, rather, if she was brutally honest, that somehow she had expected more for herself.

And as Christos shouted she fell into a safer place: the comfort of her memories. After working at the carpet factory for a couple of years she had begun to draw up designs of her own. She took them to old Konstaninos and, after long and careful consideration, he made a few using her patterns, and they sold well and she was given a bonus. But it was a declining business and the factory closed when she was only fourteen. By this time some of her childhood friends were betrothed, but Rallou had long since made the decision that an early marriage was not for her and, after two years back at home, just after her sixteenth birthday, she got a job in a *kafenio* in town and moved back to live with Vasillis, who now had two children. She enjoyed that job and would probably have happily stayed had it not been for the offer of another job in a *kafenio* in Athens, at double the wage.

How exciting life had seemed back then. Anything could happen, and she really thought it would.

'Are you even listening to me?' Christos shouted at her.

# Chapter 5

No, she was not really listening to him. She was wondering what happened. The Athens job had been such fun. Maria, the bar owner's wife, took a shine to her and for a while she became the mama for whom Rallou had so yearned. She lived with them in Athens for two years but, at Maria's suggestion, she did not stay working in the bar for more than a month. Instead, she got a job at a travel agent's and that sparked a wanderlust that remained with her.

'You know what, Rallou. If I was young again, as young as you, I would go.' Maria was wrapping rice in cabbage leaves and packing the parcels tightly into a pan.

'Go where?' Rallou was back from work for *mesimeri* – siesta time, which would give her enough time to eat and maybe even take a little nap before she had to return at five.

'Wherever you like! You work in a travel agent's, don't you?' The leaf she was rolling split and the rice poured out. She took another leaf, laid it flat on the chopping board and ran a knife along the length of the thick stalk, thinning it out so it could be bent without it snapping, then spooned in rice and dill and rolled again. It had never occurred to Rallou until that point that she too could travel.

The planning was almost as exciting as her final departure. Maria encouraged her and suggested that travelling with a package group was probably the safest way to go – at least this first time.

At the time it had felt almost unreal – so exciting, such an adventure – but later, looking back, it almost took on a dreamlike quality, as if she was no longer sure which bits she had imagined and what had really happened. First she went to Paris, where she visited the Louvre and Notre Dame, and wandered through the backstreets and then lingered in the cafes with their tables on the pavements. Then the group flew on to London, where she saw the Houses of Parliament, and London Bridge. She was only going to stay a week in each city, but sometimes life will not be contained, and as it turned out she spent over two months in London.

'Rallou!' Her husband's voice brought her back to the argument. His hands were on her shoulders and he was shaking her.

'What?' she snapped and he let go, but it didn't stop his rant.

'You are lucky we live in these times and that I am as easy-going as I am,' he was saying. 'There are men on this island who still do not let their wives go out to work, and perhaps with good reason.'

'What am I supposed to say to that – thank you for letting me work?' She stepped out of the light of the open back door so she could see his face more clearly.

'Most women are satisfied with children and a house to clean, and a man to look after. There are women out there who would love to be in your shoes. We may have been married for twenty-eight years ...'

She had been so flattered by his interest in her after her return from her travels.

It was Harris who pointed him out, initially.

'Have you seen Christos since you got back? Grown at least a head taller. And the way his hair used to stick up – well, you'll see, he's had it all cut. You should have seen him combing the olives.' She paused to look towards the village as if he could be seen now. 'Will you help me take up one of Mama's dresses?' she added excitedly.

In the time Rallou had been in Paris and London, just a few short months, he had become one of the tallest and strongest of the boys from Korifi, and so good-looking, or maybe she had just not noticed him before she went away. He would lead the hunts up there on the hill, and whilst his friends would return having only caught one bird he would have three. How exciting it had seemed to have his admiration.

'I am worried for you, Rallou.' Harris had come to help her as she daydreamed whilst collecting the eggs from the chicken coop. She was just replaying an event from the day before in her mind, recalling Christos drawing water from the well for her, the sleeves of his T-shirt rolled right up over his shoulders, the sun on his arms. 'You are paying with fire,' Harris continued. 'Do you know that he was practically engaged before you came back? To a girl from Corfu. Educated, too,' she added. 'Training to be a nurse. What if she comes back? What if Christos is just playing with you till she returns?'

But Rallou could only see Christos by then. Their love – she already knew it was that – felt like a continuation of the same whirlwind that took her to Athens, Paris and London, and so she went with the flow and they were married within six months. She could not have realised that it would, in fact, mark the end of the freedom, of excitement.

'Twenty-nine years,' she corrects him.

'Twenty-nine,' he agrees, without thought. 'But you seem to forget how many women wanted to marry me back then. Not just up in our village – here in Orino town too.'

'What are you saying? That I should consider myself lucky? I seem to remember that it was you who chased me when I returned from London. And how exciting you promised our lives were going to be. We were going to open a shop, build a house, become the talk of the town with our popping to Athens whenever we felt like it. We were going to travel, have children. But you have never travelled any further than the edge of this island! The only thing in your list of promises that came true is the children, and precious little you had to do with them!' She shouldn't have said that. That was unfair. But was it? She struggled on her own with them when they were babies whilst he carried on as if nothing had changed in their lives. The only thing he did more of was whistle. His incessant whistling. As she became more and more tired he seemed to spend ever more time up in the hills shooting at birds and trapping rabbits. He would whistle as he stepped into the house as if he had none of the cares but all of the energy in the world. His edible trophies would be displayed to her and she was expected to applaud and admire, and then cook the rabbit or bird, or whatever it was he had shot. At one point, when one baby was teething and the other refused to suckle, she was so exhausted that she went to Vasillis and his wife for help, or at the least just a word of comfort. But Eleftheria had started with her depressions by then and there was nothing they could offer. Their world had become insular and dark. Their own children were staying with Eleftheria's mama for the winter. So Rallou retraced her steps, passing by what would later become Harris's house, in another two years or so, when she married Stephanos.

'I provided for those children! I put a roof over their heads,' Christos snarled, and her eyebrows shot up of their own accord.

Some provision! At first the disputed house seemed like an adventure – their own little place. A place to laugh and love and curl up with one another. Harris moving in opposite was just the icing on the cake. When Christos was out she would chat with Harris and the world was a perfect place. But what was meant to be just somewhere to make do before they bought their own house no longer seemed exciting when the first child came. As Harris pointed out, you cannot have holes in the roof and the wind blowing in through the gaps in the windows and under the doors all winter, not when you have a baby.

The house had been Christos's grandfather's and he didn't make a will, and so, like so many houses in Greece, it was inherited by Christos and thirteen cousins, and no one could agree what should be done with it. Several of the cousins were for selling the place as it was but could not agree on the asking price, whilst another felt that this was foolish, and that they should renovate first, so as to maximise the profit. One thing they all agreed on, apart from Christos, was that the house was not really habitable in the state it was in. But Christos and Rallou were used to rough living, being brought up in Korifi, and, at the start at least, it was an adventure. For a while Rallou held out hope that Christos would make improvements to the house, but as he pointed out – and Rallou did have to admit that he had a point – it made little sense to spend time and money on a property that was not wholly theirs. Besides this, if the cousins saw improvements made to the house, who knows, perhaps they would make trouble and try to get Christos out so that they could use it instead. This might all have been fine if Christos had provided in other ways, but the cupboards, as her own children grew, were as bare as when she was a child. As soon as food came through the door it was eaten. As Harris was quick to point out, Rallou never dreamed she would have to bring her own children up the way they themselves were raised, not now she lived in the town. One consolation was her job with the Americans; that gave her enough to spoil the children a little. Not that they were neglected. They were cared for and kept clean and loved. How often had she spent the day washing clothes – all by hand back then, before she bought the washing machine, which was paid for, of course, out of her wages. The hours she spent, digging the soil and generally tending the allotment in their garden, cleaning the perpetual dust from the house as well as sewing clothes for the children and keeping them entertained! She struggled with the daily chores on her own, minding three children under six, with never a rest, continuing until she was ready to collapse. Then, what eventually became her most hated sound in the world would stir her from her fatigue: the happy sound of his whistling as he came down the track behind the house and in through the back door, all bouncing with energy, excited by his day, a rabbit in his bag.

'He means well, Rallou,' Harris commented, and to a degree she was right. 'Surely it is better that he creates excitement with the children rather than ignoring them altogether? How is he to know that you had spent the last hour or so calming them to the point that you could at least sit down? He is only a man after all, and you cannot expect him to be so sensitive.' As Rallou started to reply, her newly married sister held up a silencing finger and pointed out, 'Now, I know what you are thinking. But you must remember that Stephanos is a unique individual.

'It is natural for Christos to expect for you to continue just as you did before any of the children arrived. And besides, shouldn't your focus be on the children now, rather than on what Christos does?'

Sometimes it did not feel like Harris was helping at all. Was Rallou supposed to jump up at his return, skin the rabbit, or whatever it was he had brought that day, and cook it whilst he washed and rested upstairs after his day in the hills? Perhaps that was what a good wife should do? But then to serve him his food and wash up, all before getting the toddlers ready for bed – surely, if you put it all together that was expecting too much of her? How was Rallou meant to know? Harris was too young to be a real role model. One thing she never discussed with Harris was her pleas of exhaustion when she and Christos finally got to bed. What was once a time she wished the clock would run fast towards, and which she would stretch out into the early hours of the morning, became a time that she dreaded.

After the children started school, life became easier for a while. But when the third joined the other two each day it did not feel like the liberation she had anticipated. For a month or more it was a shock. It felt as if her role had been taken away and a vast emptiness had come to replace it. She felt she was not needed, and it gave her time to breathe and look about herself and digest her situation, and it was not what she had expected it to be. And then the homework started. First one needed help, and then the next, bringing home reams of homework every day, and double at weekends. She took to preparing the food whilst they were at school so she could sit with one after another at the kitchen table from when they came home until bedtime, struggling with maths, geography, ancient Greek.

Christos had never spent even a day at school and could not help, and so it was left to her. But as soon as her precious children found a degree of independence it was as if the Americans caught a whiff of her freedom. How exotic they had seemed, how worldly and exciting. Who wouldn't have snatched the job they offered her? All they wanted of her was to ready the house a few days before they arrived each year and to make the keys available if a plumber or an electrician came to service the boiler or the air conditioning. It wasn't until they got to know her more that they asked more of her, but the truth was she did precious little for her substantial monthly wage. She had even said as much, at one point.

'Ah, but it is to eliminate worry,' Lori had cooed. Lori did not look like she had spent a second worrying in her life, with her painted nails, long kaftans and strappy, thin sandals that would break if she were to step off the cobbled pathways of the town.

'Yes, I guess that is really what it is, so we know the place is safe when we are not here and ready for when we come,' Ted had drawled, taking his hand out of his white linen trousers so he could tuck a tip in her apron pocket. Lori had given her a lingering smile and nodded in agreement.

Rallou took some deep breaths and returned her thoughts to Christos. It would be better not to argue, let him have a rant, then allow him to cool down. When they were both calmer they could talk over the situation.

'Yes, you did provide for them,' she said, 'and we can be proud of them. Look at them now!' Rallou hoped this would distract his thoughts, change the direction of the conversation. Their young son was at university in Bristol, in England, and the eldest daughter, Natasa, already a doctor, was married to an Italian and living in Bari, where he had an important job at Karol Wojtyła Airport. To everyone's excitement, Natasa was pregnant with her first child. Their younger daughter had married an Australian and they had moved out there. Together they ran a business that had something to do with underwater barriers to protect the beaches from sharks.

Christos faltered, as if catching his thoughts, but Rallou's diversionary tactics had not worked, and he turned on her with renewed energy.

'You spread your poison to the children too. They are not satisfied to stay here with normal jobs either,' he spat. She had not seen that coming. He had never uttered a word of disapproval regarding their children's choices before. It surprised her that she had been blind to his feelings on the matter – assuming that it was something he had felt before and not just something he was saying to spite her in the moment.

'What? How can you resent what they are doing? They will never have to carry firewood to light the stove or worry if they can afford clothes for their children or new clothes for themselves!' After they were married she never had the sort of clothes she dreamed of until she took the job with the Americans and, in the very early days, she spent much of her time altering the children's clothes so they fitted as they were passed down from one to another because they could not afford to keep buying new.

'Is that what it is about then?' Christos sneered. 'New things, whatever money can buy? Is that how the American son has you, then?'

And that was it. Without even reaching for her bag she stormed out of the back door and up the track, her lungs burning with the effort before she even reached the top, and then she walked the length of the ridge to her childhood home and her baba, her safety net.

They have reached the hives by the time Rallou finishes her synopsis of the argument, and she lets out an exaggerated sigh. 'I see,' her baba says.

# Chapter 6

The bees are busy, a group of them crowding the entrance to the hive, and one or two lazily flying around Rallou's head.

'How were the frames, did you need to do much repairing this winter?' Rallou asks.

'No, no – well, one or two, but it was pleasant enough, you know, sitting by the fire. It whiled away a few evenings when it was cold.'

Rallou feels she should ask about the winter evenings, whether they feel too long, and does he get lonely, but she is not ready for the answer. Last winter he came to them for a week or two, a journey taken on Yanni's donkey that he said he would not repeat in a hurry, but he was quick to return to Korifi, complaining that the town was too busy, that he found it difficult to breathe.

Baba lifts the lid of one of the hives and they stare in together at the activity.

'Have you seen those new hives with man-made honeycombs?' Rallou asks. 'With a turn of a handle the comb can split,' she enthuses, and puts her hands together and then slides one down a fraction to demonstrate. 'And the honey runs out to a central channel and then you just turn on a tap and out it pours.'

'No!' Her baba opens the lid of the next hive, which is not so active and in which there are fewer bees. He frowns.

'So much less work and of course not so many bee casualties and disturbance.' Rallou walks to another hive, noting that the lid is not quite on straight, but as she gets closer she can see it is empty.

'Flew off,' her baba says.

'You should think about getting one of those new hives.'

'Ha!' he says gently. 'Even Greece is importing cheaper GMO honey now.'

'Don't be silly, you cannot have GMO honey. Honey is honey.' Rallou looks out across the sea. Today is definitely warmer than yesterday, and she will not be surprised to wake up tomorrow to the first sounds of the cicadas.

'Yes, it sounds crazy, doesn't it, but the world is a little crazy these days, I think.' He would never insist he was right.

'Tell me?' Rallou is intrigued.

'Well, when Yanni brought up the supplies last week he told me about it. So, what they do is, they modify the plants to produce more pollen for the bees. The bees can then make honey with less effort and the whole process is quicker and cheaper, so they can sell it at a lower price. But this is not quality honey. No rich wild pollen is being used, and, of course, the pollen of the plants they use is present in the honey, so you are ingesting it.'

'Interesting.' Rallou encourages him to say more, if there is more to be said. He takes the bait, enjoying the safe subject.

'But, and here is the problem, they do not have to say that the pollen plants are GMO on the label of the honey. So people do not see the difference between that and, say, the honey I produce. All they see is cheaper honey.' He stops walking and leans back, his hands on the small of his back.

'I don't really know what the fuss is about with these GMO foods.' Rallou also stops. Perhaps they should turn back; she does not want to tire him.

'So many ways,' he says, and turns as she does. 'They modify the plants to be resistant to things, like the weedkillers they use. So then they use as much weedkiller as they want with no ill effect on the crop, but, for example' – he glances at her briefly – it is the look he uses when he is concerned that he is boring her, and she loves him for his thoughtfulness – 'apparently the insecticides they put on GM corn can get into the blood, even to the baby, if a woman is pregnant. And another thing, the genes they insert into soy beans can cross into the DNA of the bacteria that live inside us. And that can't be good, can it? Interesting man, that Yanni.'

'Hmm.' Rallou considers all he has said.

He smiles and she reaches out to take his arm as they walk on. He is not shuffling now, and his legs seem strong, as strong as he has always been.

'Well, seeing as the chickens were kind enough to supply us with eggs again, shall we have eggs for breakfast?' She will cook for him as if the years have never passed, as if he has not spent the last eighteen up here in semi-solitude.

'It won't be long before you have company up here,' she says.

'You are right. As soon as the sun warms up all that stonework in town and the stone flags begin to reflect the heat, those who still have houses up here will come scuttling back to the cool of the hills – and the men, no doubt, will linger for the hunting in the autumn. But, like every other year, when winter bites, they soon hurry back down.'

'But you will be pleased to see your old friends.'

They have reached the back porch and Baba sits by the table, slumps a little.

'Shall I make some more coffee before I cook?' she asks.

'No, water please, water would be nice.' He sounds slightly out of breath as well. After a long drink he puts the glass down and smiles up at her.

'The trouble is that the people who return are not the ones that left. Those my age do not bother to make the journey back up here so I never see my friends. Now it is sons of sons, and daughters of daughters. Some have foreign twangs to their voices. We are mostly an adaptable lot, us Greeks, and we have no fear of moving countries if it will profit our children, but my guess is that there are little ghost villages like this all over the country.' He sits back and looks across at the twenty or so solid stone houses that nestle in the cleft on the summit. Rallou glances at the familiar sight and then turns towards the sea. The view is just breathtaking and it still surprises Rallou every time she focuses on it. The islands dotted one behind the other look almost like they have been cut out of coloured paper and stuck on, a hazy gauze drawn over them to blanch their colour, and there is a fine line of white that stops them sinking into the sea. Blue sea, blue islands, blue sky.

'So, eggs?' Her baba startles her into action.

# Chapter 7

Rallou takes the apron, with its pockets still full of eggs, into the tiny kitchen. She is glad that her baba has succumbed to the convenience of the gas stove that sits on a little table in the corner. As well as making cooking so much easier, it also means Yanni will have to come up with a gas bottle every once in a while, check on him, make sure he is in need of nothing else. Whenever she sees Yanni and his donkeys going up or coming down the track behind her house in town, they nod their acknowledgement of each other, and if they talk it is always, and only, about her baba.

She tries to lift the large gas bottle, to see how full it is. It doesn't move as she tugs; it must be new. The gas hisses and she strikes a match. As the stove bursts into life the flame catches the fine hairs on the back of her hand and they shrivel and turn black.

There is no fridge, and the icebox that stood in one corner of the kitchen rusted away some years ago. Now it stands outside by the entrance to the goat pen, a handy set of shelves for bits of twine, the hammer, a cup full of nails, medicine for the goats and endless other bits and pieces that might come in useful one day. The doors have been removed and used to block up holes in the chicken coop where mischievous paws have dug away for an easy meal.

In the kitchen, where the icebox used to be, is another of her baba's contraptions. It looks like a pallet has been carefully altered, reassembled into a box, and sanded smooth. Once he would have had no time to sand it, but this chest has been made beautifully, and he has obviously taken his time over the finish. She lifts the hinged lid to reveal a polystyrene cool box. There is vague smell of fish.

'You want feta in your eggs?' she calls.

'Have you seen it?'

'What?'

'The feta.'

Rallou looks again. The feta is sitting there in a dish looking – well, just like feta.

'What about it?'

'It is from Yanni. From his mother, actually. Sounds like she is going like me, soft in her old age. She didn't want to kill a kid to use the rennet to make the cheese so she has found a way to use fig sap.' He shouts a little, but there is no need with the back door standing open. Rallou examines the feta again.

'What, the white stuff out of their stems?' She sniffs the cheese but it does not smell of figs.

'Yes, that. It irritates my skin, and I come up in a rash if I touch it. Oh, you will remember, that time we went down near the shore, where that tiny enclosed inlet is.'

'Oh yes, with the fig tree that overhangs it so you have to crawl to get to the water. You didn't follow us, did you? It's an amazing, tiny little cove. But I do remember your hands were as big as melons, and all red and scaly. Poor Baba.' With this she steps out and kisses the top of his head. It may be white but he still has a good head of hair for an old man. Returning to the kitchen she sniffs at the cheese again. There is no evidence of its figgy component, but it does smell vaguely of fish.

The bucket is empty, so she takes it up to the well and back. When she returns she finds her baba trying to read the label of a medicine bottle.

'Rallou, I cannot quite make this out – does it say once a day or once a week? It is for a goat.'

Rallou puts the bucket down and smiles. He has no idea if it says once, twice or every half hour: he cannot read a word. She takes the bottle from him.

'No, it says mix three capfuls with water.' She reads.

'Oh, they will drink it?'

'It seems so.' She gives him the bottle back and takes the bucket inside. Christos was the same. Never a day at school, couldn't read a thing. He hid it well in the first year or so of their marriage, and even if she had known it would not had bothered her in the least; many people of the island and most people in Korifi cannot read or write. But it seemed to bother him. Especially when the children got to the age when they were bringing home so much homework every day. To all appearances, the school expected more learning to go on at home than inside the classroom.

'Rallou are we ever going to have supper?' Christos would come in after a day on the hills to find her and one or more of the children at the table, books spread to cover the surface.

'Can you not see we are doing homework?' she would reply.

'There is more to life than you can find in books – what they learn by playing will last a lifetime. When do they get to be children?' With which, he would dump his canvas bag on top of whatever they were studying and take his temper to the bathroom where he would wash his face and neck and return to stand over them.

'Well, are we eating?' he would say and Rallou felt she must hold her tongue for the children's sake. She knew that he would not act that way if he could sit and help them learn. It was almost as if he resented that she could.

Rallou breaks from her thoughts to find her baba is now dozing in the morning sun, his chin on his chest, arms folded in his lap, the bottle still in his hand. That will be how she will find him one day, maybe not with the bottle in his hand, but out here in the sun, eyes closed, chest not moving, and she will feel him and he will be cold.

'Stop it,' she tells herself and takes the water inside. 'You are just being macabre because you are feeling negative. Anyway, the chances are you won't be here when that happens and it will be poor Yanni who finds him, or Tolis, or Takis.' She wonders how they will tell her.

'Stop it!' she demands of herself again and then wonders why she went to fetch water when she is going to scramble the eggs with feta. She is pleased to see that there is half a loaf of bread in the *fanari*, but she will have to make some tomorrow or the day after, depending on how much they eat today.

The kitchen has not changed much. The broad rough beams overhead support the canework that provides the bottom layer for the upstairs floor. A shelf runs around the room at head height. Long ago it was painted blue and has remained so ever since, but where it meets the plasterwork across the bowed front of the fireplace it is as white as the walls.

Outside, the cockerel tells the time, wrongly, but he repeats himself just to make sure everyone heard. The chicken cluck their scorn, or agreement – who knows which.

The main table, which stands in the centre all winter, is outside with the chairs so there is plenty of room for Rallou to move about. The gas stove is propped up on a circular metal table with three legs, under the arch of the fireplace. In the winter the table that is outside will come in, the round table will be crammed against it and the fireplace will become functional again.

She hates the fireplace. It would be better if it was modernised, or filled in. It is a reminder of both Mama and Evgenia.

'Oh, stop it now! You are picking on things to make yourself miserable,' she chastises herself. 'But I *am* miserable.' she moans, but then shakes her head and stands erect. This is not the first time that pointless negative thoughts have tried to pull her down. She watched Eleftheria go into a very dark place without even a fight, and she almost pulled Vasillis with her. Ever since then, Rallou has worked on a way to maintain a distance from such a possible spiral. She can't remember where she read about it originally – some magazine perhaps – but so far it has worked, even on the evenings when Christos does not come home and she is alone, lying in the vastness of their empty bed. Then that motionless, spiritless place has seemed so seductive, offering a promise that everything will stop.

'I am miserable, I am miserable.' She begins her technique. '*I am having the thought that* I am miserable, *I am having the thought that* I am miserable.' Pausing between each sentence to really give it impact, she focuses on what she is saying. '*I notice that I am having the thought that* I feel miserable. *I notice that I am having the thought that* I feel miserable.' Then, with no warning, and flapping a tea towel in time with herself, she sings the word 'miserable' to a jolly tune she has heard on the radio recently. The word begins to lose its power and with it its effect.

'There!' she congratulates herself, putting down the tea towel and feeling slightly out of breath.

'What?' Baba mumbles, not quite awake.

'Nothing, go back to sleep.' She faces the kitchen again. The clock on the wall ticks out the seconds.

It was amazing how much silence their mama left behind: a silence that was filled by the ever-hungry Evgenia's cries. Harris just could not cope with the child; she knows this now, but back then the baby's screams were as if the sounds of her own heart had escaped, but with none of the relief. The silence her mama left felt as if it lasted for lifetimes. Her baba seemed to spend so much of his day away with the goats. Of course, life went on, and he could not neglect them, but perhaps he spent just a little longer than was needed with them. It was his way of coping, she realises now. Besides, she was so small then that it probably felt like he was away more than he really was. Her eldest brother had been spending a good deal of his time down in the town at that point, and after this unhappy event he very rarely returned. The other two brothers – well, they seemed to busy themselves with collecting the sap and tending the olives, and it felt as if each was retreating into his own sphere of silence and work. That left Harris, Rallou's playmate. But she was gone too, replaced with a girl who looked like her but was full of the frustrations of trying to deal with a newborn baby, and struggling with the demands placed on her by her new role of mother, cook, cleaner.

'Bring the wood. Fetch the water. Give me that towel, and go get the eggs. Have you fed the chickens?' Harris would bark at her in a way her mama never had. It was mystifying and unpleasant, and she tried harder and harder to please her sister in return for just a little love, and this was at a time when her heart was already torn open and bleeding. It took her a long time to realise that it was an impossible thing to demand of a six-year-old, to look after a baby, because that's all Harris was at the time. But then, how had it been for Rallou? She can hardly remember. All that comes to mind is the silence, and the space. She can recall looking out over the island and then beyond to the sea that went on forever in every direction, and the feelings were hard to understand. It was as if there was nothing to stop her falling off the edge of the world. And there would be no arms to catch her. Mostly she is grateful that she can no longer feel how it was inside her head at the time. She is left with an image of herself, so tiny, standing in the porch, small and powerless, the huge world around her getting bigger and bigger. She was three.

But, as time passed and three winters came and went, the silence of her baba and her brothers and the cries of Evgenia lessened, and the perimeter of the island shrank until everything once again became normal. It was a new normal, with less laughter but with more cuddles from Baba. But that normality seemed to last only a short time before Evgenia fell into the open kitchen fire and was burnt so badly she never recovered. They buried her little body on the hillside. It seemed the best thing to do seeing as they were so far from the cemetery, which was a day's ride on the donkey.

Rallou stirs the eggs at they begin to congeal and the feta melts. At some point since she was last up here her baba has burnt the handle of the pan and it is sharp under her hand where the plastic grip has melted. Maybe she could remember to get him a new one, or find a way to bind it with rope.

Her brothers and Baba always maintained that she was the hardest hit by her sibling's death, she and Evgenia being so close in age. But to her mind, whenever the subject comes up, it seems that hers is the dimmest of all their memories and so the whole incident has the aspect of a family tale rather than a reality she has lived. Losing her mama, on the other hand, left a hole that no one could fill. Harris, at the tender age of six, had no choice but to fill all the roles left vacant by their mama's absence. All the roles except one, the one Rallou needed most. Harris cooked and cleaned and learnt to sew and milk the goats. She also learnt how to make cheese and she took care of Evgenia. But Rallou still needed the security of her mama, and she needed cuddles that Harris would not give. Nor would Harris cuddle Baba or her brothers. It seemed she only had time for Evgenia, whom she played with like she was a doll until the baby cried, and then she would get cross and lose her temper with her little sister and everyone else around her.

'You want some bread with your eggs, Baba?' She looks again to the *fanari*; perhaps there is more of the staple than she first thought.

As her baba does not answer she presumes he must be still dozing in the sun. She cuts two slices of bread; it crumbles at she does so, the yellow of the olive oil dominant. A plate in each hand, she takes them outside and puts them down on the table more noisily than is necessary.

'Oh, er, what, was I sleeping?' He stretches, blinking several times. 'Oh, that looks good.' They eat in silence, looking across the strip of water that separates the island from the mainland. Yachts with billowing sails make slow progress, the white of their canvas forming bright pinpricks that stand out on the blue sea, and taxi boats criss-cross the water, leaving a ribbon of froth in their wake. A fishing boat sits motionless and the islands continue to float in between. Out to the west the strip of water opens out to the vastness of the sea, which stretches all the way down to Crete and beyond, to Libya. It travels to places she once thought she might get the chance to visit but which are now just missed opportunities.

# Chapter 8

In the few days Rallou has been there she has slipped easily into the familiar routine of work that mountain living demands. When she remembers, she waters the little yellow flower at the base of the balcony step as she passes with buckets of water from the well. She has also been taking the goats for at least one of the two outings a day they require, to give her baba a rest. But the jobs are not as pressing as they were when she was a child. These days Baba can afford to buy some things on the small pension he now draws. The tins of beans, tomatoes and sardines that Yanni brings up from town must make his life so much easier. His pension is small and cannot afford him many luxuries, although he has paid into it his whole life, but he can treat himself occasionally.

Sardines are his favourite, and he says they keep their flavour well. He still grows his own tomatoes, too, but admits it is a relief not to have to get involved in the tedious process of boiling them and storing them in jars for the winter.

Since Rallou arrived, her baba seems to have spent a great deal of the day sleeping on the porch, but then, why shouldn't he? It gives her some satisfaction that her visit has had the consequence of being able to give him a break?

The days have slid by so easily. She does not remember which day the cicadas began to sing but they are doing so now, at full volume. The summer is here! But there has been no sign of Christos. Not that she really expected him to follow her up here. For what? To beg her to return? He would not do that. As she is absorbed back into familiar routines she is surprised to find how much she really wishes he had followed her, and with each day that he does not appear it feels as if a band is tightening round her heart. Life may be less stressed without him around, without arguments about where he has been and how long he has been away, or taut silences, but in the growing warmth of the summer sun, which eases out the knots in her shoulders, and the peaceful solitude of her surroundings she finds that, without him, life feels like it is missing some of its flavour, some of the spark that his presence imparts, and she discovers that she is wishing he were here after all.

One evening, whilst she is preparing the food, her baba comes in to show her a hardened lump of tree sap he has found, with a fly stuck in the centre.

'In a few billion years that will be amber,' he tells her and returns outside, examining his find, turning it over in his fingers. It reminds her of Christos coming home that time with the black stone.

'Look at this!' He came in clearly excited. 'I think this is volcanic rock! Why else would it be black?' He showed it to each of the children in turn, their small fingers feeling the rough texture, eyes wide at the possibility that it could be something special. He began to explain to them about volcanoes and to talk of Santorini, where the sand on the beaches is black. But all Rallou could think about was, firstly, why he had never taken her there, and, secondly, that the children were hungry, and that the hungrier they got the more fractious they would become.

'Can I feed them, please?' she said, and pushed past him to set the table. For a moment their small faces, Christos's included, looked disappointed, but when she told them that she had made a special moussaka they forgot the black stone and began jostling each other to get to the table. Christos took his stone outside and sat on his own under the pomegranate tree. When she offered him food, he said he wasn't hungry, and he went to bed without eating at all that night. The stone remained by his bed for months, perhaps years.

Rallou sighs, sad he has remained in town.

She knows that being up here is not a long-term solution. For a start, she misses the electric kettle, and her hot morning showers. But more pressing than that is that she will need to return to ready the house for Lori and Ted in a few weeks, and Greg will want his sheets changing soon. It is not them she wants to be away from, anyway. She likes her work, and she likes to be needed, she knows that. Without her, the American family flounders on the island. Her job, which originally involved just a couple of hours of cleaning each week, has evolved and now she is in charge of ordering and arranging fresh food deliveries and cooking some of their meals. She has helped Ted set up instructions with his bank to have the bills paid automatically, sitting with him at the computer to translate the Greek. Some bills, such as the water, cannot be paid online, and she makes sure that these are dealt with each month so that their supply is not cut off. She orders and takes delivery of the flower arrangements Lori likes to see on the hall table, fresh every few days when she is here, and, on several occasions over the years, she has accompanied them to Athens when the need has arisen for a native speaker to translate for them. Once she was even sent on her own to the tax office in Piraeus with some official papers. She has become a manager of sorts, and this gives them the freedom to swim and drink coffee, eat at tavernas and sit and read newspapers on the balcony when they are here, and it spares them worry about the house when they are absent. It gives them a complete break and it gives her pleasure to be able to offer that.

If they are around when she is doing her work they talk to her of 'back home', and she listens with wonder at all America has to offer. Lori's view of home and Ted's are remarkably different. They live somewhere called Amelia Island, which, apparently, is a section of a beach called Fernandina in Florida. She has seen photographs of their house with its garden down to the beach. On the map their home is close to the border with the next state, Georgia. Once or twice a year they visit their second-eldest son, Scott, who at forty is already semi-retired (whatever that actually means) and lives in West Palm Beach, Florida, in a group of houses that, for some reason, have an electric gate separating them from the road. Even the names of the places sound so exotic, so magical, to Rallou. Lori tells her how she likes to drive along the east coast when her husband is away on business. The bit she likes best, she says, is the miles of open land with nothing but greenery on either side, just palm trees and tall grasses. It makes Rallou wonder sometimes why they make such a long journey to be on a tiny island in Greece in a place without cars or bikes or even its own water supply. But they say Greece offers them a trip back in time, a life that is simpler, more enclosed. She doesn't quite understand.

Their middle son Bryce lives, coincidentally, in Bryce Road, or was it Street, or maybe it was Valley? – anyway, somewhere in California – and travels extensively in his job as a representative of a high-tech company. It must be a demanding job because when he is in Greece he sleeps a lot. Then there is Greg, who lives in New York and was a stockbroker on Wall Street, and who owns a three-bedroomed house in somewhere called the Hamptons in New

York City. He now deals in property, but judging by the amount of time he spends in Greece it seems this new career is not very demanding. He came to the island a month ago and she is not sure he has even left the house in that time. When she goes in to change his sheets and clean the kitchen, Greg will often be wandering about aimlessly in his shorts, if he is up at all. Or he will be slumped on one of the sofas with a book about modern art. He arrived one day unannounced when she was flicking a duster over the place. His entrance made her jump, and he muttered something about his wife walking out on him recently and that they were getting a divorce. But he obviously does not want to talk and she has been thankful that the place is big enough that she can avoid him whenever it is necessary for her to go over.

How she would love to take Lori and Ted up on their offer of a trip to America! The message they sent making the offer had come as a surprise. Rallou does not have access to a computer, and so when they want to contact her they will send an email to Andreas who runs the photographic shop in town, and he will print it out for her. Generally they will let her know the date that they will be arriving, and whether there will be any guests with them, and they provide a list of groceries. But last month, when Andreas stopped her in the street he informed her that she had been invited to America. 'Not as a housekeeper, they say, but as a friend. Come to the shop later, and I will give you the email.' Later that afternoon, when the shop was open again after Andreas had finished his *mesimeriano* – siesta – Rallou went round to the shop and found that it was true. As well as sending the usual instructions, Lori said in her letter that it would be excellent if Rallou would come back with them to see a little of America at the end of the summer, and not as their housekeeper, but as their friend. She said that she knew how interested Rallou was in the place and that it seemed like a lovely thing that she and Ted could offer, 'as a thank you for the years you have kept the house on Orino Island for us.'

The offer made her gasp, and she swallowed hard as she read through the email again at home, her heart beating faster and her mind spinning with the possibilities. But then Christos came in and rummaged roughly, and noisily, through the cutlery drawer for a sharp knife and she knew such an adventure was impossible. He had not been invited, and nor would he want to go, and he would not approve of her going alone. He would stop her – not in so many words, but he would gradually let his opinions be known clearly enough, without stating them directly, until they filled every room in the house with unspoken resentment. It would make her life hell. No, she could not even think about going, or mention the offer to him.

That was before the argument. If she went now it would be an even bigger slap in his face and she wonders if he would even be there to come back to. Not that he would go anywhere – he wouldn't want to lose face; but she could imagine him moving into one of the children's bedrooms and closing the door.

# Chapter 9

Counting the days off on her fingers, Rallou comes to the conclusion that she cannot stay up here on the mountain much longer. She must change Greg's sheets, tackle the mountain of washing-up that he will have created, and sweep up the eternal dust that gathers between the stone slabs on the living-room floor.

'It's funny how in life things go around and back again, isn't it, Baba?' But her baba, in the chair on the porch next to her, is sleeping. She was thinking of how Lori and Ted's stone-flagged floor used to be covered in threads and wool dust years ago, when the house belonged to the carpet-makers. Her loom had been by the far window, where Ted has put the old Turkish chest he brought back from Constantinople. The rug in front of it is not one they would have made there. It is Chinese and the pattern is somehow cut so the leaves and flowers lift higher than the background.

So many hours she sat there, the tall window providing natural light. Three other looms filled the room, each by one of the tall windows. Now the windows offer one of the best views all the way down over the terracotta roof tiles to the port. The house is in a commanding position, and the whole town can be seen from the balcony that runs the length of the house at the front. They could, if they were here at that time of year, watch the mayor's speech from outside the old naval school at Easter without having to move, the excessively large speakers echoing his droning monologue around the basin that contains the town. They will witness the festival from here, though. Every summer there is a celebration to mark a naval battle, led by a sea captain from the island, which contributed to the War of Independence.

Rallou smiles at the thought. She likes the festival, the re-enactment. A plywood barge is constructed each year, to represent the Turkish fleet, and is pushed out into the bay, stuffed to the gunwales with fireworks. All the taxi boats, fishing boats and visiting yachts sail out to surround the Turkish boat, which is illuminated in the bay. The Greek boats sound their horns and release flares, and the Turkish boat is set on fire to triumphant cheers from the people lined up around the port, on the hills, on their own balconies. Rallou has seen fireworks on television, the fireworks of New Year's Eve from London, Sydney, New York and Paris, but none fill the sky like the display that follows on the island, and her chest lifts with pride at the thought.

But what had she been thinking, before recalling the festival? Was there something she had to do? The eggs, the goats, the cheese, gather some *horta*? No, she has already done all those things today. Oh yes, it was Greg's sheets. Could they not wait another few days? No, perhaps not. But it is a long way to go down and back in a day just to change the sheets and do a little cleaning. She is not ready to see Christos; she doesn't even want to think about him, let alone see him – not yet. So she cannot sleep at home to break up the journey. There is no way she is going to Harris and she does not feel ready to explain her position to Vasillis, no matter what mood Eleftheria is in.

She would not feel comfortable, at this point, explaining to anyone what she is or is not doing. She has no real idea herself yet, so how can she explain it to others?

Yanni's house is closer to the town than her childhood home, all the way up here, but it is still a heavy stretch of the legs and directly up from town, an hour's walk. However, from Yanni's she can walk to her baba's straight along the ridge and neither Yanni nor his mama or baba would ask any questions. They would just make room for her, sharing what little space they have. But she has never stayed there before and she does not really feel she knows them well enough to ask. Her baba would say just go, but she has lost a bit of that mountain attitude. In the town she would have to know them pretty well to presume. Or maybe that is just her way.

There are always Tolis and Takis, though. Their house down by the boatyard is big enough and they only use a few rooms. It is a good two hours from the town, but it is at the bottom of the steep climb up the mountain and would break up the return journey.

If she were to stay there the night, she could enjoy the walk back up the next morning. The track snakes past the boatyard into the pine trees, up and up, zig-zagging left and right until it finally breaks out through the trees where the cliff on the left-hand side keeps the valley in shadow until quite late in the morning. From there it is relatively flat until the road divides: left into a dell, where two whitewashed cottages are visible, or right, where you think you are just heading to a single, honey-coloured, two-storey stone house on a ridge. But, as you draw level with this building, you can see down a second dell behind it to the two dozen or so houses all crowded in together in the shade of the hillock. It is then the shortest of walks to go through and beyond this hamlet to where her baba's house stands on its own. She has followed this route many times from town, but usually reaching the boatyard when the sun is high and the rest of the walk up the hill is a slog against the heat. If she stays the night with the Kaloyannis brothers she could get up at dawn, and in the first light of day the walk would be cool, refreshing even.

She resolves to make bread so Baba is provided for and tomorrow she will make the journey as discreetly and as quickly as possible.

# Chapter 10

Although part of her has not really wanted to leave the cocoon of her baba's world, marching down the track early the next day feels like a freedom. He has entrusted her with one of the loaves of bread she made and a block of Yanni's feta to give to Greg, and she is also burdened with eggs, which he has instructed her to take to Costas Voulgaris at his *kafenio*.

He has also given her a bunch of flowers twisted round with a grass stem. They are for her.

'Oh, Baba, that is so sweet, thank you, but how do I carry them? They will wilt before I get into town. She has seen these flowers before. They only grow high up on the tops of the mountains. Christos came home with a big bunch for her some years ago, but by the time he arrived home the sun had set and the flowers had closed up.

'Ah, what a pity,' he said. 'The flowers are so small, so intensely blue, and I want you to see them. Perhaps if we put them in water they will open again tomorrow.' So he put them in a glass of water but they did not open the next day. They had wilted even more.

'They look like dead weeds,' she said. Perhaps it was not tactful, but it was honest. There was nothing attractive about them at all.

She lets the memory fade.

It is nice to be moving and it is easy to recall the feeling from years ago, before she was married, before she had children, when she experienced the same feeling of freedom and was brave enough to travel to Paris and London.

In retrospect, she was even braver than she knew, as just after she left France it became a very unsafe place to be, with people getting killed. She can remember reading in a newspaper in London soon after she arrived there that the French police had arrested nine people, including five ultra-leftist activists, in connection with a series of bomb attacks. Because she had no knowledge of French, this was the first she had heard of these attacks, and at the time a little shiver ran down her spine to think of all that had been going on around her whilst she was staring at Notre Dame and the Eiffel Tower. When was that, she tries to recall? It must have been around September. September, she muses, trying to calculate the year.

She was twenty-one at the time, so it would have been ... 1986. How could so much time have gone by? She is very proud of her children, but what has she achieved for herself in all these years?

Yes, 1986, and yet she can still remember phoning the boatyard, to get a message to her baba to tell him that she was fine, as if it was yesterday. Tolis seemed very glad to hear her voice.

'Thank goodness,' were his first words. 'It is all over *Ta Nea*. Here, let me read.' This was followed by a sound of shuffling papers. 'Nine people have been killed and one hundred and sixty-three wounded in a series of bomb explosions in Paris,' he continued. 'Responsibility for the attacks has been claimed by a group calling itself the Committee for Solidarity with Arab and Middle Eastern Political Prisoners, which is demanding that France free from prison a suspected Lebanese terrorist leader, Georges Ibrahim Abdallah' – his tongue twisted over the foreign syllables – 'and two convicted terrorists.' He paused and then added, 'There are big demonstrations.' The paper rustled again and he added his own view;

'You see what happens?' he said. 'Algeria and France. Once you have a history with someone you cannot erase it and it can come back and bite you if you have been unfair. People do not forget.'

She cut him short, telling him how much the call was costing her, and made him promise that he would climb the hill and tell her baba that she was safe and in London. She rang a couple of weeks later, too, when she knew she would not be delayed any further getting home. She didn't want to worry anyone, especially her baba, so she lied, and told Tolis that the tour had been extended.

Walking on towards Orino town, she repeats aloud, '"But once you have a history with someone you cannot erase it." How true is that, Christo?' But something brings a picture of Harris to mind.

The upper edge of the pine woods is marked by an old fallen tree, and as she passes it the sound of the cicadas is even more deafening. Their rasping love song is sung loudly and desperately, their brief lives above ground lived to the full: a few days to find a mate before their energy is gone and they fall to the ground. The forest is alive with them and nothing else can be heard. This stage of their life is an emergency and their rasping serenade seems to respond to this fact.

Despite the noise, it is peaceful under the trees, insulated and shady. Rallou's footsteps are softened by the pine needles that carpet the ground, and the sun's direct heat is kept at bay. There is no one for miles. Before she knows it she glimpses blue sea between the branches, and she knows the small plain of the boatyard will be visible in a moment and – there, yes there, is the track that goes down the other way and leads to a remote olive grove. If she were to follow that track and go further she would pass the fig tree that guards the tumbling rocks down to the hidden cove.

It cannot be very late yet. She waved goodbye to Baba before the sun was fully in the sky. It might set her back an hour, but wouldn't it be worth it to see the cove again? Her childhood pulls at her, sparking a desire to feel unburdened once more.

The track through the trees is little used and the way is not clear. It looks like it has been a long time since any man or beast has come that way, and when, after quite a detour, the pines give way to the olive trees she is nonetheless surprised to see them overgrown and neglected. Takis's and Tolis's baba began to cultivate the trees, but he has either lost interest or has found that it is too much work for his advancing years or, more likely, just not economically viable these days.

Up ahead, the fig tree looks healthy. There are no figs yet, of course – it is far too soon for that – and the thought occurs to Rallou that Yanni's mama must have found a way to store the fig sap that she used to make the feta. She might ask Yanni about this the next time she sees him. The sun reflects on the big, dark-green leaves. The tree is bigger than she remembers it, but then it would be: it has been growing without her all these years. The branches that once arched to show the way to the entrance down to the cove are no longer curved. Instead they are tangled and dense. But if she goes to the side of them there is a way through.

Her foot touches the first stone of the descent. She cannot see the cove yet for the branches of the fig tree. The rocks are nowhere as near as steep as she remembers, but then she was so much smaller the last time she was here.

She grips a branch and steps down. A tangle of vines has crept over the stones and it is tricky to sweep it away with her toes before planting her foot and still keep her balance. Maybe this was not such a good idea. This part of the coast is known for its rockfalls. The coastal path often gives way in the winter when the water rushing down from the top erodes the surface, creating gashes in the path, or else seeps underground, washing away small tunnels waiting for unwary footsteps to cave in the surface, the pebbles as slippery as ice.

Rallou keeps hold of a branch or a part of the rock face at every step. Baba told her to always maintain three points of contact, two feet and a hand, whenever she tried to climb something that felt difficult. Between the branches she can make out shimmers of light and sparkles of blue, and what looks like a dark rock that must have fallen and landed in the centre of the small patch of sand down by the water's edge. Concentrating on keeping a steady footing, she decides to wait to really look at the cove until her feet are on firmer ground. It will be easier going back up, as she is clearing the way as she goes. Just the last bit and – there, that is sand under her feet. Pushing the hanging fig leaves out of her face she turns to view the hidden cove of her childhood, and her hand goes to her chest at the sight that greets her. 'Ah!' she exclaims. 'That is so sad.'

# Chapter 11

What looked from above like a large dark rock, lying there in the sand, is in fact a donkey. Just its head, front legs and shoulders are out of the water. The animal is motionless, its coat smooth and glistening, wet. The current must have only just washed it up for it to be soaked like that. Its hindquarters are still immersed. The water gets deep here suddenly, Rallou recalls.

But it does not shock her, particularly. Growing up with herds of goats and sheep, and having always kept chickens, she is used to animals dying. But a donkey! It brings back the sadness she felt when Mimou died. Mimou was old, very old, and had been Papous's donkey before he died, and that was before she was even born. Their baba had explained to them all that the donkey was very old and that they must treat it as gently as they could before it died, so no jumping on its back, and they should give it a treat once in a while. Even so, when it happened, it felt as if life would not let her forget the pain of death, the isolation of life – that her mama was gone, that her little sister was gone. It seemed as if death waited at every corner for the ones she loved.

She is older now, and the lifeless donkey on the sand arouses ambivalence in her. Animals and people die; it is a fact. But still, the sight of this poor creature touches something in her: the sadness of life passing, the waste perhaps? Or maybe the urgency created by the awareness that life can be cut so short with no warning, and must be lived. Rallou knows.

The water splashes against one of the animal's hooves, covering it with a thin layer of sand. Rallou lets her bags, with the bread and eggs and feta, slip from her shoulders softly onto the sand and on impulse she strokes the animal's muzzle. They always look so soft, but she was nipped by a donkey as a child and has since kept a distance from their downy lips and nostrils.

The poor animal is still warm. It must have been in the sea for a very short time; donkeys do not have the grease in their coats to keep water from their skin that horses do, and she had expected the creature to be quite cold. Curiosity brings her to her knees as she studies its face. She has never really examined one so closely before; on the island donkeys are there to do a job, and for years – since she has lived in Orino town, anyway – she has seen them without really seeing them, as she might a pickup truck, or any other device for carrying heavy loads. But, with its soft muscle against her fingers, the warmth of its skin indicating the recent passing of its life, she finds herself recalling her experience in London.

'Today's activities,' said the tour guide, who was plump and chewed gum endlessly, in a voice designed to cut through the chatter that accompanied breakfast at the hotel, 'will include' – she looked at her notes – 'a trip to the British Museum.' Rallou thought this sounded rather dull. There was a museum on her island with displays about the ships' captains who had lived there, and after her third visit she had found it very boring indeed.

'This will be followed,' the fat girl continued, 'by a visit to Madame Tussauds.' Rallou had heard all about Madame Tussauds, and it appeared that she was not the only one, because a wave of excitement spread through the group at this announcement.

Once at the museum, though, she found herself in room after room full of ceramics from Greece: red-and-black Attica ware, Mycenaean pots with geometric patterns and pictures of octopus painted on them, and frescoes from the Minoan palaces in Crete showing brightly coloured dolphins and tall young men leaping over bulls. In the next room were Egyptian mummies in ornate caskets, with their twisted, blackened fingers and taut, dead cheekbones, and by the time she found her way back to the entrance the group had gone and she had been left behind. She chided herself for her stupidity and felt a momentary sense of panic, which was soon replaced with excitement. Being alone in this big city, with no one in the world knowing where she was, seemed to open up endless possibilities, freeing her from all constraints. Ever sensible though, and lacking the funds for a greater adventure, Rallou looked around for a taxi. She could have asked for Madame Tussauds but if the group were no longer there when she arrived that would necessitate a second taxi back to the hotel. With limited resources for such extravagances she decided one taxi straight to the hotel was the wisest thing to do. 'There you go, darling,' the cabbie called back over his shoulder, indicating the house her group had stayed in the night before, the signs outside advertising *Bed & Breakfast* and *No Vacancies*.

Alighting on the pavement, she debated whether she could put off going straight into the place, with its gloomy hall and breakfast room. If the group were not back yet she could spend some time getting to know the immediate area, the 'real' London – maybe meet some genuine Londoners. That could be even better than the waxworks. These thoughts were crossing through her mind when she felt a sudden sharp tug at her wrist. Looking down, she realised in an instant, and with horror, that she had shut her bag in the door of the taxi and, worse, that the strap was wrapped around her forearm. As the car began to move off she shot forward with amazing speed, only to be stopped by a lamppost, her left shoulder taking the impact. Her head snapped backward and the last thing she remembered thinking was that the postcard she had written for her baba was still in her bag and if she did not get it back she would not be able to post it.

Then lights seemed to go on and off, but at one point she was aware of a handsome man inside a white vehicle telling her to lie still, his fingers on her wrist. It might have been the case that she asked him to go to dinner with her, or maybe that was just a dream. Then it was all dark again. The next time she opened her eyes it was dark, and the same man stood by her bed.

'I just came to see you were all right,' he said, and everything went black again.

Then, with no warning, Rallou awoke again and felt herself rushing upward and backward in a wide cylindrical tunnel, the walls of which were pulsating red, pink and dark orange light. She could feel the wind on her back, her arms and legs splayed out in front of her as if a string attached to her spine was being retracted to its place of origin, pulling her, allowing no resistance. The colours in the shaft shifted as she travelled and she had the sense that she was moving with tremendous speed. Now and then the colours lightened as if the tunnel walls were thinner there, but she knew if she reached out there would be nothing solid to grasp, and in any case the tunnel was wider than she could reach, even if she were able to hold her arms out to the side against the force that was propelling her. She had no power to resist the momentum, and it was clear that she was being taken somewhere. Then just as suddenly as it had started, the movement stopped, and the walls of the tunnel on either side of her grew lighter and widened into white, light area. Rallou turned around and found that she was on the edge of the tunnel, in an elevated position, with a good view all around. From here she stared amazed at the scene before her. In front of her and slightly below her was what appeared to be an endless space full of people busily engaged in some activity, the details of which were unclear. The floor was white, the backdrop was white and the sky was light. But it was the people that she could not take her eyes from. They were not made of flesh and blood, they appeared to be made of light, each glowing.

It was beautiful.

But the greatest impression was how she felt. It was as if her mama's arms were around her again, she felt so loved. No – it was even more than that, more than any love she had ever felt before. She felt totally and absolutely accepted for everything she ever had been and everything she ever could be. Every aspect of her was love here. It was as if she hadn't realised that a part of her was missing, and that that part of her was in this place; here, she felt whole, complete. She felt accepted. She felt love. If ever the word 'bliss' was appropriate then this was it. She was in absolutely bliss and every worry she had ever had, every insecurity she had ever felt was not only extinguished but also understood, by her and everyone around her. How could her life not have been confusing before this experience? Now everything made absolutely sense now and she sighs the deepest and longest sigh or pure flawless contentment.

A being, or maybe a person, appeared at her left-hand side. He, and for some reason she knew it was a 'he' even though his features were obscure so much light as pouring form him, increased the feeling of being loved and accepted and she did not have to ask who he was or what he wanted. Nothing needed explanation, the sensation, the feeling she was enveloped by made sense of it all. The person, the being, the glow of human shaped light began explaining everything and as he did so he gently took hold of her arm, his fingers encircling her left wrist, and the light that he was made from began to creep into her up her arm and down to her fingers. Two more people, beings of light, appeared in front of her, to talk to her. There faces glowed so their features were not discernible, but she knew that she knew them and that they loved her and she loved them.

As she talked with them, the feeling of love grew. This was where she belonged; she had never been so certain of anything ever. This was her home, the pieces of hers that was missing were here, she was complete. But just then, a flicker of memory of the home she grew up in, on the island, images of her father made her doubt herself. It was such a small doubt, so tiny it would have been forgotten in the next second. But it was enough to bring her rushing back down the tube, at a speed faster than she arrive with, until she was left awake and in her bed.

Her body felt heavy, awkward and uncomfortable and she fought to be released but her skin had her trapped. The ward was dimly lit, and Rallou watched a woman in a nurse's uniform walk past the end of her bed. The colours were drab and dim, the place felt alien and she felt very alone and unloved. She closed her eyes and tried to force the tunnel to reopen, force herself to travel up it, to get back to that sanctuary of peace, get back to herself. She wished and wished, and once, in the next forty eight hours she made it part way up the tunnel, and for a moment she was elated that she was going home. But it was not to be. She fell back into her body and awoke in the lightless word.

'She's awake,' a nurse called to a man in a white coat.

It went dark again at that point, and her memory of the next couple of days was hazy. A few days later the man in the white coat stood at the end of her bed with a group of people her own age who looked nervous, and who also wore white coats.

'Ah,' the doctor explained to the group. 'Now here we have a lucky young lady. Cracked C2, broken clavicle, and ribs, four, five and six. Came in in a coma. Didn't seem to have the will to live at one stage and we thought we were going to lose her. But, as you can see, alive and well … But if that break had been a quarter of an inch lower, well, it could have been a different story.' At this point he smiled at her and wagged his finger as if to suggest that she had done something wrong, or that she hadn't taken enough care. Then the smile was gone and he turned to the group to ask, 'Any questions?' There were no questions, and the carnival departed.

'It is a lovely place, donkey. I hope that you can go there,' she says wistfully. She has never told anyone about this experience. It feels too important, too special, to dilute it by putting it into words. 'But you won't go there if you are not ready,' she adds.

With one finger she delicately traces the soft fur around the animal's eye. An involuntary tiny tick seems to spasm the muscle in its cheek. Did she imagine it? Was it a reflex, a cadaver's twitch of a nerve to the spinal cord? She jerks back and looks at the animal. Nothing has changed and her hope drains.

Then – there! It did it again.

The animal coughs and water comes from its mouth, momentarily turning the sand beneath its jawbone darker before draining away. It coughs again and wheezes. Its eyelids flicker and open. It is alive! A hoof digs into the sand but it has no strength to lever itself out of the water.

'Hang on,' she whispers. With one leg either side of the donkey's neck she curls her hands underneath and tries to pull, but it is a dead weight.

'Come on, donkey – help!' With this, she jumps into the water and rummages for buckles and clasps, releasing the wooden saddle with its blanket covering, pushing it off onto the sand. Feeling along the donkey's back, she finds its hind legs. The last time she was here, in this cove, she would have been out of her depth in the water that now seems relatively shallow. She bends her knees and puts her shoulder under the donkey's rump to push. 'Move!' she shouts, and slaps its haunches, and immediately regrets this as the water around the donkey's back end begins to turn red with blood. But the slap creates a reaction, and the animal weakly struggles. Her heart pounds and it is as if her strength doubles. She pushes as the front hooves momentarily scramble and the poor creature manages to pull itself more fully onto the beach.

'Good girl. Go on!' She wonders if the exertion has killed it, but then its chest labours.

'How did you get here?' she asks it breathlessly as she pushes its rump. Perhaps it has fallen from the coastal path that leads to Orino town, and floated here. If that is the case then it must have had quite a fall.

It is harder to get out of the sea, given the steep gradient, than it was to get in, but she has energy she did not know she possessed and is crouching by the donkey's head in seconds. She has not managed to move the animal far up the beach, but it is mostly out of the water now, and the sun will warm it once its coat dries out.

'Just lay there, my beauty,' she tells it. Maybe she should run to the boatyard for help. With tender fingers she slips off the bridle.

The sun is still rising and now it peeps past the top of the fig tree, casting its warm and healing rays on the shoulder of the beast. Another five minutes and its head is in sunshine, its fur drying fast. As the donkey warms up, its breathing becomes more even, less laboured, and the panic that was in its eyes dims.

It would be better if she could get its back leg out of the water to see what the damage is. The animal also needs to be out of the water so it can dry fully, stay warm.

Looking around the cove, she searches for anything useful that might have been washed ashore. The inevitable beer bottle is half buried, and by a rock sits what looks like a black fly swat and the pink of a plastic clothes peg. Further along the short stretch of sand lies a sun-decayed plastic bag and a half-buried aluminium pan without a handle. As if to mock the situation, sitting upright by the water's edge, bright in the sun, is a modest-sized yellow rubber duck, the kind sold for children to play with in the bath. Its orange beak is slightly the worse for wear. There is nothing else, useful or otherwise.

A slight breeze reminds her that her own clothes are wet now.

'Scarf!' She rouses herself as she unwraps the length of material from around her head and neck. She does not have to get back into the water to loop it around the donkey's rump and, with one end of the scarf in each hand, she tries once more to slide the donkey all the way onto dry land. As she does so the animal's head is repositioned relative to its body. After dragging the beast sideways onto the shore, she is much relieved to see that the donkey is alive enough to move its head so as not to twist its neck.

The back legs are all black with wet, which accentuates the pink and bloody split in its skin and muscle. Rallou clicks her tongue against the back of her teeth. They may be tough little beasts when they are well but that is a wound that will be hard to recover from. What is worse is the gash lower down, near its hoof. If the tendon is gone then there will be nothing much anybody can do for the poor ass.

# Chapter 12

She needs to get some help, find out whose the donkey is, and get in touch with the owner. After laying her wet scarf over some low-slung fig branches to dry, she heads for the path that leads out of the cove. Halfway up, moving with speed, she grabs a handful of the fleshy, slightly spiky leaves growing from a crevice for support. The whole plant comes away from the rock face, leaving her off balance. At this moment, a new thought hits her.

'No!' she cries, and, using her instability to her advantage, she twists and, more quickly than she ascended, part-runs, part-slides back down to the donkey to look again at the animal's leg.

'There's a good chance they will shoot you in your condition, little donkey,' she says to the animal, the verbalisation of this thought helping her to come to terms with it. 'If I get help and they think the damage is too great …' The sentence trails away.

Maybe she can help the animal to recover sufficiently so they would not consider shooting him. She has the patience to help it heal. She can remember nights sitting up with one or another of the children, mopping fevered brows, reading stories, telling tales, and changing the sheets as they sweated out their illnesses. She would never leave their side. Harris saw this, and praised and encouraged her. Christos also commented, but not in the same way. Yes, she could help the donkey heal. But every owner is different, and who is to say what this donkey's owner would think of that? She crouches and strokes the mule's forehead, pushing its fringe from its eyes.

'How well will you have to be to assure your future, my furry friend?' she asks it.

Still in her other hand are the fleshy leaves that came away from the rock face.

'Samphire,' she announces and puts the plant to the donkey's lips. 'Are you hungry?' She asked the same question of little Natasa, her forehead so hot, her eyes so wide, hugging her bear before the fever broke. How she sweated and cried, poor little thing. Rallou sat by her bed day and night, ready with a glass of water and morsels of food to tempt her back to her happy little self.

'You not coming to bed then?' Christos had asked. She didn't bother to answer. 'You will be good for nothing if you are too tired. Go to bed and I will sit with her for a while,' he pressed.

But sitting with little Natasa 'for a while' was not good enough. What if she woke in the middle of the night with no one there, or got worse? No, she had to stay. That's what mamas do. If Natasa fell asleep she would wake at the slightest sound, whereas Christos would sleep through anything.

Maybe this is the same situation. Maybe this donkey also needs a mama's touch, that extra bit of care, just until it can get on its feet again. The mule's lips curl over the succulent plant and it makes an attempt to chew, but lying on its side seems to make this difficult. Perhaps she should treat the wound first. Help its recovery first, then tempt it to eat.

'I need *myriofyllo*, or aloe vera, or even sempervivum,' she tells it. There may be some *myriofyllo* left in the shade of the trees further up the hill if she is lucky, but spring has come and gone and the heat and sun may have shrivelled any remaining plants. Her best bet is probably the aloe vera that Kaloyannis's grandfather has planted around the edge of his abandoned olive orchard. There must be a dozen plants there, now growing wild. Leaving the donkey bravely trying to chew, she heads off up the path out of the cove again, her legs moving with purpose, finding her footing. The olive grove is not far along a rough rack, which is overgrown with long grasses. Brightly coloured grasshoppers jump and whir out of her way as she passes, making a wave with each step. She finds the plants and takes two or three leaves from each, pulling them back on themselves to tear them free, being careful of the spiky edges. She gathers an armful and carries them back to the cove, and notes that, although she tried to be careful to avoid the thorns, her arms are coming up in a red rash.

Back in the cove she searches her bags to see what her baba has put in apart from bread and feta.

There are the eggs, of course, and he has also popped in a tin of sardines and a sharp knife.

'Bless you,' she calls to him and pictures the wind whipping her words up the valley to the top of the island.

She tentatively puts her hand above the gash by the animal's hoof and is relieved to find it is not hot and there are no signs of infection. This gives her hope. Using the point of the knife she carefully lifts the flap of skin to examine it more closely. The gash looks horrible but it is not too deep, and the donkey does not react. Maybe it is not as bad as she first thought.

Cutting both ends off one of the aloe vera leaves, she deftly strips off the thick green outer coat to reveal the transparent gelatinous interior. This she slices thinly, then she lays the pieces side by side to cover the whole wound. When she runs out she begins on a second leaf, then a third and a fourth. Once both wounds are covered with the aloe vera gel, she continues to strip the leaves and then scrapes out the viscous secretion that lies just beneath the outer coating, to form a layer over the more solidified gel strips.

Once the wound is awash with aloe vera goodness in all its forms she allows herself to relax. This will speed the healing process, form a protective barrier and keep flies from landing on the raw flesh. She rubs her hands together and wipes what's left of the sticky gel on her face. It will do her good too.

The serum dries quite quickly, first on her skin and then on the wounds. As time passes, the gelatinous strips oxidise and turn a dull pinky-red, becoming firmer to the touch. In a few hours she will very carefully remove the strips, if they will lift, and replace them with fresh pieces. She has brought enough leaves to the cove to repeat this several times.

Hunger begins to remind her how long it has been since breakfast and she contemplates boiling some of the eggs. She could use the abandoned pan that is half buried in the sand and boil them in seawater, but does she have matches? As it turns out, she does not, neither in her bags nor in her pockets, so she settles for the bread and feta. With a full stomach she decides that a second application of aloe vera will not harm the donkey, and maybe the fresher the serum is the quicker the wound will heal. The sun is now quite high and it is hot, but the aloe vera strips will keep the wounds cool and the fig tree provides some shade. She shuffles backward and leans against the saddle to survey her charge in the relative cool, and soon sleep takes her.

She wakes slowly, thinking at first that the donkey is actually Natasa and that she has failed to be vigilant. But as she comes to her senses she remembers where she is and recalls the whole situation, and wonders how long she slept.

The wound on the animal's hindquarters has now taken on a pinkish tinge and is firm to the touch, oxidised. She wonders if she should apply fresh gel, but she has used up all the leaves, and the discarded green shells are now curled and hard where she piled them. The gash above the donkey's hoof looks even better than she had hoped, and perhaps it won't be a problem at all.

Rallou's next hour is spent gathering more aloe vera and treating both the wounds, and in this time the donkey lifts its head once or twice to look over its shoulder at what she is doing. The plant is so gentle it causes no sting or suffering and she can already see the difference its medicinal properties are making.

The donkey occasionally tries to nibble a little at the samphire but with no great enthusiasm. The afternoon is passing quickly, and it would be better if they could move away from the water's edge before evening as the night will be very cold on the beach at this time of year. Even in the hottest days of August the nights are chilly right down by the water.

'Why aren't you trying to get up?' she says to the donkey on several occasions, but it continues to lie there, blinking, occasionally sighing, but making no attempt to stand. She needs to take some action, make sure its night is comfortable enough and that it is warm enough to sleep. Rest is the best medicine.

'Sleep, my little Natasa,' she whispered. 'Sleep my little doll.' The child's fever broke eventually, and colour returned to her cheeks but the whole ordeal frightened the life out of Rallou.

'You need to sleep too.' Christos put his head around the door.

She did need to sleep, she really did, but what if Natasa got worse again? What if she cried out and Rallou did not hear? No, she had better stay here.

'Rallou, come, you must sleep, you cannot keep up this vigil,' Christos urged, but she did not answer him and he shrugged and left, and his snoring could be heard shortly afterwards. He was right, she was overcome with exhaustion; but in her mind it was not her own daughter's light breathing she could hear in the night, but the whimperings of Evgenia as her burns continued to eat into her skin as the days after the accident passed and nothing could be done for her.

The donkey shivers.

'Oh, my little *koukla*,' she says softly. 'Hang on, I will get you a blanket.'

The walk to the boatyard is not a long one, and the light in the windows of the Kaloyannis house glow like orange eyes in the near dark, casting a subdued light over the yard. The grounded boats are held on their keels by wooden supports on either side as if they each have six or eight legs: an army of giant wooden insects ready to come alive when the sun rises again. If she does not hurry, the light will fade completely and she will find it difficult to get back down to the cove unless there is a full moon. She ducks from boat to boat, making sure that if anyone is looking from the window they will not see. The Kaloyannis brothers and their family are good people and it is natural that they would phone around the island to find the donkey's missing owner, but that would come with such a risk! She keeps moving until she finds a fishing boat, one that looks like it is being recaulked, which has a tarpaulin folded neatly inside it. With this tucked under her arm she makes her way back. The waxed sheet is heavy but it will keep them both warm. The donkey needs a name. She called it her little *koukla* – doll – earlier. Adults are always calling children their little dolls. She misses her own little dolls, and the role she played as their mama. At one point, motherhood felt like her mission in life, and there is a gap now the children are all gone. She never thought about how it would be once they had all left home until it actually happened. Now the reality is there for her every day, and she is becoming increasing aware that there is very little left to fulfil her life. Except the Americans. But is that really a good use of someone's life, she wonders for the first time – to play servant to the rich, no matter how nice they are?

It is almost dark as she reaches the descent to the cove and as she nears the bottom she can see the donkey scrabbling a little. It must be very aware that it is bait for dogs just lying there.

'It's all right, my little *koukla*, it is only me.' The donkey is also afraid of the tarpaulin as she opens it out. It is bigger than she thought and she doubles it over to make two layers. Curling into the mule's back, transferring her warmth to it and vice versa, she feels sleepy but strangely happy. There is no moonlight and she does not know if the donkey closes its eyes first or if she does.

# Chapter 13

The next day she repeats the aloe vera treatment a few times, again pouring the viscous liquid between the jelly-like strips to make sure the wounds are fully coated, and she swears she can almost see the healing taking place. But she worries that the donkey has not tried to stand yet. Maybe it has hurt itself internally, or it is wounded on its other side, the side that it is lying on. As she ate most of the feta yesterday, and she fed most of the bread to the donkey, there is not much of either left. She cleans out the saucepan that was half buried in the sand in case she decides to boil the eggs but then remembers that she has no matches. She is well aware that Greg will now be sleeping in fairly dirty sheets. The last thing she wants is for Lori and Ted to think she is shirking her responsibilities. She looks at the animal, unsure that she can leave it. Apart from being a living creature, it is also someone's livelihood, someone who is on the island, not half a world away in America.

But in reality there is not much more she can do. It is just a waiting game. If she keeps applying the aloe vera, she feels almost certain, the wounds will heal, all will be well. But the beast has not tried to stand, not really, and the bread it ate was such a small amount.

On the waves of the sea the memory comes to her of a conversation that she once overheard between Baba and Yanni. It ripples up the inlet to her like a gift. She looks up and out to the entrance of the cove, the shoreline of which is so convoluted she cannot see the sea.

In her mind's eye she can see the two men standing, facing each other, hands in pockets, talking.

'Ah, you see, if donkeys don't eat they are very susceptible to ...' And the wave recedes, leaving the sentence unfinished as her memory fades. She cannot remember the word, but when she blinks slowly it comes back to her.

'Hyperlipaemia, especially after stress,' Yanni's voice says.

It was a time when her baba visited her in town. Every day he sat in the back yard looking a little lost until Yanni passed by on his way into town for his day's work hauling things from the port to people's houses and shops, or later, in the early evening when he began his return journey home. Her baba would call something out to him, a cheerful *kalimera*, causing him to stop to answer, and a conversation would always develop. Rallou knew Yanni's mountain mentality suited her baba more than her own way of thinking, which was now more aligned to that of her neighbours in the town.

'Not much chance of them living if they get that,' Yanni had continued. 'More so if they are old or overweight.'

Rallou looks at the donkey; it is not fat, but it does look like it could be old, with its white muzzle and whiskers around its eyes.

'Don't die,' she tells it gently as the rest of the conversation comes to her: if a donkey does not eat but expends a lot of energy then it turns to its fat reserves like all animals, but, as Yanni explained to her baba, donkeys are not able to turn off the fat release process and their blood can become saturated with fat, leading to liver and kidney failure.

'That's a strange reaction,' her baba had said.

'But how soon does that happen?' she asks the absent Yanni.

'People don't understand donkeys,' Yanni had gone on to explain. 'They say they are stubborn, but that is because they have this cut-off mechanism so you cannot work them too hard. Their systems will just stop and they won't move if they are overtaxed. Horses do not have this, and you can work them to death, but it is not so with donkeys.'

'Ah, now, I didn't know that.' Her baba had been feeding the chickens and had the apron on, the string done up in a bow at the back, so this conversation must have been up at the house at Korifi. A different conversation.

'But these cut-off systems also work against them. Like, after a shock donkeys tend to stop eating, so that is when they turn to their fat reserves, which is when they can get hyperlipaemia.'

'Is it hard to pull them back from it? How do you know they have it?'

'They get sad, they don't want to eat. The only way to get them out of it is to make them eat so they have more in the system so the body no longer has to break down the fat.'

'How on earth do you know all this?' her baba had asked him, with a laugh behind his words, clearly enjoying the mental stimulus.

Rallou returns her thoughts to the present. 'You need to eat!' she tells her *koukla*, her doll.

The cove is lined with rock, and samphire grows everywhere. She grabs a handful and offers it to the reclining mule. It does not even sniff.

'Come on, you have to eat.' Her own stomach rumbles. The eggs will need boiling if she is to stay another night. Maybe donkeys cannot eat if they are lying down. That's a possibility. Maybe what she needs to do is to make the animal stand, encourage it to the next stage. It would be a good idea to put the bridle back on now, then. This proves more difficult than taking it off. The animal's head is heavy and is lying on the sand. The buckles have stiffened with dried seawater, which has left a fine layer of salt on the brown leather. But the donkey shows no resistance and, once the last buckle is firm, she strokes its nose to tell it she means no harm, and then she gently pulls the animal forward. At first there is no response, then its neck stretches and its head comes forward, and, as she continues to pull, it drags one front hoof from under itself and then the other, straightens them out as best it can and makes a feeble and shaky attempt to stand.

'Well done, Koukla – go on, girl!' She wonders if this is what it feels like to be a donkey man. 'Come on, keep trying.' She pulls harder and, after a final tug, the animal is on its feet, although rather unsteady.

'Oh, you are clever,' she tells it, and steps towards it and pats its neck. Now it is on its feet she knows she definitely recognises this donkey. There is something about the way it stands, the flick of its forelock. Of course! It is Yanni's donkey.

'Dolly?' she says, hardly able to believe the situation. The animal flicks its ears. 'Dolly, is that you?' The animal makes no response. It has locked its legs but is swaying ever so slightly.

As if knowing the donkey by name has given her power, she snatches handfuls of samphire from the rock faces and thrusts them under Yanni's beloved animal's nose. At first it responds tentatively, but soon with some relish. The swaying stops and the animal begins to look just like any other donkey, except for the gash on the leg, from which all the aloe vera strips have fallen now it is vertical. The viscous goo remains, however. Rallou gathers armfuls of samphire and places them in a heap in front of Dolly, then she gathers up her bags.

'Right!' she says. 'There is no way in the world Yanni is ever going to shoot you, so I am off to tell him where you are.' Dolly slowly lowers her head and takes a mouthful of the plump leaves. A frown crosses Rallou's brow. What must Yanni think has become of his favoured workmate? Surely he was leading her, if she was on the coastal path? He must be distraught to think he has lost her to the sea. Poor Yanni.

Her legs do not propel her fast enough and the coastal walk into town seems longer than usual. The sun is high in the sky and the heat is slowing her down. The calm waters along the coast are the most magnificent blue-green and so clear it is possible to see the bottom; the sands there are rippled and dotted with pebbles, small fish darting over their surface. The temptation to jump in and cool down is huge but there is no time for that. At one point, just before she is on the straight stretch into town, the track narrows, as if the ground has collapsed at this point. Maybe that is where Dolly fell?

The first house appears at the smaller inlet and the path dips down and then back up the other side as she passes silent houses and tavernas. It is later than she thought, already *mesimeri*, and everyone will be sleeping the midday heat away. A rather red-skinned woman wearing a brightly patterned, see-through kaftan over a bikini and carrying her flip-flops is coming the other way. She is not Greek: German maybe, or English. As they pass each other, Rallou can smell her sun cream and a whiff of something else, a more complex scent. There will only be tourists about in town at this time of day.

Shopkeepers will be hiding at the back of their shops, general workers will be at home, and there is a very good chance that the donkey men will be home too. Maybe one, or even two, will remain, hopeful of trade, looking out for tourists who want rides. But the one-day-tour ship that comes from Piraeus will have left by now so even that is not very likely. Those that wanted rides, or transport for their suitcases to their hotels, will already have been catered for.

If there are no donkey men, who should she tell? The first name that comes to mind is Christos. Yanni will pass the back of the house, and Christos could let him know where Dolly is and that she needs attention. Rallou must get word to Yanni, but she must also get on with her life, change Greg's sheets, make preparations for Lori and Ted's arrival, and get back up to her baba's before it's too late in the day and she has to find her way in the dark. There are no street lamps in the hills. But asking Christos, her husband of twenty-nine years, to let Yanni know where Dolly is so he can properly attend to her wounds somehow seems like a lot to ask, even for Dolly's well-being; there should be no question, and yet there is.

# Chapter 14

The coastal path turns right and the view of the town opens up before her – the houses fanned around the port, from the water's edge and up the hill, arranged in a semicircle facing out to sea, like an ancient amphitheatre, with the port itself forming the stage. Even though she has been up and down to her mountain home hundreds of times, that last turning into civilisation always affects her deeply. When she was a girl the town thrilled her, and when she first got married, too: it was to be their future home. She had expected the nights of passion that started on their brief honeymoon, taken at Mandraki, just along the coast from Orino town, to continue once they moved into their home. The excitement was mixed with fervor and she expected this feeling to trail endlessly into the future in this town. But the white of the wedding dress had all too quickly become the white of the first child's christening gown, and the nights of joy that had once been theirs became a sleepless time of tending to and feeding the baby.

As she turns the corner into the town this time, it strikes her how removed from nature town life is – her life too – and how that distance knocks people off balance without them even noticing. But no sooner has she had this thought than it is replaced with another. 'What do you know?' she says to herself. 'Maybe there are some people who feel out of balance when they are in the country.' But she does not believe her own words; even humans are animals at heart.

Talking to herself is keeping her mind from her aching legs, however, and from her empty stomach. It is a relief to be in town now because she really needs to stop, catch her breath.

There is not a single donkey man on the front. She looks down the right and left arms of the enclosed harbour. No, not one!

'*Gamo* ...' She begins to swear to herself.

'*Yeia sou*, Rallou,' a voice calls out from the shady interior of one of the shops, its owner hidden in the depths.

'Oh, *yeia sou*,' Rallou replies, but does not slow her pace. Maybe the donkey men are at their favourite *kafenio*, but then why are the donkeys not tied up on the corner?

'*Yeia sou*, Rallou,' another voice calls. It is Aris in his jewellery shop. He was such a slim boy when they were at school together, and now he is like a barrel.

'*Yeia sou*, Ari,' she calls but keeps going. It is only when she reaches the corner where the donkeys usually stand that she allows herself to stop. No donkeys at all. What is she going to do?

From under the shade of an umbrella at the nearest cafe, a lean figure neatly dressed in cream linen stands and raises a broad-rimmed white hat in greeting. 'Rallou!' The man's address is unhurried and he smiles as he speaks, his eyes glinting and a day's growth of stubble giving an edge of ruggedness to what is otherwise a civilised and educated face.

'Oh! Hello, Mr Greg,' Rallou replies. This is bad timing.

'Do you have a moment?' says Greg. 'There are a few problems in the house … Nothing big, just little things that I am sure you will solve in an instant.' It does not sound like he really has any concerns about the house. His speech is slow and he lowers himself back into his chair. A bright slice of sun cuts through the space between the awning, which stretches from the building nearly to the water's edge, and that of the neighbouring cafe. The cafe Greg is at is only two tables across, with blue-painted woodwork.

'Well, I – actually …' she begins, but as she speaks she realises that she cannot put the donkey first right now. There is no one to ask about Yanni. Nor is there anywhere for her to go. She has no intention of going home, not yet. Not until she is clearer in her mind. So maybe it makes sense to change Greg's sheets and attend to the little jobs he is referring to. She can also sweep the Americans' yard and water the plants. She has plenty of time until the donkey men are back. She can deal with Christos later, if she wants to deal with him at all.

'Oh, you are busy – never mind.' Greg picks up his frappé and sucks on the straw.

'No!' She takes a breath. 'No, it is fine. What can I do for you?'

'Well, I have just finished here.' He stands again and pulls some euros from his pocket and drops them on the table. 'Shall we go up to the house so I can show you?'

She doesn't answer, but she sets off in the right direction, up past the lace shops, where Kyria Anna, Kyria Georgia and Kyria Vetta are sitting outside their tiny emporiums, their fingers twitching and spinning the lace webs with hardly a glance at what they are doing. They each smile at her and wish her good day, and she feels their eyes follow her as Greg falls into step beside her.

'I haven't seen you around these last few days,' he begins again after a pause. His pace is slow and after her determined march along the coastal path Rallou has to consciously reduce her speed. As she does so the sense of urgency that has accompanied her all the way to town diminishes slightly. Yanni will be told and Dolly will be treated well and she will heal. As far as the donkey is concerned, all is well in the world.

'I went up to see my baba,' Rallou says lightly, entering into the lightness of Greg's mood.

'Ah, good, how is he?' Greg puts his hands in his front pockets. The tension that surrounded him when he first arrived on the island seems to have gone and he looks well rested. The creases around his eyes do not age him; rather, they make him look at if he is laughing all the time. The indentations either side of his mouth are so deep it is as if he is smiling even when he is not. All in all he looks a lot like his father, Ted, but he has Lori's colouring, his blonde hair greying just above his ears. There is no way he could be mistaken for anything but an American. She wants to ask how he is feeling about his wife, or ex-wife, but she is not sure such a question would be appropriate. It is one she might ask of her closer Greek acquaintances, but he is not Greek, in any way.

She is just about to answer his question and say that her baba is fine, but it makes her think twice and she wonders how he really is. She was so full of herself and her problems with Christos when she was up there that she avoided any serious conversation with him.

'I think he is lonely.' A lump forms in her throat.

'Yes, I can imagine. Does he not want to come down here and live with you and Christos?'

'There is a little – how shall I put it …? Friction. He does not like the town.' Rallou says.

'Hm, like father, like son-in-law,' he quips.

It does not make her smile.

As they near the house she looks first across to her own whitewashed home to see the grey-blue, paint-peeling doors and shutters all shut tight.

Christos will be sleeping, his snores echoing through the house, Arapitsa curled up in the shade on the floor by the back door, her chin on her front paws: resting, but with ears alert. A glance towards Harris's house reveals that her windows are open, and a shadow, a silhouette of a person passes through the interior. Rallou hopes it is not Harris herself, to whom she would feel obliged to explain her recent absence. No, best not to be seen, not yet. In fact, she does not really want to be seen by anyone, greeted casually and asked how she is, where she has been, as if it is any of their business!

'Here we are.' Greg politely steps to one side for her to enter first through the tall wooden gate, a white slash in the grey stone wall. In view of the rumours, perhaps being away for a few days and then going straight to Lori and Ted's house with Greg will look bad if anyone is watching. Maybe she can make an excuse to go home first, step into the house quietly, not wake Christos, be seen to be doing the right thing: be more discreet, as Christos puts it. She glances over again to Harris's window and thinks she can make out the silhouette retreating deeper inside. She hesitates before entering.

'Everything all right?' Greg asks, the gate still held open.

'Yes, fine.' Rallou shakes her head. She will not be pulled into the gossipers' games. She enters the garden and walks along towards the house. But there is something about the building that does not seem right, and for a second she cannot put her finger on it. Skipping through her mental notes she checks off all that she needs to do before Ted and Lori arrive. The sheets are done ... Well, no, that is not true – there are the pillowcases that Christos trod underfoot, which will need washing and ironing again. For a moment she dwells on his behaviour, her breath shortening, but she stops herself and draws her attention back to the house. The plants all need attention, the dead leaves and flowers need removing and the soil raking out underneath. The balcony needs another good sweep and a scrub, and the kitchen – well, she has not cleaned all the cupboards yet and little insects will have crawled through crevices and made tiny homes or left little trails in the silent interiors. She told Greg she had not done this yet and he did not seem to care in the least.

'Oh!' Greg murmurs as they walk around to the front entrance. At the top of the steps the heavy double doors are wide open, the dark interior a sharp contrast to the bright white walls that reflect the sun outside. The vivid orange geraniums in their heavy terracotta urns either side of the door cast heavy shadows. Rallou puts a hand up to shield her eyes from the sun, to see if she can see anyone or anything inside. Just for a second – and she has no idea why she thinks this – she wonders if Christos has broken in, perhaps with the aim of checking whether the rumours are right!

# Chapter 15

Rallou's eyes adjust to the dark inside the house, and she blinks several times. Greg, slightly in front of her now, must be doing the same because he does not move. Inside the house, everything has been moved slightly; some of the cushions she carefully arranged on the sofa have been piled on the floor, but that could have been Greg. The blinds, which have remained closed since Greg's arrival, are now pulled wide open, exposing the balcony and the view down to the port. Most notably, to Rallou, the Turkish chest that sits on the Chinese carpet is open, its lid thrown back.

'I knew you would turn up sooner or later!' There is no doubting the voice and both Rallou and Greg turn to see Lori coming out of the kitchen, whisky and soda in hand.

'Mom!' Greg breaks into a broad grin and loses all his adult mannerisms, rushing to her like a boy. When he reaches her, though, it is he who pulls her in, instead of the other way round, his arms around her protectively, her head pulled in under his chin as if she is the child.

'My poor boy,' she says, pulling away to study his face, and Rallou presumes she is referring to his divorce.

'Ah, Greg! There you are!' Ted is right behind Lori, also with a drink in hand. They shake hands and hug.

Thoughts of the pillowcases that Christos stood on, that need rewashing, the flowers that need deadheading, the dust on the balcony and in the kitchen cupboards all rush at Rallou, and her cheeks flame hot. Her neglect of her duties is apparent and for one dizzy moment she wonders if Lori will release her from her position for her lax behaviour. If she were to explain why things have been left undone, that would mean divulging the state of her relationship with Christos, and the intimacies of her life with her husband are not something she has discussed with Lori. There is no doubt Lori would be understanding, and certainly supportive. But how would she explain? The words to describe how she is feeling do not come even when she takes the time to contemplate the situation. Besides, Lori's world is not full of messy relationships, long-harboured resentments and unspoken anger. As far as Lori is concerned, Rallou is happily married to her childhood sweetheart, who is a fine hunter and one of the men on the island who can turn his hand to any job that needs doing. He has been employed by the *dimos* to mend public pavements and fix telegraph wires, and by locals to rebuild walls and replace window frames, and also by foreigners to paint their houses and fix all manner of problems. He has done work for Lori too, at Rallou's request, but never in the owners' presence. Their image of him is of a hard-working, rural islander. Blinking a few times, she wonders why she has considered this an *image*. Is that not who he is? Does everyone on the island see him this way? Everyone except her, maybe?

'And Rallou!' Lori cries, and her arms open in greeting. Her wide smile is full of warmth. It seems she has not seen all the things that need doing, or that she does not mind that they have not yet been done. That would be typical of her. Arriving earlier than anticipated, she would perhaps not expect the house to be ready at all, and Rallou is aware that she has had a little panic for nothing. It was her own harsh judgement that she reacted to and it has nothing to do with Lori's generous nature.

Lori's smile grows as she reaches towards her for the customary kiss on each cheek. But as the distance between them narrows Lori's smiles changes, the corners drop and she begins to grimace. Her eyes narrow as she looks right and left, frowning, and her face distorts. Rallou reaches out to grab the door frame. Her legs become boneless and the ground turns to water.

'Outside!' Rallou commands. The ground is moving so much that Lori's glass slips from her hand and smashes on the tiles, and Lori follows it, her knees making the first impact. The glass cuts into her and blood seeps over the marble floor.

'Lori!' Ted shouts, grabbing the table for stability as he reaches for his wife. Greg shuffles to his mother, palms flat against the wall.

'Outside!' Rallou repeats, shouting this time as the tremor grows. It feels like a big one. Holding fast to the door, she reaches out to Lori and slides palm against palm, only their fingers gripping. Lori's other hand is held by Ted. Greg has hold of his mum around her waist and the three of them, Rallou acting as the anchor, sway on wavering legs, slide their feet across the floor towards the door, the urgency showing on their faces. In the kitchen, plates and cups rattle. Something heavy crashes to the floor in the rooms above their heads and the lid of the Turkish chest slams shut.

They all grab the door frame round Rallou. One of the terracotta planters wobbles on its narrow base and topples sideways, and Rallou quickly steps out of the way to save her toes. The pot rolls past her, thuds heavily down the steps. Trees between buildings are rustling madly, and there is the sound of a branch cracking and falling. Screaming can be heard from every corner. Dogs bark frantically and a donkey calls its terror.

'To the street!' Rallou is halfway to the gate. Greg and Ted still hold on to Lori as the blood from her knee runs down her shin, covering her foot, curling under the sole of her sandal, and as she tries to walk her foot slides in her own life source. Tiles begin to slip from the roof and one lands on the flags beside them, adding an urgency to their movements.

More screams are heard from all corners of the town. Rallou casts a glance around her. Everything is shaking, swaying, and there are voices shouting for help in every direction. Another donkey brays, a tremoring wail of fear, and Rallou crosses herself with her free hand and hopes that Dolly is safe, that fear forces her up the path from the cove. She will be safe in the olive grove. And Baba! What of him?

The tremors grow worse. Crashes can be heard inside the house and inside the other homes around them. A thud comes from the depths of Ted and Lori's upper floor, through the windows that have been flung open, glass shattering. Visible through the gaping front door, the hall table crashes over, spilling flowers and water over the tiles.

They are not the first to arrive on the street outside. The neighbours who are already there are shouting to each other, arms gesticulating, legs wavering; children and the elderly are being supported by parents and offspring. They are in nightclothes, housecoats, shirtsleeves. One man is wearing just a pair of shorts. Unseen islanders are still screaming in the lanes behind and to the side of Lori and Ted's house, and Rallou looks around for Christos. Surely he will be there any minute. She will be in his arms and they will be safe. Neighbours up and down are still hurrying from narrow passageways to take refuge in the wide causeway where nothing can fall on them. People stream like rats to the central artery and, once there, watch their feet for cracks that might appear and stare in disbelief at the falling buildings, mesmerised by the horror of it all. They huddle with their backs to each other as tiles cascade off rooftops and buildings crack diagonally. Walls begin to crumble and fall, thunderously booming as they impact, and the sky fills with dust, lacing the air with a smell of age, plaster and fear. Whole sides of houses shift, rumbling as they move in an unearthly manner, leaving black open seams at corners of building where no openings should be. Dogs come yelping, seeking people's legs for sanctuary. There is not a cat in sight; they have their own ways. The Americans' house is shimmying to such a degree that the two central pillars between the three main windows both crack, the render splitting away and falling first, leaving exposed stone. Then the stones fall, first one by one, with a trickle of sand and mortar, then as a mass, bouncing as they land on each other. From the end wall, centuries-old plaster shears off, disintegrating as it hits the floor in a cloud of dust.

Lori screams at the sight, breathes sharply and then lets out a shout of surprise and disbelief. Other similar shrieks can be heard to the left, to the right, in front, behind: the air is filled with shock.

Beneath their feet the stone paving creaks, and people cling to each other. A small girl in a blue dress urinates down her leg and her mama pulls her close, pushes her child's face into her stomach, her arms around her for protection.

As another wave rattles through the earth, Lori's legs give way and she is on the floor again, as is old Kyria Vetta from next door but one. Kyria Vetta's son is also on his knees, holding and trying to calm his mama. Kyria Vetta is screaming, her arms outstretched towards her house.

'Baba, Baba, Baba!' the girl in the blue dress cries. The girl's mama has lines of tears on her dust-covered cheeks. Greg and Ted are by Lori, supporting, holding. Rallou looks back to Harris's house; it hasn't moved but it shimmers like a mirage, and looks unreal. As the trembling subsides, her anxiety is no longer focused on herself. Where is Christos? Where is Harris?

'Baba, Baba, Baba!' the girl continues to scream. The rumbling is quieting, which allows the shouting from all parts of the town to be heard more clearly.

A man covered with debris comes out of a cloud that was his home. He clutches four kittens. The mama leaves the child, runs and hugs him. The girl shouts 'Baba' again, but this time with relief.

But where is Christos? Her legs want to run. But in which direction? Where is he?

Another tremor.

'Aftershock!' someone shouts. The people on the street freeze for a moment, then they turn to each other with fear in their eyes as they take hold of one another for support and reassurance. There is a high-pitched splintering, friction of wood on wood. Behind them is a telegraph pole; it begins to topple, the cracking and screeching increasing as it gains momentum and crashes across the breadth of the street. People dart out of its way; a man grabs a boy who would otherwise have been crushed, his legs dangling from the ungainly hold the man has on him. Rallou watches with her mouth open as the telegraph pole's end smashes straight through Harris's roof, accompanied by crackles and fizzes and sparks of electricity. The earth's vibrations increase again. Where is Christos? Rallou's nose is thick with dust, and her mouth opens again, partly so she can breathe but partly at the sight of her home, which is wavering, threatening to fall. Then slowly, almost gracefully, one wall falls outward and half the roof collapses. The dust that was created by the collapse of the first wall hides what is left of the house, but Rallou can hear the rumble that tells her the whole lot is going to go.

'Christo!' Rallou's scream is automatic. Greg grips her arm, stops her, before she has even realised she is running towards her home.

Tiles slide off the roof, which is now at an odd angle, and the wall by the front door is cracked, a jagged black line that grows before her eyes. Now she can see through it to the blue walls of her kitchen and now out to daylight and the pomegranate tree in her back garden, next to the washing line, with Lori's sheet still hanging, flapping.

It will collapse. The whole house is going to fall. Where is Christos?

'Christo!' she shouts again and tries to wriggle from Greg's hold as her stomach knots and twists.

Greg coughs from all the dust in the air. Rallou's nose is now completely clogged and her heartbeat is in her throat. Where is he? He is not in the street. He has not run out of the building. Her house is going to fall! What is left of one wall crumbles, and another seems to concertina vertically. The walls that remain fall inward and, with nothing left to support it, the roof crashes down. It breaks apart, the wood and the tiles separating, sliding and shearing over one another until the end of her old brass bed is left poking through the roof beams, with rubble and tiles and dust on her mama's bedspread. For a second the front door is left standing. Then it falls backward in a cloud of dust at the foot of the bed. Rallou's nails dig into Greg's fingers and her feet propel her forward.

# Chapter 16

'Christo!' It is her own voice screaming his name into the dust and rubble. Rallou falls sideways after a new tremor, scrambles forward on liquid ground, her feet fighting to gain purchase.

'Christo!' she calls for the tall, capable, good-looking, caring Christos she married, the man she knew on her return from London. Other names are being shouted all around her.

'Dimitri!'
'Anna!'
'Constantino?'
*'Moro mou!'*

The cries come from every corner as if a roll-call is being carried out. The voices sound strained, choked, full of fear and the dread of loss. The dust hangs in the air, the town engulfed in a thick mist even now the ground has solidified. Rallou makes progress, on her knees, onto her feet, every step taking her nearer their home. She must get home, open the front door that now lies flat on the floor and let him out.

'Christo.' The call is more to herself, to hear his name. The ground is quite solid now but the shouts from all corners do not diminish – quite the opposite. New calls start and people begin to run now the ground no longer moves, but this time towards the buildings, not away from them.

'Mama?'

'Theia?'

'Nectario?'

'Papous?'

Rallou reaches what was her home and starts to climb over the debris, the stones and plaster pieces, roof tiles and wooden beams. Ted, who has followed her, grabs her arm to pull her to safety, but the terror in her heart gives her strength and she jerks free to grab the knob of her own front door and wrench the horizontal slab of wood up and open, then drops it with a dull thud, creating a cloud of dust. The open frame reveals more rubble, one of her best shoes with just the toe showing, a piece of blue plaster from her kitchen, the corner of a pink cushion from Natasa's old bedroom. Her life, broken.

'Christo!' she shrieks at the top of her voice, throwing her head back.

Similar cries can be heard all around the town.

'Oh my God!' Ted is by her side. 'Greg!' he calls behind him to his son, who comes running, leaving Lori where she is sitting by the side of the road. Kyria Vetta's sons also run and Kyria Vetta attempts to stand. Rallou pulls up stone after stone. He has to be here somewhere. Did he seek refuge under the kitchen table, under the stairs? None of this remains standing. She pulls out from between roof tiles one of her scarves, a pale dusty version of itself. They must get to him before the air runs out – wherever he is. Stone after stone she lifts and hurls away. Her skirt, her hair, her face are white with dust. And where is Arapitsa? She would not have been caught inside the falling house, but would have run out, and should be barking.

Rallou pauses in her futile task to look around for the dog.

'Arapitsa? Arapitsa!' If she finds the dog she will find Christos. Other people are also shouting for loved ones. Their cries become increasingly hoarse as lovers, children and parents do not reply. Wails of grief begin to flow and fill the silence the earthquake has left. The echoing sounds pull Rallou up short in her own search and she turns atop her own pile of stones and mortar to look upon Orino town. A cloud of dust hangs in the air, pillars rising here and there, and between them there is still clear blue sky and the sun is still shining. Here and there, too, structures are still failing, crashing sounds confirming the damage done. Where taller houses once stood, pillars of rubble now act as markers. Where rows of tender flowers in pots once lined the path, bricks, stones and piles of debris now mark the way. Electricity lines fizz and worried dogs run this way and that, but of Arapitsa there is no sign. Accepting her absence, Rallou suddenly has the darkest of feelings and sinks down abruptly, on the edge of her own flattened front door. She idly plays with the handle that she will turn no more to enter her home. That choice has been taken from her.

'Rallou?' Greg asks, a stone in each hand. Ted is pulling away rubble as fast as he can and now that the ground has stopped shaking Lori is there too, showing strength Rallou would never have imagined, pulling away stones she herself would struggle to move.

'It is no use,' Rallou says.

'There is a chance, if we dig quickly enough ...' Greg pulls away another stone. Underneath it, broken, is the photo frame that held a picture of Christos's mama and baba with her own children. It hung on the kitchen wall, beside the socket where she would plug the iron in. Greg pulls out the photo, blows the dust from its surface and passes it across. All that time and energy Rallou spent devoted to those children, to the exclusion of everything else. Why did she not save just a little of that energy, put a little of that effort into being with Christos? The sight of Christos's baba, so like Christos, bring tears to her eyes, which roll down her chin; she can feel them cutting through the grime. She must dig! She cannot give up. On her feet again, she renews her effort with vigour. She wants the chance to give him the focus she never gave him, devote to him the energy that until now she has used up on everything and everyone else. She wants it to be like when they were first married.

'Rallou.' The voice is behind her.

'Harris!' There is a brief wave of relief that her sister is unhurt, before the crushing weight of needing to find Christos returns.

'You are safe,' Harris states.

'Help us,' Greg puffs. He does not stop pulling at the rubble.

Harris frowns, a look of confusion. Her hair is all white too, from dust, and there is a tear in her blouse that shows her wide bra strap. But she does not hesitate, she is on her knees pulling at stones.

'Who is under here?' Harris asks as she digs.

Rallou finds she cannot answer. Her nose is blocked with dust, her throat is closed with fear; the terror in her heart has sealed her mouth shut.

'Christos!' Ted replies. Rallou's vision starts to blur afresh.

'No, no. It is okay. He is not here.' Harris sounds relieved and stops digging. Rallou looks from one of her sister's eyes to the other. Hope allows her heartbeat to stabilise, but she is breathing fast. Behind Harris, Lori pauses, a heavy rock held in both hands, her back arching with the strain. The shouting from around the town has calmed. Now the people of the town begin to wail and cry. Lori's face is smeared with tears and her nose is running. She drops the rock and drags a hand across to wipe her face dry. Rallou notices that her neatly painted nails are broken, stone dust whitening her tan.

'Thanks and praise to all the saints and gods,' Lori says and crosses herself several times. 'Where is he?'

Rallou's world is spinning, the tightness in her throat is releasing. Her love, who she thought was dead, is alive. The thought gives her lungs air, the hope brings strength. Her voice is released and she lets out a wail of relief and sinks back on her heels, her hands loosely in her lap.

'Oh my, oh my.' It is Stephanos, Harris's husband, who comes running, in the direction of Harris. Then he sees Rallou's house. 'Oh my.' He seems unable to say anything else as he looks at her flattened home 'Oh my!' he repeats once again and then adds, 'Thank goodness you are safe. Where is Christos?' He turns to her, his face anticipating the horror of what she might say. She in turn faces Harris.

'I saw him yesterday. He said to tell you he has left a note on the kitchen table.' Harris says, turning to look back at her own house. Rallou's heart leaps. She can feel its pulse in her parched throat. The reprieve flows like cold water through her veins and an involuntary shivers runs down her back. He is safe. He is not in the rubble.

'So where is he?' she asks.

'Where is he?' Ted echoes her question. They have all stopped digging now and have turned to face Harris. There is an urgency in Ted's voice that Rallou appreciates, and it brings more tears.

'He mentioned something about Corfu. But he said he explained it all in his note. He didn't seem to want to say any more.' But she is distracted as she speaks. Buildings are still falling. People still running, voices still wailing.

'Hey! Hey!' Harris's husband steps in, as his wife's legs begin to give way. 'Oh, my love, you must sit,' he says, helping her to the ground and fanning her with his hand.

'Corfu?' Rallou feels the earth move again but she knows that this time it is her own balance that is at fault. 'But he has never been off the island in his life!'

Harris mutters something.

'What did she say?' Lori asks Stephanos.

'I didn't quite make it out. Something about young love or new love. Did you say *neos* or *nea*, Harris?'

Harris's eyes roll in her head.

'Oh, my love. Someone help me to get her in the house to lie down. This heat will not help.' Stephanos has such a quiet voice. Even when he shouts it is breathy and faint.

'The house? It might not be safe.' Ted is at Harris's feet.

'The kitchen at the back is untouched. Put her on the table there.'

Greg takes Harris's shoulders from Stephanos. Harris's husband is so slight he would not manage. People are still calling, but not so urgently now, and the dust is starting to settle.

Rallou walks by Harris's side as they carry her. Her concern for her sister mingles with the need to know why Christos is in Corfu. But at least he is safe. What of her brothers? Her baba?

'Okay, so Christos is safe. Thank goodness. Harris has fainted but is alive. We should see who else we can help,' Lori interjects. She touches Rallou's forearm.

'I will go to find our brothers,' Rallou tells Harris, but Harris's eyes are closed, her eyelashes encrusted white with dust.

Lori is on one side of Harris, Ted on the other. Rallou crosses herself as she passes the rubble that, just this morning, was her home. It is unreal, as though if she blinks hard enough everything will return to normal. How else will life carry on? They have no money to rebuild the house, and nor, these days, compared to when they were first married, do they have the energy. All her life force seems to drain out of her and she hardly sees any point in putting one foot in front of the other.

Greg calls from behind them, 'Pa, there is a man here who needs our help. His wife is trapped under a beam, I think he said.'

'Okay, Greg. Rallou, will you be all right? I must go and help.'

Rallou nods her permission. Now she is alone: completely, utterly, devastatingly. Her legs move but it is not by her will. They continue their slow tread to the port automatically. She should be delighted. Christos is alive! He is not buried in the rubble that was their home. But he is alive and in Corfu, not here with her to tell her that everything will be all right, to tell her not to worry about the house, to tell her that he has the strength for both of them. Why on earth is he in Corfu? What was so momentous that it would persuade him to leave the island? What did Harris say? A new love, a young love? They have no connection to Corfu. No family, no friends. The only connection they have ever had to Corfu is … But surely Harris did not mean that girl that Christos once knew, the one training to be a teacher – or was it a nurse? Yes, it was a nurse. Surely that is not what this is about? They may be going through a rough patch but this cannot be his response, can it? When people have been married as long as they have there are going to be times that are rough and those that are smooth. He must know that there is no truth in the gossip about her and Greg – surely he knows her better than that? But she shouldn't have to flatly deny it, should she? Hadn't her walking out stated loud and clear that she was disgusted that he even thought there was any truth in such a rumour?

She coughs and her phlegm is thick with dust. She spits. Others are also making their way to the port: a place to find each other. How many other people are homeless?

If he did not take her walking out of the house as a disgusted denial, what did he think it meant? Her legs stop moving. Surely not! He cannot have thought she had left him?

The last walls of her life, the emotional walls that hold her together, collapse, and the world suddenly seems like a very large place with no boundaries, no limitations and no safety nets.

He has gone. Everything has gone.

There is no point in making any more effort so she sits where her feet have stopped, right in the middle of the cobbled lane. All the jumbled emotions inside have evaporated, and she is numb. Everything is functioning; her lungs operate, her heart beats, her eyes see and her ears hear but she watches herself function as one might watch an ant climb over a twig. It is impressive in one way, but unremarkable in another.

Kyria Vetta's son is now talking to a man who owns a small shop on one of the side streets. He is looking for his own son. They assure him that the last time they saw him he was down at the harbour in a cafe-bar and that he will be fine. They move off together, supporting Kyria Vetta herself, but they only get a short way when they are stopped by another man who grabs their arms and pulls them. He is shouting. Someone must help him roll away a large rock that has trapped his dog.

Meanwhile, Ted has reappeared from a side street, the underarms of his shirt stained, his black trousers white with flakes and granules of plaster. An old woman in black calls to him and he in turn calls to his son.

'Greg, a woman here says her husband is stuck.'

Greg appears and turns onto the side lane, Lori behind him, eager to help.

Rallou continues to just sit there.

# Chapter 17

Slowly, her thoughts begin to press her for answers. When did Christos go to Corfu? Oh yes, Harris said she saw him yesterday. How long was that after she went to Korifi? Three days, five, a week? Why does the mountain do that – twist time until days and nights no longer have meaning? But whenever it was, Christos did wait some days. Maybe in that time he began to believe that she wasn't coming back? But the only connection Christos has ever had with Corfu was the girl he was seeing when she was in London – the nurse.

When she and Christos first started courting, Harris did try to warn her. Didn't she say that he and this girl from Corfu were close? Maybe there was more to what she said than Rallou gave her credit for. Is it possible that he has been in contact with the girl all these years? Well, she will not be a girl now but a woman, and not such a young one, just like Rallou herself. But the difference between the woman from Corfu and herself is that Christos has not witnessed this ghost from his past age and wrinkle. In his head she will still be young and perfect.

Rallou tries to swallow but her throat is lined with dust. Has he really taken her absence as the end of their marriage, and gone off to see what he has been missing all these years?

'No – please, no!' she says out loud.

'You all right, Rallou?' A hand on her shoulder. A neighbour is talking to her. 'You and yours safe?' The neighbour releases her shoulder and puts her hand to her head and pulls lumps of plaster from her knotted curls.

'Yes,' Rallou stammers. The neighbour's face is masked with debris, little flakes of whitewash in her eyebrows. But she grins, an act of forced confidence, perhaps, and as she does so the red of her gums and the white of her teeth contrast with the film of grime on her skin. The interruption to her thoughts brings Rallou back to moment. All around her is rubble and chaos, people are crying and shouting, buildings are still collapsing, and the town is engulfed in a cloud of dust.

'Your brothers, your baba?' the neighbour asks.

'My baba!' Rallou shrieks at the sudden horrifying thought.

'He is up in Korifi, isn't he?' the neighbour says, clearly alarmed at Rallou's reaction.

'Yes!' Rallou cannot take in all the people around her. Where have they come from? It is like a festival, everyone on the street, but no one is laughing.

'Korifi will be fine,' the neighbour assures her with another grin that creases the parched skin all the way up her cheeks but gives no light to her eyes. She looks scared, despite her forced positivity. She does not explain why Baba will be safe in Korifi, but she pats Rallou's shoulder and marches on, leaving her dazed and unsure what to do next.

Her brothers. She must find Vasillis, make sure he and Eleftheria and their children are safe, and Costas and Yorgos, Grigoris, their wives and children. She scrambles to her feet and starts down the main lane, turning down a side street towards Vasillis's home only to find it blocked by a fallen wall. She tries the next, which leads to his shoe shop, but this too has been filled with rubble and roof tiles. Many people, all with white hair and dusty clothes, all looking as dazed and unsure of their movements as she feels, are filtering to the main lane down to the port. Everyone is heading to the central point.

As Rallou nears the waterfront, she turns off towards the small hospital. If any of her brothers or their families are hurt they will be there.

The square in front of the small building is milling with people. Some are moaning and holding their arms, or legs, or heads. There are cuts and sprains and blood. A mama pushes for attention for her offspring. Her daughter has suffered a bump on the head. Her fussing is brought up short by the sight of neighbours and friends in a worse state than her little ones, and she helps an old woman with a torn blouse to find somewhere to sit. To Rallou it seems a remarkable piece of unselfish concern. When her children were hurt or sick she had no room for anyone or anything else. How often has Harris told her what a dedicated mama she was? How can this woman think of others when her own child needs her attention?

The woman pulls her child in towards her and bends to talk to the girl and give her a kiss on the forehead. Then the two of them, the woman and the child together, comfort another old lady next to them. Is that why she and Christos have been so far apart? Did she direct all her energies towards the children's needs and in the process exclude Christos? Is it even possible to care too much for one's children?

Everyone in the square is talking, but not loudly, as if they have agreed that to remain calm would be best. The dust in the air is beginning to thin. People are coughing less. The doctors are there working methodically through the crowd, attending to those in most need first. Normally they share the job, working shifts around the clock. Rallou also recognises a German man who has been coming to the island for years, who is a doctor. He is busy treating people too, aided by the three nurses from the hospital, and in amongst all this is Lori, somehow still managing to look elegant despite the dust and her tear-stained face. Her sleeves are rolled up and she is attending to people with great authority, clearly in her element. Rallou had no idea she had any medical training and has always assumed she was simply Ted's wife. She feels slightly shocked and just a little ashamed of her assumption.

'Rallou!' It is Vasillis. 'Oh, thank goodness.' His voice brings her out of the stare she has fallen into.

'Eleftheria? The children?' she asks, once again animated as Vasillis takes hold of her forearm so the bustle of people moving around them does not separate them.

'Fine. I have just seen Yorgos too and he is fine, and he has seen Costas and his family are safe.' He is pushed close to her by someone making his way behind him.

This news is a relief but it also feels surreal. What has happened is just not sinking in – the whole situation, all these people outside: it's too much to take in. She is not sure what she should be feeling, or what to do. Her mind feels blank, her emotions on hold. She wishes Christos was here but …

'Grigoris? His family? Baba? What about Baba?' She tries not to shout. At the thought of him being harmed, panic runs through her chest, curls around her stomach.

'I don't know. I have heard Korifi was not so badly affected but we won't know until someone actually goes up there. Don't worry, Rallou. The houses up there have been standing forever and there is plenty of open ground. Grigoris is fine, his wife hurt her shoulder, but the kids are safe. I have to go – I am looking for Eleftheria's mama. She was not at her home when it struck – she was at her friend's house by the port, I think.' With a quick squeeze of her arm he is gone, into the crowd, and Rallou is left as an observer. She knows all the people around her, by sight, by name, by little pieces of shared history, but no one is a close friend to her, no one special. She came to town as a besotted new wife, with eyes for no one but Christos and a desire to stay in the house and keep him with her. But then, so quickly, she became a mama, and then her children took all her energies, her time and her focus. At that point in her life, when would she have had the chance to make friends, real friends? At what point in her life should she had taken her eyes off her children, compromised their safety and focused on Christos or anyone else for that matter?

'Excuse me, Rallou.' Someone pushes past her.

Maybe she had better leave the hospital square to those who need it – her brothers and their families are safe. If she goes to the port, perhaps she can find out if anyone knows anything about Korifi. Pushing her own way through the crowd, she briefly catches sight of Lori making a tourniquet around someone's arm. The thought that even Lori has done more than just raise her children passes through the back of her mind as she makes her way to the port.

Down at the harbour, even more people are milling about, shoulder to shoulder. One side of the port is unrecognisable. Whole buildings are missing. The statue of *The Old Captain* has shifted on its plinth and he looks in danger of plunging into the harbour. The Venetian-style clock tower, originally built in three sections, does not look right and it is only after a second glance that she realises that the top layer is leaning, the columns on one side missing.

Where should she go now, and who can she ask about Korifi? She heads to the coastal path. A crack wide enough to step into has opened up across the walkway. How is the donkey doing? In all this she has forgotten about the animal. Just hours ago its well-being was the most important thing in the world, and now it is all but forgotten. If the rocks around the cove have collapsed in the earthquake, the poor thing could be buried. But animals are wise, they feel these things before humans do, and maybe the ground moving was enough to give it a surge of adrenaline that would have carried it up the stony path to the olive grove.

'Rallou! Have you seen Vasillis?' It is Eleftheria's mama, who looks very shaken, her thin little legs hardly holding her. She does not have her stick with her.

'He is looking for you. Eleftheria and the children are fine. Take my arm – which way are you going?' It feels good to help.

'I don't know where I am going. Home? If it is still standing! Where is Vasillis, did you say?'

'Looking for–'

'Ah, thank God.' Vasillis appears, crossing himself, and then his arm is around the old lady and her weight is transferred from Rallou to him.

'Vasilli, have you heard any more of Korifi?' Rallou asks.

'Come, Mama,' he addresses his wife's mother. 'Yes!' He turns back to Rallou. 'One of the Kaloyannis brothers has gone up to Korifi. He will call Costas Voulgaris as soon as he gets there.' He nods in the direction of the *kafenio*. People are crowded outside it – drawn to it, perhaps, as a central point of congregation. 'I will see you back here. Wait for me if I am not back in time to hear the phone call.' Then he is gone, carefully leading his mother-in-law through the crowds.

Costas Voulgaris is open for business, except no money is exchanged for the strong Greek coffees and glasses of brandy that the waiters are passing out to the crowd on the waterfront. Rallou turns away from the cafe, wondering what to do, where to go next.

'Rallou!'

She looks around to see who is calling.

'Rallou, you all right? Over here,' It is Costas Voulgaris himself and he is holding out a glass of brandy. He has always been sweet to her. 'Drink, it will steady you. Are your family all right?' The question is beginning to sound like a normal greeting, with everybody asking everybody the same thing. When she does not answer he says, 'Drink, girl.' She takes a sip and the liquid loosens the dryness of her throat. She wipes her hand across her nose. It is hard to believe that the sun is still shining and the water in the bay is still twinkling under a cloudless blue sky. Then Costas's arm is around her shoulders, and he is hugging her tight as she drinks. It feels so supportive. The brandy, in her empty stomach, takes effect presently. Reality takes a little backward step and her overloaded mind calms.

'Have you heard from the Kaloyannis brothers?' That is the one thing she needs to know.

'No. It will take them a while to walk up there. There is only your baba up there, right?' Rallou nods and takes another sip. 'Here, come here.' He leads her to the front of his shop and pulls a chair out from inside. 'Sit here, Rallou, just sit. Wait.' Someone calls his name and he is gone, and Rallou is left on her chair, watching the strange chaos on the harbour very slowly subside as time passes. The table next to the chair, surprisingly, still has a holder for napkins on it. Perhaps it has been casually replaced by one of the waiters. Either way, she takes one and blows her dust-clogged nose and the relief is immediate. People are talking all around her. News is travelling fast from one person to another. As far as she has heard, no one, thank the heavens and the stars, seems to have been fatally injured. News like that would have already travelled like wildfire.

Some people are beginning to leave the harbour, and others arrive. At first the question people asked was 'Have you seen …?', naming their missing loved ones. But as time passed the question changed to, 'Is your family all right?' – and now this has become, 'I've not heard of anyone seriously injured, have you?' To that question the answers include broken arms, broken legs, bad cuts, sore bruises but, so far, not one person reported dead; then, later, this becomes the greeting: the miracle that no one has died.

But all Rallou wants to hear is that Korifi is safe. Then and only then will she allow herself to think of Christos.

# Chapter 18

The quake was so sudden and so violent that the world itself seemed to be coming to an end, and the silence that follows feels like a mockery. It seems ridiculous that gulls are still flying above the port, that the yachts are still floating. In a few hours it is ascertained that in the whole town there has only been one fatality, and she was a very old woman who was confined to bed, and who was not expected to be long for this world. People cross themselves when they hear the news, and consider it a miracle that there were no more deaths.

Rallou goes on waiting for news from the mountain.

A large woman, whom Rallou recognises as the wife of a local builder, bustles onto the harbour's edge, telling anyone who will listen how she cried herself sick with worry, searching for her husband.

'I thought he was dead! Buried under the rubble of that house he has been renovating for the Swiss man. Her face wears a furious expression. 'Have you seen the huge stone lintels and ancient heavy wooden beams in that old mansion? Any one of them could have crushed him like a walnut!' And she crushes the knuckles of one hand into the palm of the other and twists them with force.

She is talking to no one in particular, just anyone who turns to face her as she keeps walking.

'But it turns out that he was not at the mansion at all! No! He was avoiding work and loitering in a *kafenio* here by the harbour, eating fish, drinking ouzo and playing *tavli* with Pan!' There is no relief in the woman's voice, just anger, and indignation, as if a cruel game has been played on her. Pan is a big bearded man who, for a price, will dive into the harbour to untangle the anchors of the visiting sailing yachts. He turns at the sound of his name and, seeing the woman, ducks into a *kafenio* out of sight. 'Where is my husband?' she demands, and someone tells her that he has gone looking for her. At this news there is a softening of her stride, and she bustles away again, still in search of her lazy spouse.

Suddenly there is a wail that rings throughout the town. The relative calm that was beginning to settle is instantly replaced with a feeling of tension. But within minutes it is reported that the wail was that of a young bachelor, and that his cry of distress was over his mama's four-year-old ashes, which had been in a jar in a little niche in the kitchen wall in the house his papous built. The house and the ashes have become one as the house has just collapsed. Those in the harbour area once again begin to remark that it is a miracle that no one was seriously hurt, and everyone agrees that they have come off very lightly.

Rallou continues to wait and as she does so she cannot reconcile the sunshine and the warmth, the sparkle of the sea and the cloudless sky, with the damage around the harbour.

The buildings have not fared as well as the people and those around her begin to compare the buildings that have shaken to the ground with those that still stand. Then the offers of rooms and beds begin. Those who have been the most fortunate are eager to help those who have not. Dust is still being brushed from clothing, and hair ruffled free of debris. Space to sleep will be found for everyone, it seems; no one will be left without shelter, and promises of help to rebuild follow this. It seems to Rallou that everyone has someone and everyone has someplace to go. No one is to be left without a bed or support. No one except her.

Her heart feels so heavy, and she cannot remember feeling this alone since Mama died. The reality is she could stay with any of her brothers but she just does not want to. She does not want to find herself in a position where she is discussing the whereabouts of Christos, and Vasillis is sure to ask that very question. Tears prick her eyes and she blinks. If she thinks about Christos now she feels that she will fall apart. Better to focus on the question of where she will stay tonight.

There is no choice; she must return to Korifi.

The phone inside Costas Voulgaris's *kafenio* rings, and Rallou listens, alert. She pushes inside to see Costas pick up the receiver.

'Hello, yes, yes, yes, oh yes … Oh, that is good news.' He nods his head to all those who have gathered around him. Their mountain homes are still standing. People who have homes up in her baba's village nod at Rallou in recognition and some come up to her to exchange a few words. Costas Voulgaris turns to Rallou and, putting his hand over the phone, says, 'Your baba is fine. Tolis has been sitting with him for a while but the old man said he has seen worse quakes than this one. Tolis has invited him to the boatyard for some of his wife's fish soup.'

'Tell him I am fine. Can I speak to him?' Rallou asks. Costas nods but turns back to the phone to continue talking.

'They are fine,' he says. 'Yes, all of them. Rallou is here – oh, and Vasillis has just come.' Costas looks over the heads of the crowd to Vasillis, who is pushing himself to the front.

'Costas and Yorgos, Grigoris?' Costas Voulgaris asks, and Vasillis smiles and nods his head. 'Yes, yes, they are fine too and there are some people here who want to know about their houses.' There is a general increase in the volume of talking in the bar.

'What, nothing has fallen at all? Well that's good to hear.' Costas is still on the phone 'The well top? Well, yes, but you can rebuild it … Sure, but someone will go down and pull all that out … Yes, you will. Ha ha!' Costas laughs at something Tolis has said. The way he chuckles makes him sound like a boy.

'So glad we have the house up there,' says a voice by Rallou's elbow.

'Where else can we go now the town house is gone?' These and other comments prompt Rallou's realisation that there will be several new neighbours for her baba now, at least for a short time, with so many town houses damaged.

'Can I talk to Baba?' Vasillis reaches for the phone. 'Baba? Baba? You there? Ah, there you are, everything all right?' The throng in the *kafenio* filters back outside and Rallou presses her ear up to the other side of the phone, nose to nose with Vasillis. She is so relieved that her baba is safe. She has nothing pressing that she wants to say to him; she is just glad she can hear the sound of his voice. Vasillis asks about the house, the chickens, the beehives. It seems nothing has changed. The tremor was a strong one and the treetops oscillated wildly, but he stood in the pasture and watched the birds fly up in alarm and the chickens flap about. Then she hears Tolis Kaloyannis's voice again, asking to speak to Costas Voulgaris.

'Toli, is the boatyard safe? Oh, I am glad to hear that … What? No, don't joke with me. What? … Seriously. You expect me to believe that? You have to be kidding me? No! I don't believe you!'

The people in the *kafenio* sense something extraordinary and they hush.

'But that is not possible.' Costas looks around his audience. 'Ah, you are joking with me. Really? Serious? If I believe you then that is a miracle, to be sure, Toli.' Costas rambles a goodbye and the hushed crowd wait to hear the latest phenomenon.

'Okay, listen to this!' Costas says, and steps onto a chair so everyone can see him. 'Tolis declares that there has been a miracle.'

There is a hush. One or two of the older men and woman cross themselves.

'He has just told me, and he swears on his mother's life, that Dolly, Yanni's dead donkey, has just walked into his boatyard, alive and well!'

'But why wouldn't she? With a quake like that they can run for miles,' Spiros, who owns a modern forty-two foot yacht, says.

'Ach. You have been away around the Cyclades. You wouldn't have heard. Dolly fell over the coastal path edge where it has given way,' Pan answers.

'But she was seen floating out to sea,' another voice says, incredulous.

'Well, Tolis says he should know her – her and Yanni go past them at the end of the month on their way to Korifi, stop every time for a chat and a refill of water,' Costas Voulgaris answers.

Rallou opens her mouth to explain. But then, how would she explain, what would she explain? That she had looked after the donkey herself for a time because until she knew who the owner was or whether the donkey was well enough to stand she had a fear they might shoot it? That would not go down well, no matter how true it is. Besides, it might sound like she was trying take the donkey for herself. Most people know that she had been pressing her baba to get an animal for years to make him more mobile, and they all know that with the lifestyle on the mountaintops being what it is he could never afford one.

'Maybe the animal itself is a saint,' someone quips.

'It's true, a nicer nature beast would be hard to find, and one so willing to work.'

'Yanni will be pleased. Where is he?'

'Off the island, buying a donkey.'

'Well, if the animal has flown out of the water and into Tolis's boatyard perhaps he should rename her Pegasus!' another voice quips.

Raucous laugher fills the *kafenio*, the tension of the recent event dissolving, the promise arising that life will return to normal, there will be jokes and banter again. Only Hectoras, one of the other donkey men, coughs nervously. Rallou understands. The competition for work is based on how many animals a man has. He has three, the most any man on the island has, so he gets all the work that demands three beasts. His fear is that Yanni will also end up with three. He is anxious to maintain his monopoly.

'So, your house? It is all right?' Vasillis breaks into her thoughts. 'Gone,' she replies, and quickly forgets that she has missed her chance to say anything about herself in connection with Dolly's recovery. No matter, let them think it is a miracle. Besides, when Vasillis asks about her house it suddenly occurs to her what is coming next … She tries to think quickly what she will say; she will tell him Christos is fine, of course – but should she tell him that he is on Corfu? Or does she lie and say he is up on the hills? She could be caught out. Better to tell the truth. But then he will ask why Christos is there. What will she say?

'Well, you and Christos must come and stay with us. Where is he?' Vasillis looks around and then back at her, his eyes wide. 'He is not hurt, is he?'

'No, he's fine.'

'Oh, for a minute there … Where is he?'

What can she say?

# Chapter 19

Rallou feels like she has been waiting for hours. She looks up at the clock tower. With the top portion leaning, and iced with dust, the hands are stuck at four twenty-three – the time the quake struck yesterday afternoon. She shields her eyes to judge the sun's position in the sky. It is still only morning. A gull circles high overhead, its calls only just audible.

At Vasillis's insistence, she spent the night at his house after all. It was odd to be in her old bed again after all the years that have passed. It was hers before it was passed to Vasillis's and Eleftheria's second child, when he became old enough to need a room of his own. Now he is grown and married. Eleftheria made her feel very welcome.

When Vasillis pressed her about Christos in the *kafenio* the question was deflected by Costas Voulgaris offering more brandy. But it was inevitable that, in the evening, almost as soon as she arrived at their house, Eleftheria asked the same question, and Vasillis, who had been assessing a cracked wall in the next room, came in to hear the answer. Rallou stumbled over her words and made a couple of false starts, and in the end she resorted to an out-and-out lie.

'His second aunt is very unwell,' she said, and told them how he had had to make a trip to Corfu. It sounded so false to her.

'He has an aunt on Corfu?' Vasillis asked. 'I know he had second cousins or something up in a small village near Saros, but Corfu?'

'One of his aunts from the village moved to Corfu.' Rallou felt sure her flaming cheeks would give her away.

'Ah, it is a shame he could not wait for you to return from your baba's,' Eleftheria said. 'Then you could have gone together. She must be very sick.' She crossed herself three times, then smiled. 'So you will be following him tomorrow? It's all happening, isn't it?'

And there she was again, stuck with another question she didn't know how to answer. The easiest thing was to agree.

'Yes, yes, of course, that is why I came down from Baba's.' But the moment she said it she realised that they could catch her out with this lie. How would she have known to come down? Who would have told her? There is no phone in Korifi, and Yanni was not due up there until the end of the month.

But thankfully Eleftheria's mind was on other things. 'I can only serve us fish soup,' she said. 'I'm afraid I have nothing else prepared.'

'That will be great! Thanks, Eleftheria,' Vasillis said, but he was still looking at Rallou.

Eleftheria had not appeared so animated for years. The disaster seemed to have shifted her away from her normal grey outlook; apparently such things can happen. But even with Eleftheria's new-found enthusiasm the evening proved very long. To add to which, she cooked the soup in the kitchen instead of outside, and everywhere stank of fish. It can't have been fresh, Rallou concluded.

'The back kitchen was damaged in the quake and will have to be rebuilt.' Eleftheria sparkled with energy for the future. 'But I think we will rebuild it properly and extend it. With units from Athens, and have you seen the worktops you can get now? Unbelievable! No need to put up with smoothed and painted concrete any more!' Eleftheria's imagination seemed fired by her thoughts, and there was little Rallou felt she could say in reply. In the end, Vasillis, very gently, reminded Eleftheria that Rallou had lost more than her back kitchen, and perhaps it was not a subject to dwell on in present company. It was very sweet of him but Rallou hadn't minded; it was better than the silence that followed. It also took her mind off Christos, and steered the conversation away from more questions about him, for that matter. As she made her way to bed, Eleftheria said she would see what she could put together by way of food for her to take with her the next day. Rallou had been within a heartbeat of asking where she was supposed to be going when she remembered her lie. Or was it? Maybe she would have to go now, to back up her words. They were not the only people who were going to be asking.

General sounds of activity woke her very early. The sun streamed in through the shutters – which Rallou noted had recently been painted a very attractive shade of light blue – along with shouts and calls and the sounds of stones being moved. The air was clear and bright and the sky a deep hue, and all the dust from the day before had settled, but here and there little clouds rose again as rubble was shovelled and rocks rearranged. The clearing up and rebuilding process had already begun and every man and donkey was at work with the dawn.

Eleftheria was not up when she left but she thanked Vasillis heartily for her bed and food, and for the few euros he pressed on her to help with her journey, which left her feeling obliged to continue her deception.

Now she is waiting for the boat, all because she is not good at lying. She waits and yawns, after a disturbed night, during which she had visions of houses falling, rebuilding themselves, falling again. Arapitsa barking, Christos laughing and stepping out of the front door and then the house falling again. Christos still laughing as the dust rose around him. The dog trying to catch flying bits of stone as she jumped in the air. The same loop of action played over and over.

The glare of the water on the harbourside is now almost too bright to look at.

The harbour wall, at least, stayed intact. The arm at the end, jutting across the harbour's mouth, almost enclosing the port, looks unscathed. The port is crammed with sailing yachts and gin palaces, jostling for space, every corner taken; some are two rows deep, one moored to the back of another. There is activity on the decks of several of the vessels, the crews readying for departure. The halyards click against the masts and crews call to each other gently. Rallou watches as one yacht glides silently away from the harbour wall and into the middle of the harbour, people on the neighbouring boats ready to fend off. A single squashed buoy floats near where the ferry boats dock. Beneath the surface, little fish swim about, unaware that anything significant happened yesterday.

Three red-and-white water taxis are moored up in a corner of the harbour that is reserved for working boats, but there is no one on board any of them. Maybe no one will work today. More likely they will all stay at home and shovel dust, repair cracks, rebuild kitchens.

The distance over to the mainland seems so short, and it only takes twenty minutes or so on the high-speed taxi boats. She could call either Costas or Yorgos and they would happily take her there. But they have their own houses and families to think of, and in addition to this she doesn't want any awkward questions about where she is going or why. But the question remains: why is Christos there? If it is a mistake she needs to go and sort it out. If it is not, if he has left her, that is something she needs to sort out too. Isn't it?

But what will actually await her in Corfu? What will she find? Will she find him? Perhaps making such a journey is a knee-jerk reaction to the lie she's told, but if she is not to be exposed for a liar, what else is she supposed to do? Wait and hope he returns? That is not her nature anyway; she is not a passive person. Her falsehood gives her a legitimate reason for going. The island of Corfu, she has heard, has nearly fifty times the population of Orino. The reality is that once she arrives she will not even know where to start looking for him. The whole journey will, most likely, prove futile. But it will be better than staring at the rubble that was her home, fielding her neighbours' questions, facing her baba and seeing the sadness of her loss reflected in his eyes.

The gull that was so high up drifts downward, its wings outstretched, swooping lower and lower until it lands flat-footed on the other side of the harbour, where Christina from the bakery is putting yesterday's bread in the bin. The bakery looks untouched by the earthquake. That too is a blessing, the daily staple still being supplied. The amount of stale bread Christina deposits in the bin stops the lid from closing fully and as soon as her back is turned the gull is on it, curling its neck over the side to tear at the plastic bag squashed within. The rubbish that it pulls out it drops to the ground, and then its razor-sharp bill rips into the bread. It lifts its head, bill to the sky to swallow, and then begins to repeat the process.

'Shoo!' Christina hurries out of the bakery, flicking at it with a tea towel. The bird lazily takes to the air and flies to the nearest mast top to wait for her to go back inside.

Rallou yawns. Another hour or two's sleep would be very welcome, maybe as much to block the world out as to revive her.

The earthquake was such a strong reminder of how things can change, with no warning, in just a few minutes. Last night, she lay with the sheet tucked up under her chin and the scent of an unfamiliar washing powder in her nostrils, looking at the familiar lampshade, the one she stared at waiting for sleep as a schoolchild.

As she lost focus on the lampshade, she wished she felt sleepy. Just as Eleftheria's cloud of emotional darkness had shifted with the quake, so too had Rallou's own cloud of pessimism and antagonism towards Christos.

She had certainly had cause to think. She realised that it was extremely unlikely that Christos had gone to Corfu to be with a girl he had known so briefly and whom he had not seen for the best part of thirty years. Also, it was simply impossible to believe that he had remained in touch with her all these years and that Rallou wouldn't have seen any evidence – a card, a phone call, something. No, it was more likely that he left the island to teach her a lesson, or to frighten her, or for a million other reasons, but not to chase a childhood love. Maybe this girl was a pleasant memory and that was all it took for him to select Corfu over the hundreds of other islands he could have gone to.

She turned on her side and looked at the picture on the wall, a print of some tropical beach, with palm trees and hammocks. That was new. Outside, a dog barked, another returned its call and a third joined in. There was the creak of a rusty hinge and a wooden shutter slammed shut, creating a sanctum, within which was a lucky person whose house had not been flattened. She yawned, and as she lay there she wondered what might have been if the quake had happened the day she stormed up to Korifi. Supposing, in that quake, God forbid, Christos had been caught by a falling beam, a tumbling wall. Suddenly, all that control she thought she had over her life, over him, would have been shown up for what it really was: illusions, delusions. The belief that her life and his life were things that she could take for granted would have been gone. She is not the puppeteer: she is Aglaia, the wife, and she does not even have a central part to play. Her role has always been to remain unseen but forever nagging her Karagiozis from behind the curtains, for the twenty-nine years of their marriage, wittering away about his shortcomings. Ha! Shadow plays, a paper world kept alive as long as the candle is not snuffed out.

But it didn't even take an earthquake for her to see this; in the end it was Christos who showed that she was powerless. Why was it so easy to see, now, that her storming out of their home could easily have been the last act he needed to decide that their marriage was over? How often had she hinted at her discontent in the months, or years even, up to that point? Little digs at his shortcomings, little reminders of all he was supposed to do but never did. The drawer he was meant to fix the bottom of, the chair he was supposed to bind together and glue, the washing line he was meant to hang. And how, over coffee, Harris had convinced her that she had a point, that she was right. How tired he must have been of it, repeated day after day, when she was quite capable of doing many of these jobs herself. Of course, she never intended him to take her walking out to mean that their marriage was over. She had reacted to what had sounded like his accusation that she was having an affair with Greg for money! But maybe he was just sick of ... Of what? She didn't need to ask herself twice. He was sick of her not showing her love for him. That's what!

The orange hammocks in the picture on the wall were hanging from palm trees; balanced on the bamboo table in the foreground were two cocktail glasses with cherries on sticks across their tops. The colours were all too strong. It was unsettling in its unreal plasticness.

She turned around to look at the opposite wall, to stare at Eleftheria's grandmother's chest of drawers. Eleftheria must polish it every day, judging by the way it shone in the moonlight.

Full moons always take her right back to the early days of her courtship with Christos, when the girl from Corfu was still on the island! Rallou had returned from London and, without a thought for anyone else, she had claimed her prize. The best-looking, tallest boy in the village – on the island! It just felt like a continuation of all the excitement life was bringing her. She did not spare a thought for the girl whose place she took. Or for Christos and how he saw her, even. Everything was from her point of view.

She yawned again, tired but unable to sleep.

The island's clock strikes six and thoughts of the night before fade as she looks up to the hands that have not moved. Four twenty-three. Someone nearby chuckles. The bells are not truthful either.

Maybe, back then, Christos saw her like she sees the Americans now, as people with the keys to foreign places. Is that possible? This feels like a new thought. If that was the case he would have no idea that in those first few years it was she who was waiting for him to whisk her away to the faraway places they had talked about. But from his point of view, didn't it make more sense that she would be the one who would have initiated their travels? Why had she not taken action? Why was he supposed to do all the work?

The cargo ship that serves the island's daily needs appears at the entrance to the harbour and slowly slips into its mooring spot. Donkeys and men are gathered beside it. No doubt there will be a full cargo today, with building materials and all manner of household items. The mayor put a notice up outside his offices yesterday evening, stating that essential repairs could be carried out immediately, without planning permission, which would take too long to process. The notice went on to say that checks would be made in due course to make sure that the traditional character of the island was maintained and that no one took advantage of this amnesty to build additional rooms that were not there before the earthquake struck. To Rallou, the notice seems pointless; the people would have started to renovate their houses anyway.

With the sun on the water casting ripples of light along its length, the cargo ship ties up to the pier and the heavy metal bow gate lowers onto the quay. There is the high-pitched scrape of metal against stone, grinding another day's work into the grooved marble blocks of the harbour wall. The sound brings more donkey men and their beasts, ready to help with the unloading. But there is no Yanni. He will no doubt be here in a moment and she will tell him about Dolly before she leaves the island.

Costas Voulgaris promised her he would ring Tolis at the boatyard and ask him to let her baba know that she will not be back immediately. Costas smiled that smile of his, but with a twist to it, a reminder that perhaps he still thinks he could have made her happy. The flattery of his interest made her feel young again for the briefest of moments, but she knew that to act on such a thrill would be irresponsible, and likely a short route to a great deal of pain for everyone. First she must sort out where she is, and then decide where she is going.

But is just chasing after Christos any more responsible, or logical come to that? Is she just kidding herself that by taking such an action she is in control of her life again? The truth, is she has completely lost control of everything.

'*Yeia sou*, Rallou,' a voice says quietly and kindly, and she looks up. The speaker is silhouetted by the brightness of the sun. 'I hope you slept all right. I was relieved to hear that your baba is fine.' The extravagantly soft tones can only be Harris's husband.

'*Yeia sou*, Stephanos. Thank you, he is well.' She blinks the tiredness from her eyes as best she can. 'How is Harris?' Really she should have gone to see her but all her instincts are saying 'hide'.

'And what brings you to sitting here today?' He always speaks with such genuine concern. He responds to Harris in the same way, softer even, almost as if she is someone who needs extra-special treatment.

'Oh, I was planning to go to Corfu but actually, perhaps ...' Rallou stands, her cheeks growing warm. Her plans and lies seem grandiose and rather embarrassing now she really thinks about it. She will go back up to her baba's and wait to see if Christos returns to the island. If he doesn't, then she will decide what she will tell everyone. Realistically, what else can she do?

'Ah, of course, you were going to Corfu. You don't think you might be too late, do you?' His tone is even quieter, even kinder. But the 'too late' throws Rallou completely and unexpected tears well and blur her vision.

# Chapter 20

'Ah, Rallou,' he says, 'please, there is no need to cry. Oh, I can be so tactless sometimes. But please, she will still want you to go. I mean, you know, even if you are too late. Well, it's not too late, is it, I mean, life goes on. And Christos will still need your support.' He is stammering and stumbling over his words and now Rallou knows for sure that she has no idea what he is talking about. It seems most unusual that Christos would confide in Stephanos. And who is this 'she' he is referring to? Surely he does not mean Christos's teenage girlfriend? But who else would the 'she' be?

And what on earth has the phrase 'life goes on' got to do with her situation? Her own lie about Christos's aunt flies through her thoughts, and for a moment she half believes it. Maybe he has heard it too and believes it? Or does he know Christos has left her and is he therefore suggesting that she just get on with her own life and leave Christos to his? And if that is the case then why is he encouraging her to go and give him her support? He must have heard the lie about his aunt. It is the only thing that fits.

'Yes.' She can only hope that her agreeing makes sense to him as she feels so lost, mixed up with lies and truths, her perceived worries and realities. She feels suddenly very awake.

'Ah, look,' says Stephanos. 'Here, a taxi boat. Not one of your brothers, but as safe a ride as you will find. Enjoy Corfu. It is a simple journey, no? The bus up to Patra and the boat straight there!' He is talking fast, trying to take his leave on a jolly, upbeat note. 'Oh, and don't forget to turn right where the boat lands you.' He chuckles. She frowns. This seems a very odd thing to say indeed. 'But above all, don't be afraid.' Now she really is lost; she has no idea what he is talking about. He ushers her to the taxi's side before marching away rather abruptly.

'Hello, Rallou, you going across?' It is a new water taxi man, who has recently inherited the job from his father. He looks like his baba but for the life of her Rallou cannot remember his name.

'I – er ...' She looks down at her bag; she has been to the bank and withdrawn all the money she can. Then she looks over the water, to the mainland, hazy in the sun. Behind her, the house they called home has gone. Christos has gone. Yiayia's lace-edged pillowcases are buried. Her children's paintings from when they were four and five and six are crushed. Natasa's medals from when she was into running in her teens, the bills she worried over, their wedding photographs, grandfather's *komboli* – everything entombed under tons of dust and rubble.

Maybe she should have stayed and sifted through the stones to salvage what she could?

She has never felt more alone. There is just her and her handful of euros.

'Shall I wait longer? The mainland is not going anywhere, it can wait.' Is the boy trying to be funny? The world waiting for her – now that is a silly concept. But then what else is the world doing? It has always been waiting. Just as she has always been waiting too. For what? For the right time, the right day, the right moment? Well, there is only now. And with this thought, and not another word, she climbs aboard and pays her six euros for the short crossing.

It does not surprise her that no one else joins her in the taxi boat. Everyone is cleaning and rebuilding and trying to restore some sort of order in the aftermath of the disaster. The shouts of one worker to another echo all over town but there is a subdued tone to their calls.

The new driver casts off the ropes. The engine roars into life, and the whole structure shudders into movement and then quietens to a putter as they negotiate their way out of the harbour, hitting the squashed buoy that Rallou noticed earlier as they go. Across the water the world that is waiting for her seems a very big place and she is suddenly unsure about why she is going. To try to restore a life that is no longer hers to lead?

As it passes between the harbour walls the taxi boat gains speed, its hull slapping on the waves. The noise is very loud and the movement rather uncomfortable. Rallou grips the edge of the seat as the taxi boy increases the speed and with it the intensity of the buffeting. The stern look she gives him is intended to suggest he slow down, but instead he grins and goes even faster. She hangs on and watches the water behind them break into froth, curling into outward spirals and rippling away, line after line.

When she was expecting her first child and she and Christos were making the town house habitable, they would go down to the sea at the end of the day to swim the dust and the dirt away. Under the water, she would smooth a hand over the bump that was to be their child and he would look into her eyes as if he would love her forever. Then, with no warning, he would flick over backward and swim away, leaving her to float, the sound of the sea cracking and pinging in her ears, the chill of the water cooling all her senses, her limbs waving and loose in the water. Then he would return with treasure for her: a starfish that he would later release, the shells of sea urchins in green and purple and sometimes orange, and, on more than one occasion, a shell coated inside with mother-of-pearl. These he took home with them; he would drill a tiny hole in the edge of each of them, to hang them on a thin chain he bought for the purpose, for her. She hasn't worn that in ages. It is now under the rubble that used to be their house, under her collapsed life. She puts her hand to her throat, to feel where it used to hang.

She is relieved when the engine cuts and they idle towards the dock at the other side, but the boy-captain has not mastered the art and it takes him two attempts to tie up alongside the pier.

'*Kalo taxidi*,' he wishes her as he offers his hand, before looking around to see if he has a return fare. No one is waiting to go back with him and his disappointment shows on his face; it is the eagerness of youth taking the first of many, many discouragements he will be bombarded with in his life.

'Oh stop it,' Rallou tells herself.

With a big sigh she turns and begins to walk up the track that leads to the main road. Corfu seems a lifetime away, and almost certainly a place that holds humiliation and rejection for her. Maybe she does not need to go, and she could just stay off Orino Island for a day or two, regain her composure, work out her position? She could go to Saros town. Christos has a distant cousin in a village near there. Theo, wasn't it, who runs a *kafenio*? Maybe Christos has been in touch with him, or stopped off on the way.

'Don't be silly,' she tells herself. There is no way she is going to walk into a strange village up to a strange man and ask if her husband has left her. Wasn't a hotel built on the edge of that same village by a friend of this second cousin? Maybe she could stay there, find out casually if Christos has been around or in touch.

'Oh!' she exclaims. In all this planning and scheming, she has completely forgotten about the

Americans. How could she have forgotten! But then, they probably have no expectations of her right now. They have probably not even given her a thought. Her house is gone, theirs is substantially damaged. Everything is in chaos.

She stops walking. She should have let them know, nevertheless. She looks back across the water to Orino again. Is the correct thing to do to return, explain to Lori – but explain what? What is she doing? Surely she is just going for a day or two?

Rubbing her forehead it feels like she has a headache coming on. She doesn't often wear sunglasses but just now they would dilute the intensity of the sun's glare. But her sunglasses were on the shelf in the kitchen, and they are not there now, and neither is the shelf. A sob escapes her. 'Damn you, Christo! Why now?' She curses him out loud. She lets herself cry for a minute or two, the sun beating down on her head, her salty tears drying before they reach her chin. Then she tries to recall what she had been thinking about. Sunglasses, Theo, hotel ... Oh yes, Lori! She shakes her head; she should at least have let her know that she would not be around for a day or two.

She must send them a postcard, from the first village she passes through. Her feet begin to move again, up the track to the road. She will send two cards, one to their poste restante address on Orino Island, and one to their house in America, just in case. Maybe they will return there if their house on the island is too badly damaged. She will thank them for their invitation and explain ... But wait a minute! Everything has changed!

She stops walking again.

With no Christos around, she could take up their offer of a trip to America. She could go back and accept their offer and start planning immediately! She steps under the shade of an olive tree whilst she thinks, grateful that the mainland is not as hot as Orino town. There is more exposed earth here, and more trees, in contrast to the stone paving that covers the majority of the town. It is very pleasant – like Korifi, but less open. The olive tree has spread some of its branches over the road a little, creating shade, and a couple of upturned barrels and an old plastic chair have been placed by its trunk. One of the legs on the plastic chair is cracked right across. She sits on the upturned barrel to think things through. The edge digs into her legs but it is not too uncomfortable. The cicadas are deafening.

If she were to return immediately, where would she go? Back up to Korifi?

She puts her hand under the edges of the barrel and shifts a little, deeper into the shade.

The whole point of going back immediately would be to talk to Lori, accept her invitation to America – but then she would get involved in cleaning and sorting and rebuilding their house. Is helping them with the mess their house is now in a part of her job? No, probably not. So, if she were to go back and find somewhere to stay they might pay her extra if she helped, which would increase her resources if she were to take them up on their offer to take her back to America with them. Of course, they didn't mean for her to go and live with them forever, but would she have to tell them at the outset that she was thinking of extending her stay? Would it be possible for her to stay permanently in the States?

One cicada, right above her head, is singing so loudly it is hurting her ears. It is hidden amongst the leaves, and she cannot see it. How often Christos used to catch then, chase her with them, even as recently as last summer, to scare her, pushing the insects' little blunt faces and goggly eyes at her. Laughing, she would push his hand away, both of them ducking when the insect took wing so it would not be caught in their hair.

She smiles at the memory but her vision blurs with tears. She cannot face going back to Orino Island. Not alone. Not immediately. Maybe she could just take a little holiday. It is most likely that Lori will organise everything perfectly well. Everyone on the island will be sorting out their own houses. It is easy to imagine that Lori and Ted will get a team of builders from another island. Piros, or Syglos, maybe. That's what she would do if she was them and she had their money. It might have been helpful to them if she had been there to translate, but they will manage. Perhaps she will get back after the building work, when they just need someone to help clean.

Meanwhile, it is not unreasonable for her to take a little holiday. Yes, that is what she will call it: a holiday. And she will send a postcard accepting their offer to return to America with them as soon as she can. Meanwhile, being away from Orino might be the balm she needs. She yawns again and, as her eyes half close, the unspilt tears squeeze out.

A small lizard runs as fast as it can across the empty road and then, safely across, hides, so very still, in a small pile of browned olive leaves.

She does not see the bus coming and its horn startles her. The door hisses open and the driver waits, one hand on the wheel, one on the gearstick. Brushing the tears aside, Rallou realises that this is it: she has to decide to go somewhere – but where?

# Chapter 21

'*Ella*, kyria, are you coming?' The bus driver asks, his words drawled out in a manner that suggests there is no hurry at all.

Rallou looks behind her, down the lane that leads to the boat and back to her island. Somewhere on the hilltop is her baba. It's likely that he is no longer alone, surrounded instead by woman and children sent there whilst the men stay in town to rebuild their damaged houses. Baba surrounded by women and children – he won't complain!

Rallou steps up into the bus.

'Patra?' the driver asks.

'No, only Saros.' Saros is far enough if she is just taking a little holiday. She swallows as she pays for her ticket, a little tension in her throat, wondering if making the choice to only go as far as Saros means she has given up on Christos. But there is still his second cousin Theo, in the village near Saros. She will find Theo in his *kafenio*, discover if he knows anything, without drawing attention to herself. She can use the same lie, about a sick aunt. No, Theo will know all his aunts … Perhaps it can be a sick friend in Corfu. Yes, that's better. She will say that she is following Christos, and she will ask casually if he passed by, and just see what Theo says. If he knows nothing then he will say so and she will leave, keep it all vague. If he does know something, then – well, she will decide what to do depending on what he has to say. She will cross that bridge when she comes to it.

There is only one other passenger on the bus. Swaying slightly as she moves up the aisle, Rallou notes that the flimsy curtains that are drawn down one side of the bus do little to keep out the brightness and the heat, and she sits on the other side, in the shade. Her fellow traveller, two seats behind, has a big, red chicken on her knee, just sitting there. The old woman's bent fingers stroke its head and it blinks.

The sudden movement of the bus pushes Rallou forcefully back into her seat. The motion is not like that of a donkey, and it seems to sway more and is noisier than she remembers from London. It is just a little bit frightening, but how marvellous it would be if there was a bus from Orino town up to Korifi. How her baba's life would change then! How her life would change! It would mean she could live on the hilltop and work in the town. Others would return too, as they could do the same. Maybe she can have a word with the mayor when she goes back.

After a few minutes, the swaying of the bus begins to make her feel ill. Perhaps it is better to stick to walking on the island, after all, and suggest to Baba that he get another donkey, one like Dolly. She hopes Tolis is taking good care of Dolly at the boatyard if Yanni has not returned yet.

The other passenger gets off at the next stop, clutching her chicken, and Rallou has the bus to herself. She was enjoying a sense of freedom as the road spun past under the wheels of the bus, but now, with the vehicle completely empty, she starts to feel very alone and, with the movement of the bus, a little bit nauseous. Row after row of olive trees fly past the windows.

Back when she first returned from London she had delighted in being able to roam amongst the olive trees again. The leaves, blue on one side, silver on the other, spun on their stems with the slightest breeze, rustling gently. The thick, twisted trunks were reassuring in their timelessness. She realised that the olive groves were the one thing she missed the most – after her baba, of course. Her courtship with Christos was largely played out in the olive groves, with Christos hiding behind them to jump out, climbing them, showing off. His family's orchards abutted theirs, the trees merging with each other. To cut costs at harvest time, because each family had approximately the same number of trees, they combed them all together, helping each other, and divided the oil between them. It was the year she returned from London that they began to jointly buy in labour to do the job. The tarpaulins spread beneath to catch the crop were by now so old and patched that no one stopped to consider any longer which family they belonged to: they just belonged to the trees. Christos doesn't go up there any more; certainly he hasn't in the last three years or so, as far as Rallou is aware. Maybe he has arranged something with Vasillis, who still tends to his olives. Rallou has not seen any income from the olives over the last few years. She can remember asking the first year about it, and the following year too, but he made excuses and so she just gave up chasing and pushing him. So it is perhaps over four years since he last harvested the olives. What a waste.

The corners of her mouth pull down and she frowns. Not tending to the olives is so like Christos. He just never seems to get around to doing the things he should do and instead is too busy pretending to be a hunter up in the hills and only working the days he absolutely has to in town. When was the last time he built a wall or painted a door and got paid for it?

The whole topic depresses her more than she can bear and just in that moment she does not care that he has gone. Good riddance. But the tears come anyway. She presses her face against the relative cool of the bus window. The olive trees seem to go on forever, the leaves fluttering in the light breeze. Blue-silver. Silver-blue. She yawns and closes her eyes. She will feel better after a few days away. Maybe even just a day – stay a night and go back.

It is the stillness of the bus that wakes her. She opens her eyes and for a moment nothing makes sense. It is dusk and not even the driver is on board. The silent vehicle sits stationary at the edge of a vast area of black tarmac that is dotted with long articulated lorries in the half gloom. Men with dark skins and rough clothes are walking between them. They look like they are checking the rigs as they try handles and pull at the corners of the tarpaulins. It takes Rallou a moment to realise these are illegal immigrants, like the ones she has seen on the television.

This is not Saros!

Gathering her bag and her wits she trundles down the aisle to the front of the bus, down the steps and outside. It is still warm but she has no idea if the sky is cloudless because the orange glow of the street lights blocks all visibility of the stars.

By the lorries there is what looks like some sort of entrance, and beyond that the moonlight flickers, reflected, telling her that there is water there. This is a dock, and it is brightly lit and rather shabby-looking.

There are barriers at the entrance to the port and drivers have to stop their vehicles whilst a person in the booth checks their tickets before waving them on. Only one booth is staffed at the moment and the girl in it is distracted by a man in a port police uniform who leans against her booth door, chatting. The whole area is lit up with overhead lights, a pool of yellow in the dark expanse of tarmac. Rallou hurries past the lorries, alert for the immigrants, her sights set on the lights.

'Excuse me,' she says, slightly out of breath, to the man in the white port police uniform; the girl inside the booth is counting coins and putting them into little plastic bags.

'How can I help you, kyria?' he asks, and grins widely, with a smile that is not for Rallou but designed instead to impress the girl in the booth. 'You are looking for your boat?' he asks, and seems to think he is funny. There are many ships lined up at the harbourside, some with internal lights blazing, and others quite dark – hulks in the gloom. Rallou looks at the girl, who is making a point of ignoring the exchange, continuing to count her coins.

'Where are you going?' he asks. 'There for Bari.' The port policeman points to a big ferry alive with people milling around on every level. 'Here for the non-stop to Venice.' He points to another that looks just the same as the first, with maybe a few more lights. 'And that one is the overnight to Corfu, and it does not stop at Zakinthos, Lefkada or Cephalonia. Where do you want to go?

There is a hum of activity, and the occasional shout, from the ships. The air smells salty but is tainted with the aroma of dirty oil.

'Is this Patra?' Rallou asks. The bright lights and unfamiliar surroundings make it difficult to judge what time it is, and just hearing the name 'Corfu' sends her off balance and leaves her on the verge of tears again. The girl looks up from her coins, her mouth slightly open, when Rallou asks where she is. She slides her gaze to the port policeman, perhaps wondering if this woman in front of her booth is crazy.

Rallou is aware of what is going on but she does feel a little crazy. No, not crazy, but maybe a little confused.

'Yes.' The port policeman laughs the word gently. 'This is Patra.' His eyes flick to the girl. 'All the boats sail overnight. Do you have a ticket yet? If not, I would strongly recommend that you take a cabin.' He checks that the girl is listening, and when he sees that she is he continues. 'I took my mama once to Lefkada with only a deck ticket, but the seats were too upright and she had a very bad night. Besides, I found out afterwards that a cabin on the boat is as cheap as a hotel room, but you wake up somewhere else.' He seems to find this very funny and laughs to himself, or maybe just to impress the girl.

'The same as a hotel room?' Rallou asks for clarification.

'Well, maybe a little bit more, but then you would expect that.' The radio that he wears hooked over his shoulder clicks and hisses and a muffled voice speaks, but he ignores it. 'So, can I help you with your bags?' This is said in a more genuine manner, not to impress the girl but because he has a mama of his own. He looks back at the bus she came from.

'I have no bags.'

The man frowns under his white peaked hat and the voice on his radio becomes more insistent. He turns slightly and speaks into his shoulder.

'Well, if you are all right, yiayia, then I must go.' He grins again, taps the frame of the door to the booth, nods to the girl, and walks away.

'Yiayia, indeed!' Rallou mutters. Now the girl counting coins smiles to herself, but she does not look up.

The boats lined up in the harbour seem like forbidden fruit to her: vessels that transport people to foreign destinations, available for anyone to use, except her. Dismissing them, she turns the other way, hoping a small hotel will be just there, with open doors and cheap prices, leaving her with no distance to walk. Although she slept on the bus she feels very tired. She must have slept hard, all the way through Saros and across to Patra!

The ferry to Bari sounds its horn. That's where Natasa lives now. A wave of adrenaline, or excitement, runs through her chest. She could go there, visit her daughter. She has never been to Italy. Ah, but she has no passport. It is under a pile of rubble that used to be home, along with her *taftotita*. She has no identification at all. Her bottom lip quivers. Her emotions seem to be changing every second. There is a clanking of chains and men on the dock pull ropes the thickness of her arm from around bollards, and the towering ship to begins to slide away from the pier and off to Bari.

Fancy the berths on a boat being the same price as a hotel room! From that point of view, if she did have her passport then she could have sailed tonight, spent the day with her daughter, and come back the following night. But the boat has gone now.

She looks around, hoping the hotel she yearns for has suddenly appeared, but of course it hasn't. There are some rather grand-looking buildings beyond the confines of the port, but their entrances are small. They are not commercial places – private homes, more likely – and they are across a wide road. Rallou does not fancy dodging the traffic to find that not one of them takes paying guests. But, just to feel like she is doing something, she starts to walk, the lights of the boats drawing her closer. The tarmac lorry park, the wide road and the patch of park in front of the houses beyond are all so dark. Also, she can see people moving around in the shadows by the trucks. More illegal immigrants, no doubt, all hoping for the opportunity to steal across to Italy.

There is a sandwich board at the tailgate of each boat with the departure times written in chalk. Cars form a long snaking line, inching their way up the metal incline and into the hollow bellies of the ships, where men's voices ring and echo. It all seems very exciting. When she went to Paris and London she took a plane, which seemed very quiet and controlled, sterile even, compared to this spectacle, which is alive and pulsing and rather thrilling.

'Kyria, you need a ticket?' a man calls to her. He is sitting behind a rickety wooden stand; a coloured perspex sign hangs on thin chains at the front, advertising destinations and prices. He holds out a leaflet. 'On deck, shared cabin, two-berth cabin – although I think those have all gone – single cabin.'

She could! Go to an island tonight, not for Christos, but just because she can, and come back tomorrow.

This ticket seller also has a handheld radio and he talks into it, his accent strange to her. Maybe he is Italian. When he finishes talking on the radio he says to her, 'The boat to Venice is full. So the overnight to Corfu? That's all there is tonight, but tomorrow morning ...' He reels off a list of destinations, delivering his knowledge of what is on offer as if it should impress.

Rallou stands aside. Is she really kidding herself? Is she somehow making all this happen? Creating 'accidents' so she will end up on Corfu, chasing after Christos but allowing herself her pride?

'Eight hours to Corfu, kyria, and the ship docks there for at least two hours so there is no hurry in the morning. Here.' He tears off a ticket and holds it out to her.

Isn't Corfu actually the last place she wants to be if what she needs is a day or two's holiday? Knowing Christos is there will drive her to do something about finding him.

'Er, I'm not sure, I just overslept on the bus, I hadn't really intended to ... not really, I just needed to get away. I thought Saros ...' Rallou jabbers.

'Don't go, Natasa!' a voice calls, full of emotion.

At the sound of her daughter's name, Rallou turns around smartly. A tall youth is addressing a thin girl who looks nothing like her Natasa. Her beating heart relaxes.

'I am going, Spiro. My mama was right,' the thin girl, this other Natasa, says.

'Your mama knows nothing,' retorts the youth. There is an angry edge to his voice, a little display of the middle-aged man he will become, perhaps?

The ticket man has put down his radio to watch the spectacle.

'She knows men like you keep girls like me waiting and waiting until we lose our chances.' The girl has tears in her eyes. She can't be more than twenty, if that.

'You are not waiting. *We* are waiting.' His voice has lost its anger now, and he seems small, fragile. In appearance he is not much older than the girl. He runs a hand through his dark hair, and a steel ring on his thumb catches the orange overhead lights. Rallou thought only tourists wore those.

'And what are *we* waiting for, Spiro?' the girl spits back.

'I was waiting for tonight! I was waiting because, tonight, before you got so full of yourself and bought yourself a ticket home, I was going to take you to that cafe by the shore where we met.'

'And what difference would that have made?' She takes a ticket out of her bag and steps towards the boat.

'It would have meant I did not have to do this here,' the boy replies, searching in his pockets; then, finding what he was looking for, he drops to one knee.

'Bravo!' the ticket man shouts, and the girl, who had set off for the boat, turns around. Her eyes are as wide as a startled hare's. Her lover is on one knee, spotlighted by the ship's tail light.

'Oh,' is all she can say, her hand to her throat.

'Natasa, will you marry me?' He holds out the ring, stuffing the box back into his pocket.

Several dockhands are now enjoying the spectacle and they fall silent at this moment. A group of Japanese tourists on the aft deck begin to take photographs, the flashes attracting more attention to the couple.

It does not take Natasa even a half second to run to him. The ring is slipped on, and he stands and kisses her, lifting her off her feet, spinning her around. The Japanese tourists, the dockhands and the ticket man all cheer and applaud; the couple briefly look around them as if they have only just noticed that they are in a public place, give a little bow and, arm in arm, walk away as if they are one.

Rallou stares after them.

When Christos proposed, he got down on one knee underneath an olive tree, at the furthest end of the grove. The ring he produced was so pretty and the reality of what he was asking filled her with such happiness she could not find any words with which to reply.

'Is that a yes, then?' he pressed. All she could do was nod her head and he slipped on the ring and stood and hugged her, then kissed her, then kissed her some more, and they whispered nonsense about how different they were from other couples, how they would see the world together, escape the island. Another of Christos's unfulfilled promises.

But then, what has she done about it either? Here she is in Patra, with ships waiting to sail, and she can't even make the decision to get on one. What happened? Did the moment she walked up the aisle take away her right to make decisions for herself? For them both? Or did she pass the responsibility for making decisions to Christos, and then become angry and stubborn when he didn't meet her expectations?

But look now – who is in Corfu and who is dithering?

'Please, lady ...' Natasa and her young man are back. 'Please, take my ticket.' She offers the yellow slip, puts it in Rallou's hand. But she does not look at Rallou; she has eyes only for her Spiros.

# Chapter 22

'Ah, you see!' the ticket man says. 'When life offers you something like this it is because it has set a path for you.' He is all smiles. Rallou looks at the ticket.

Corfu, one berth, shared cabin.

'Kyria, if you cannot see a gift when it is looking at you, what more do you need? A fanfare of trumpets? Dancing girls? A police escort?' He is teasing her now, his grin even wider. He winks as he catches her eye. 'Go, have fun, and when you get bored come back!'

Prompted by this speech, she takes the ticket and walks, hesitantly, towards the boat. A man waiting at the side of the wide ribbed-steel gangplank takes her ticket and tears off part of it.

'Go to the end, up the stairs, first left, down the stairs, right past the money exchange – and here, look, the ticket says room number one hundred and forty seven.' He looks away from her to the next person.

'Up the stairs, left, down the stairs, past the money ... Up, left, down, money,' Rallou repeats to herself, and she heads inside, glad that she has specific directions to follow rather than decisions to make. 'Up, left, down, money.'

There is a jam of people on the stairs.

'Up, left, down, money.' It is a big ship, and she could easily get lost.

Halfway up the steps is a landing and an opening marked *Personnel*, from which emanates a stench of grease and oil, and the heat hits her as it billows up. It must be quite unbearable down there. A clang of metal upon metal tells her people are in the depths, working.

'How do they stand it?' she asks herself. A door opens further up and a little old lady comes towards her, with a very slow step, and her head wobbles just ever so slightly side to side. She is wearing black from head to foot: a dark blouse, a straight skirt to just below the knee, thick, flesh-coloured tights, black sensible shoes and the customary scarf on her head tied in a knot under her chin.

'Up, left, down, exchange,' the lady chants. Her fingers tremble on the handrail.

'Up, left, down, money,' Rallou says.

'Up, left, down, exchange.' The woman smiles in recognition, repeating her own mantra.

Rallou opens the door on her left, which is between them.

'Up, left, down, money,' she says, laughing now.

'Up, left, down, exchange,' the lady giggles. She is short, only up to Rallou's shoulder, and slung across her back is a large yellow bag out of which knitting needles are poking.

They go through the door and are faced with a flight of stairs, and they repeat together, 'Up.' Now they laugh openly.

At the top they exchange another word. 'Left,' And halfway down the corridor Rallou says, 'Money.'

'Exchange,' the old lady replies, and there in front of them is a sign that says *Money Exchange*, and they both turn down this corridor.

'What number are you?' the old lady asks. Her eyes are bright even though her skin is weathered with age.

'One hundred and forty-seven,' Rallou says.

'Oh, can you read the number on my ticket?' says the old lady.'I have forgotten already,' and she passes over her own yellow slip.

'Oh, one hundred and forty-seven. We are bunkmates!' Rallou feels a sudden relief at the thought of having some company.

'You are travelling alone. How brave. It took me until I was seventy to travel alone, and now I do it all the time!' She smiles. 'I am Toula, by the way.'

'Hello, Kyria Toula. I am Rallou.'

'*Yeia sou*, Rallou, we will be good bunkmates for the night. Here we are.' She opens the door into a very small room that has a neatly made bed against each wall and a small table at the end, between them. There are blinds and curtains at the window, in a caramel brown, matching the bed covers. The sheets and pillowcases are a crisp white. The walls have been painted a colour that is combination of the two, a halfway hue. Toula pauses and looks around. There is a narrow door just inside the cabin and she opens this to reveal the toilet in the same colour scheme. 'Ah, good. Not sure I could manage a whole night without,' she says, with no embarrassment, and then she fully enters the room and sits on one of the beds. The way she unslings her bag and takes out her knitting makes it look like she has done this many times before. Rallou really only wanted to find her cabin before exploring the ship but feels it would be rude just to walk away so she squeezes in and sits down too.

'I have not been knitting long. My daughter has a four-year-old, Katerina, and little Apostolis is nearly two, and she has another on the way now. I never knitted for the first two, so for this one I am knitting.' Toula has an easy manner. She pauses in her knitting to take a scent bottle from her bag, then liberally squirts herself. It is a sweet floral smell, sweeter than ripe fruit.

'Ah. My daughter is pregnant with her first. She lives in Bari. She is a doctor.' The usual flush of pride sweeps over Rallou and her chest fills and her head lifts.

'You will go over when it is born?' Toula asks.

Rallou has harboured a desire to do this since she first knew Natasa was pregnant, but she has always felt Christos would make it either difficult or impossible. But why would he? Sometimes it seems she thinks things with no real basis – just imagines the worst and then looks for it. If she looks for negatives in life perhaps it is inevitable that she will find them. What was that painted sign that Costas Voulgaris had hanging on his cafe wall? Oh yes – 'Life may give you nothing but cactuses, but that does not mean you have to sit on them.' It makes her smile. If she wants to go to see the baby when it is born she can, and she will. It is a little opening of freedom that has always been there, but for some reason she has denied it to herself.

'Yes. I will go,' she says, and it feels good to have made this decision. Trying to make a calculation, she realises she has lost track of the days. She has no idea what the date is, or even what month it is. It is not the first time that she has lost weeks just by living. But the baby will come before Lori and Ted go to America. Maybe she can do both. She must not forget to send Lori a card.

'Well, I would be glad to hear them,' Toula says.

'Hear what?' Rallou asks.

'Those thoughts that are tracing a thousand emotions across your face.'

Rallou puts her hand to her mouth as if feeling the contours of her lips will give her a better understanding of what is showing.

'Ah, you don't have to tell me.' Toula has come to the end of the row, and she takes out the needle from under her arm and changes the needles over, rewrapping the pale yellow wool around her fingers.

'Let me change the subject,' she suggests. 'Where have you come from, and where are you going?' Her needles click and clack.

With someone listening – a sounding board – and the chance of some feedback, everything Rallou has been thinking and feeling becomes more real, more enormous and far more painful. 'Orino.' It is all she dares to allow herself to say as the memory of her house sits heavily in her chest and her breathing becomes difficult.

'Oh, my God in heaven and all the saints around him!' Toula's needles freeze mid-purl. 'It was on the news. Are you all right, my dear? And your loved ones! I heard at least there were no fatalities. Or was there one? Yes, one, an old lady. I hope this was no relation?' She puts her knitting down now and reaches out to pat Rallou's hands. This is enough to bring the weight from her lungs rushing back up her throat, causing her cheeks to burn hot and tears to spring to the surface. Toula pats with one hand. Her other is in her bag, feeling for a fistful of tissues, which she offers.

'No relation. I didn't even really know her.' Pressing the tissues into the corners of her eyes seems to stop her crying.

'And your house?'

'Gone.'

With that one word the whole story comes out, in a confusing order, from the earthquake and the collapse of her house, to her setting out for Corfu, and back through her sleepless night at Vasillis's house in town, to being up in Korifi, and then on to Christos's comments about Greg. She explains the possibility that he might have gone to Corfu after an old love or maybe just to find a new one. When she gets to a point where she has no more to say she looks out of the window. If the ship has not yet cast off she will go home to her baba. The only thing she has left is her pride, and if she goes running after Christos she will lose that too.

'Ah, so you are going after him?' Toula asks.

'You know what, I think I have made a mistake.' Rallou stands.

'Where are you going?'

'Off this ship, back to the island.'

'Oh, are you a strong swimmer then?'

Rallou looks out of the porthole again to see the harbour wall slipping past, and realises that they have indeed begun their journey.

'It seems, what with free tickets and quietly departing ships, that life has plans for you,' Toula says, and her needles begin to clack again.

'Someone else already said that today.'

Toula shrugs and knits on in silence.

'You know, when my husband was alive he was a bully,' she says after a pause. 'A bully.' She repeats the words as if she needs to keep reminding herself. 'It took me ever such a long time to realise it, but now he is dead, do you know what?'

Rallou does not want to say 'What?' because she is sure Toula is going to say she misses him.

'What?' She gives in anyway.

'I do not miss him at all. What I do regret is not leaving him earlier. Waste of my life!'

'Oh! So you think I should not go after Christos?'

'Did I say that? I know that if my Apostolis had left home without giving me a clue as to where he was going, what day he would be expected back and what he would like cooked and ready on the table on his return I would have rejoiced. The fact that you are still thinking about your Christos, thinking about whether or not you should go after him, says it all. Or maybe I am wrong. But as the boat is now sailing, you are going to Corfu anyway, so let's enjoy it!'

'Are you going on holiday then?' Rallou cannot quite get to the essence of who this Toula is. She seems far too self-possessed for someone who was bullied, and now she has spilt her whole life story Rallou would like to know something of this lady.

'Sort of. I have a small apartment in Corfu. When Apostolis died I sold the lower part of the big house and gave the upstairs to my housekeeper.'

'Sorry, did I hear you right? You gave your house to your housekeeper?' Her thoughts flick to Lori and Ted.

'Oh, what a blessing she was! When I could not stand him any more I would live for the days Nikki would come. I enjoyed making her breakfast and lunch, you see – she was so appreciative, whereas Apostolis thought it was his right. So yes, I gave her the house. After all, she was the one who polished and loved it. I moved back to my family's house in the village near Saros.'

'Wait, is that the village where a man called Theo has a *kafenio*?'

'Ha, you know it! It is a small world, isn't it? Is he a friend of yours?'

'He is Christos's second cousin, but I have never actually met him.'

'Oh my, my, such a small world. Well, Theo is a lovely man, so if your husband is related he cannot be all bad. Small world, such a small world.' And her needles click.

Rallou waits for all this to sink in.

'So, you divide your time between Corfu and the village outside Saros town?' she asks.

'And London. My daughter lives there, the grandchildren are there. Didn't go until Apostolis was dead though. That's how much he controlled me.' Her mouth becomes a tight, hard line.

'My daughter is in Bari. Christos has not let me go.' But as she says this it feels like a lie, so she tries to explain. 'Well, it is not that he does not let me, it's just – oh, I don't know … It just feels like he doesn't approve. And I'm not sure he would come with me. He doesn't travel. He has never left the island.'

'Yet he is in Corfu.' Toula's forehead wrinkles and she raises her eyebrows. Click clack, click clack. Then she sighs, a big deep sigh with a slight rattle to it. 'But although I don't miss him …' – she is talking about herself again now – 'and I would not take him back, I do miss someone, you know, just being with someone, a like-minded soul. But who knows, maybe it is never too late?'

# Chapter 23

'Do you really think that's true? That it's never too late?' Rallou asks after a pause, but she is thinking of Christos, not Toula. Her eyes are still moist and she dabs them intermittently.

'Absolutely. We are social animals.' Toula takes more tissues from her bag and passes them to Rallou, and then resumes her knitting. 'We may get a little more set in our ways as we get older, a little less inclined to change and accommodate, but isolation is the thing we all abhor the most. That's why they have solitary confinement in prisons, is it not? But you know what,' she continues, 'I think men are less tolerant of that sort of thing than women. They hate the possibility of being left alone. They really are pack animals. That, or they need to be the head of their herds. Something like that, anyway. I'm sure I read somewhere that more women leave their husbands than the other way around. Not just a few more, but quite a substantial percentage.' Her wool runs out.

'Bother.' She fishes in her bag, takes out another, smaller bag, which she puts on the bed along with a change purse, a magazine, a small towel, and then, much to Rallou's surprise, a large pair of black headphones, the sort with a solid strap that goes across the top of the head. 'For the radio,' Toula informs Rallou, and then out comes the radio, a small portable transistor. 'I get the loneliest when I try to go to sleep. That's why I always get a cabin for two. But even so, I listen to the radio. Now, where is that wool? Ah, here it is.' She pulls the paper belt off the new ball and joins it by knitting the two strands together for a few clicks and clacks.

'So. What is your plan once you reach Corfu? How will you begin to search for him? Have you any idea where he might stay, any other relations he might have up here, or anywhere he has ever mentioned?' She takes a breath but not for long enough for Rallou to answer before she continues. 'Across the road from my house there are two boys who rent bikes. Ilias and Bobby. Now, they know everything that goes on on the island, and if they don't know they would know who to ask to find out.' Her knitting pace increases as if the possibility of the hunt excites her.

Shrinking a little where she sits, Rallou chews at her inner lip. It is one thing, in a moment of weakness, to tell this Toula woman her story, but it is quite another to be having her telling it to the rent-a-bike boys and having them in turn spread it around the island so that everyone will know her business.

'Actually Toula, that is very kind of you but–'

'Why do you say "but"? "But" you are going to go all the way to Corfu and not find him? "But" you are going to go back to your baba having been on the same island as Christos, cousin of Theo, "but" not talked to him? Now why would you do that?' She stops knitting again to look at Rallou with black, piercing eyes. Everything that was in her bag appears to be spread across the bed, but she breaks her stare and fishes once again in the capacious holdall. 'Can you get the two glasses from the sink in there?' She points to the toilet door. What on earth is the woman up to now, Rallou wonders, but she does as she is told. In a single pace and a long reach, the glasses are hers. But when she turns around to sit down again, she sees that on the little table separating the beds at the pillow end are feta and bread and olives and two slices of spinach pie, all laid out along with a small plastic water bottle that looks like it is filled with red wine.

'Come, we will eat,' Toula commands, and Rallou's stomach agrees with her, very loudly.

After the food and wine Toula hiccups twice and then with blushing cheeks invites Rallou to a game of cards, during which they become rather riotous, until someone in the next cabin bangs on the walls, which sets them off giggling like teenagers. Toula's bag seems to have no bottom because after the cards a second small water bottle of wine is found, and by the time they have drunk that they are yawning. Toula declares that Rallou is the best cabin partner she has had to date and that she wouldn't believe just how boring some of the people Toula has shared with have been. Before she puts the playing cards away she does a clever trick with them that involves fanning them out and making the queens rise to the top. Rallou is impressed. Toula puts them back in their box, which goes into an old tobacco tin, and that in turn is put back in her bag.

'So, we sleep,' Toula announces, filling their glasses with what is left in the bottle. 'And tomorrow you come to my little flat and we get Ilias and Bobby to find your Christos and you will have a big romantic reunion and then you can go home to Orino Island and you can invite me to stay and I can meet your baba. There – now that sounds like a very good plan.' She starts to unbutton her blouse to reveal an all-covering bodice with integral bra. It is not an unusual item of clothing for someone her age – but in scarlet, with black lace edging! Rallou is not sure she wants such a woman to meet her baba.

She goes into the toilet cabin and climbs out of her skirt, glad that she has one of her better slips on underneath. 'Your only slip, now,' Rallou tells herself in the mirror, and for the first time she realises that the only clothes she has in the world are those she stands up in, and her whole situation takes on a surreal quality. She shakes her head at her reflection and opens her eyes wide before making a mental calculation of how much she can afford to spend if she needs to replace – well, everything. The answer is that she should not be spending any of what she has saved, but then again she will get paid at the end of the month. But how will she wash and dry her clothes if she has nothing else to put on in the meantime?

'Stop panicking,' she tells the wide-eyed Rallou in the mirror. 'I am panicking,' she whispers to herself. 'I am panicking. I am panicking.' Tears prick her eyes. 'I am having the thought that I am panicking. I am having the thought that I am panicking. I am having the thought that I am panicking. I notice that I am having the thought that I am panicking. I notice that I am having the thought that–'

'I am going to sleep now, Rallou,' Toula calls out to her. 'Let me know if my headphones are too loud and turn off the lights when you are ready.'

'All right,' Rallou calls back, and looks back to the mirror; the woman reflected there does not seems quite as panicky now, and there is just a trace of a smile left in her lips from when she answered Toula.

Back in the cabin Toula is lying on her back wearing an eye mask with *Qatar Airlines* embroidered across it, and the headphones, which look ridiculously big on her. Rallou climbs into her bunk, which is much more comfortable than it looks, and finds that the pillow is full and soft. She switches out the light and closes her eyes.

The boat seems so noisy and the rocking is more noticeable now she is lying down. It was perhaps not such a good idea to have drunk so much wine, but Toula was so fun to play cards with, like a child, so easily excited. And it was lovely to be distracted from the jumble of emotions that are battling for dominance within her.

'All ashore!' Someone is ringing a bell, walking down the corridor outside the cabin. 'All ashore!' they shout again. The sun pierces its way through the blinds, slicing the room into light and shade, and the boat is no longer rocking.

Bleary-eyed, Rallou sits up. Toula is lying on her back, her headphones still in place, her eye mask still on. Rallou felt close to her last night as they drank wine and played cards, as though she had known her all her life, and now, although there is very little that is familiar about her, the sight of her makes Rallou smile. 'All ashore – Corfu.' The bell is rung again. Rallou slips into her skirt and pulls on her blouse, hurriedly doing up the buttons before Toula awakes. She needn't have worried because the old woman sleeps on, and Rallou debates whether to wake her and let her carry out her plan for finding Christos or just slip away. It almost seemed a good idea last night, but now it all feels a bit mad. She doesn't even know the woman.

Taking a comb from her bag, she goes into the toilet cubicle to use the mirror there. Her hair is thick, and a brush would be easier. There is just a trace of white at her roots. She gets this stuff, herbal, natural, not really a dye, from the chemist every month or so and uses it to wash her hair. It just restores the natural colour, it says. It looks like it is time to do it again, as soon as she gets home. At this thought the face in the mirror crumbles. The mouth goes first, almost like a grimace, but as the eyes squeeze half shut and the tears flow her mouth looks more sad than angry. There is no home. It is so strange that she can be having these emotions and yet watch herself having them at the same time, almost as if they are nothing to do with her.

'Have I overslept? Has the man been around with his bell?' Toula calls.

'No and yes.' Rallou's voice sounds completely normal so she washes her face and then steps back into the cabin.

'Been crying again, eh?' Toula says kindly. 'Not really surprising, is it? You've been through a lot, losing a husband and a house. Well, the house I cannot do much about, but the husband we will restore to you.' She is out of bed now and putting her blouse on, with her heels together, feet at ten to two, her toes splayed for balance. There is something just slightly comical about her and maybe that is what made Rallou laugh so much when they played cards last night.

'Don't worry, *koukla*, everything will be fine, just you see. I am a firm believer in the power of life. Life will give you what you need and take away what you don't need, mark my words.' And with this she gives a very pronounced wink which makes Rallou realise she was thinking about her own *koukla*, Dolly the donkey.

'All ashore!' The man with the bell is back.

Toula repacks her bag efficiently and with great speed, and the two of them step together into the corridor, which is heaving and jostling with people.

'I can't find Teddy!' a little boy wails in English.
'Did you get the toothbrushes?' his mother asks her husband.
'Mum, Mum, I can't find Teddy!' the boy wails again.
'He's here, look.' The mother takes a soft toy from one of her many bags. Rallou squeezes past them, Toula following, and they make their way to the aft deck.

The air seems different here. It is nowhere as near as hot as Orino, more like spring than summer, and more humid.

Looking over the aft rail, the first thing that strikes Rallou is the amount of greenery. Trees are dotted between the buildings, big and tall and lush green giants, like the trees in the park in London. A little flutter of excitement grips her solar plexus. The people on the dock waiting to board mostly carry rucksacks and look like tourists. But there are Greek women too, with suitcases on wheels. Everyone looks so smart. Looking down at her blouse and skirt she wonders how many years she has been wearing clothes like these: practical clothes for cleaning in and feeding chickens in. What must it feel like to wear frivolous clothes? Do the wearers worry about them all the time, worry about snagging the fine material or dirtying them?

Maybe she can stretch out her savings to treat herself to a new top?

'All ashore. Last call.' The man with the bell is insistent and the people looking over the rails continue to make their way to the steps that lead down and out. Rallou allows herself to be taken with the throng, Toula right behind her. Down the metal steps, along the painted metal corridor, down the ridged metal gangplank and over the thick rope mat that allows the cars to roll off without scraping on the concrete.

Rallou looks across the road to a row of ornately decorated buildings.

Toula follows her gaze and points. 'They're lovely, aren't they?' she says. 'It's the Venetian influence, and one reason why Corfu is so popular with tourists.' Toula walks slowly now, her head bobbing side to side slightly. 'That, and it's cooler and greener than the other islands. That's why I prefer it in summer. Here in summer, the village in spring and autumn, and London in winter. My daughter's central heating system works very well and I love Christmas in England, it's so magical.' They have not walked more than twenty paces when a car pulls up beside them.

'Welcome home, Kyria Toula.' The driver, a smartly dressed young man, leans out to greet her with a smile.

# Chapter 24

'Oh, Ilia, you are too kind,' Toula says, giving the impression that she was not expecting him or the lift he is offering. The boy's sunglasses are so dark they completely hide his eyes, and Rallou tries to get the measure of him from his oil stained T-shirt and notes that he is wearing a steel thumb ring like the youth in Patra. It must be a current fashion. Ilias springs from the driver's seat to open the trunk of the car, his plastic flip-flops slapping his tanned feet. He swings Toula's bag into the trunk as if it has no weight at all and slams the lid shut. Inside, the car smells of stale tobacco and hot plastic.

'Ilia, this is Rallou, and you are going to help her,' Toula states as he starts the car.

'Sure.' He laughs but does not ask for clarification. He glances back at Rallou, briefly lowering his glasses to look at her, offering just a glimpse of clear eyes and wrinkle-free skin.

'Rallou,' Toula continues, 'this is Ilias, the newest recruit to the bike rental shop. Isn't that right, Ilia? Been here – what, two years now?'

*'Yeia sou,'* Rallou says, relieved that Toula has not launched into the whole story. She would be so

embarrassed. But worse than that would be if this boy actually found Christos and he and Toula were watching and waiting for the outcome. What would she say to him? It would look like she was hunting him down. The hunter being hunted; he would not like that. And what if she hunted him down and he did have a new girlfriend?

'Rallou' – inside her head she speaks to herself sternly – 'it is most unlikely that he has a girlfriend already, and if you did meet him then that would be for the best. Whether it is good news or bad news you need what Lori would call *closure*.' She says this word to herself in English, unsure of the Greek equivalent. Her self-talk gives her some comfort, but the word 'closure' frightens her a little. She begins to sing the theme tune to a Greek soap opera inside her head using the word 'closure' over and over until its meaning is dissolved a little. But the tightening around her heart remains.

'Did you hear me, kyria Rallou?' Young Ilias is looking through the rear-view mirror and must be addressing her. A moped speeds past. The driver has on a leather jacket and leather boots but no helmet, and a cigarette is trapped between the fingers of his accelerator hand.

'Sorry?' Rallou focuses back inside the car. There is a St Christopher hanging from the rear-view mirror and a coffee cup on the dashboard.

'Your husband, this Christos, I have not seen or heard of him, but I am sure we can find him.'

Rallou blinks and looks at Toula. In the space of such a small distraction she has blurted out the whole business to the boy. Her cheeks grow hot.

'You can put the word out, right?' Toula asks.

*No!* Rallou hears herself shouting the words in her head, looking at the boy's face in the mirror, but nothing comes out of her mouth.

Toula turns to look at her.

'Ah!' She scans Rallou's face. 'That is one thing I am grateful for, now that I am old and grey.' She gives a little laugh as if to say that this description doesn't actually fit how she feels. 'I no longer get embarrassed because I no longer care whether I live up to what society asks of me or not.'

Rallou is still digesting this when the car stops.

'Here we are,' Ilias says, leaping out with energy reserved for the young.

Another boy, with an open countenance, bright eyes and oily hands, is squatting beside a motorbike. He looks up from his work to greet them.

'*Yeia sas*, Kyria Toula,' he says. 'Welcome home.'

'*Yeia sou, paidi mou,*' Toula responds warmly, as if he could be her son. 'Coffee, anyone want coffee?' she asks.

The apartment is not as Rallou had expected. It is on the top floor of an unpretentious whitewashed two-storey town house with a tiled terracotta roof. The entrance is up some steps at the back that lead straight into a narrow kitchen the length of the building. Off the kitchen is a door to the sitting room, and beyond that, at one end, are a bedroom and a bathroom. All the doors are wide open, everything on display. For some reason Rallou imagined Toula's place would be fussy but everything is minimal, spacious even, and the furniture is worn and practical. There are no ornaments, no clock on the mantelpiece, no pictures on the walls, and not only the shutters but also the windows are wide open. The furniture is mostly wooden but where there are covers or cushions these are in bright, jolly fabrics. The dominant colours are yellow and orange.

'How long have you been away?' Rallou asks, pulling a chair out to sit at the narrow kitchen table that is up against one wall. A shock of pink bougainvillea frames the kitchen window, its translucent leaves lit by the sun. It makes a very pretty picture.

'Oh, I have been in London for the winter, my daughter lives there. No, I told you that already. Well, I came back here a couple of weeks ago, to air the place, then down to the village for a long weekend to catch up with my friends. I am just coming and going all the time. Sometimes I get exhausted with it, but mostly … Well, I see *people* as my home so wherever I have friends I am happy.'

'Toula,' Ilias calls up the stairs. 'Do you need more wood carrying up?'

Toula looks through to the neat front room, where a great deal of wood is stacked up beside a smart, shiny wood-burning stove that looks decidedly out of place.

'No,' she calls, and takes down a *briki* from a nail on the wall. She lowers her voice to address Rallou. 'I got myself a stove from – er, Norway, I think it was. A nice man in a shop here in town helped me. Not that I am here much when it is cold, but it is nice to have the choice.' She fills the *briki* with water and sets it on a portable gas stove. Her hands shake as she lights the match and Rallou wonders if she should offer to help, but then it is done and Toula adds spoonfuls of sugar and coffee to the water. The coffee granules float on top.

'I'll tell you who makes a great cup of coffee. Theo in the village! On your way back you should drop in, give him my regards and ask for a coffee. I don't know how he creates so many bubbles on top and the grounds are never gritty.'

Rallou thinks of all the coffees she has made Christos in exactly the same way as Toula is making it now. One spoonful of sugar for him, though: he doesn't like anything too sweet.

'There!' Toula says and pours the coffee into a waiting cup and then sets about making another one. Rallou is looking forward to the coffee now. With no breakfast and all that wine last night it would really help.

When the second cup is ready she prepares herself to stand, to carry both cups to the table, but Toula shouts 'Ilia!' and running feet can be heard on the steps and it is to him that she hands the cups.

The whole process of coffee-making is repeated as if Toula has all the time in the world, which she probably does. This time she puts a cup on the table in front of Rallou and then sits, smiling contentedly.

'I won't have one, dear,' Toula says in response to Rallou's questioning look. 'Not this early, but maybe in the afternoon.' No sooner is she seated than she is up again, wiping down the surfaces. 'Apostolis liked his coffee, but do you know what, he preferred instant, he just didn't know it.' She chuckles.

'Really?' Rallou leans towards her, encouraging her to talk more.

'Yes. I would make a Greek coffee first thing in the morning, and when he asked for a coffee later I would make him a little instant one and add some of the Greek coffee grounds. It saved me so much effort.' She chuckles. 'But now – and here is the funny thing – I make as many cups of real Greek coffee as the boys here can drink and I don't mind doing it at all.' She sighs and lays the dishcloth, folded, over the taps.

'So, how are you feeling now you are here?' Toula asks. 'You know, I think you are mistaken to think he has run off,' she says. 'Men basically don't like change or unnecessary effort.'

She has a point. If Christos was the sort of man who would stop bothering to harvest the olives because it was too much effort and because he knew they could survive on her wage, then he is not a man who is about to walk away and change his life, with all the effort that entails.

'Toula.' It is Ilias again. He strides into the kitchen with two cups and saucers neatly piled up. He is not wearing his sunglasses now but the sun behind him obscures his features. 'I have to go up to the Bella Panorama Hotel,' he says. 'A bike has broken down. But we were thinking that if this Christos didn't want an expensive hotel then this might be where he would go. So, you want to come?' His last sentence is addressed to Rallou.

'Oh!' is all she manages to say before Toula answers for her.

'Of course she will want to go! Anthea will be sure to help.' Toula clears away her cup.

Rallou looks around for the car at the bottom of the steps, but it is nowhere to been seen.

'Kyria?' The boy calls, and Rallou is rather perturbed to see Ilias sitting on a moped, the engine running, indicating for her to hop on behind him. His shorts have ridden up as he sits and the tan line on his thin little legs is exposed.

After a pause, Rallou sits side-saddle behind Ilias, which seems more modest than the alternative, although not entirely secure.

They seem to wind through streets for ever, stopping a few times: at a kiosk, for cigarettes, and at a fast-food shop where Ilias conducts a shouted conversation with those inside without once dismounting or switching off the engine. After that, they are out of the town and the houses give way to trees, and then to Rallou's delight she can see the sea, which shimmers and sparkles in the sun. They travel parallel with the coastline, which seems to be nothing but sandy beaches, with not a cliff or jagged rock in sight. With no warning Ilias turns hard right up into a square and guides the bike along some very narrow paths between the houses, and finally comes to a stop in front of glass double doors at the end of one passage.

'Hi there!' A woman greets them with a wide smile in perfect English. She has energy in her movements and salt-and-pepper-coloured hair.

# Chapter 25

'Hi, Anthea! I am here to fix the bike and Rallou is here to find her husband,' Ilias blurts out, sliding off the bike, taking care not to kick Rallou in the process. Rallou shrinks, her eyes darting. Who else is here? Who else may have heard? But there is no cause for concern; they are alone, apart from the woman. Meeting Anthea's gaze feels invasive, makes Rallou feel vulnerable.

'Oh, okay. The bike's round the side,' Anthea says, and Ilias nods and leaves. 'So, your husband,' Anthea adds without a trace of surprise or intrigue, or even much interest. 'What does he look like?'

At first the question catches her by surprise. Rallou has never been in the position of having to describe what Christos looks like, or to consider which are his most prominent features. Everyone on the island knows him. Sometimes he has been described to her though. 'So handsome,' is a familiar comment. 'Tall man?' That is often the children's point of view. 'Like an ox,' one foreign woman said with admiration when he rebuilt her garden wall.

It's no use saying that he has dark hair or dark brown eyes, as that would hardly narrow it down.

'Er, well …' Rallou starts. 'He's loving, and patient and …'

'No, I need to know what he looks like.' Anthea doesn't laugh at her. Everything about her seems to want to be helpful.

'No, yes, of course. Tall, broad-shouldered, but lithe … Well, almost skinny, I suppose, although he has muscles … So yes, lithe.'

'His face?' Anthea's head leans to one side slightly, the smile still there, still genuine.

'Right! Straight nose, always a day or two's stubble, which has patches of white. Er … really nice smile, a full bottom lip. Oh, and one eyebrow is slightly higher than the other. And if he is concerned or worried, that one lifts up in a sort of arch. His hair is short. Well, no, it needs a cut actually. It is over his collar at the back and there is always this bit that breaks free and curls backward on his forehead, sort of thing.' Rallou struggles.

'He sounds pretty gorgeous to me.' Anthea laughs. 'But, unfortunately, no – no one of that description has been here. I think I would have remembered.'

On the one hand Rallou is very pleased that he has not spent time with this woman. Anthea is far too attractive and vivacious, not to mention slimmer than her. But on the other hand it would have been nice if he was staying here as she feels drawn to Anthea's company.

Anthea offers Rallou coffee and when she declines she gives Rallou a tour of her rooms-to-rent instead, of which she is quite rightly very proud. When there is nothing more to see they wander round to find Ilias.

Rallou considers whether she would have enjoyed Anthea's situation: to have spent her life running rooms for rent or a small hotel – to have something that she had built up and of which she was proud. Maybe, but Christos would have hated it. Besides, it does seem like a lot of work with all those beds to make, floors to sweep and mop, and thirty breakfasts to cook each morning; when would she ever be able to take a break? At least Lori, Ted and the boys are only five people and they are only on Orino in the summer.

'Perhaps you should try the Hotel Atlantis. Your Christos might be there,' Anthea suggests. 'It is directly opposite the port, so anyone who does not know Corfu and just wants somewhere cheap, that is the place they would go. Of course, it is not as reasonable as us – nor, I think, as pretty – but, well, you could try.'

'Good luck,' she adds as Rallou remounts the bike, and with a wave they set off rather jerkily before they quickly change into second gear and return the way they came.

Sitting side-saddle offers such a good view of the sea on the return journey. There are pink-skinned children diving in and out of the waves, shrieking and laughing. When Rallou was that age the sea was a good walk away, but it was all downhill and they would run in the heat, eager to reach the cool of the water. The beaches on the south of Orino Island, down the back, were sheltered from wind and wave and there was no way to get to them from Orino town back then unless you had a fishing boat or walked up and over the top through Korifi. Now a pleasure cruiser offers lifts there and back every day in the summer months. Some days, if the wind is in the right direction, the sounds of the bathers laughing and shouting drift up the hillside. Occasionally she feels a slight resentment at the intrusion, but she knows of another little cove a bit further along that is too small for a boatload of tourists, and, although she rarely swims these days, it is comforting to know she still has her own private place. She might swim once or twice in the summer when she is visiting her baba, but only in August when the temperatures soar. There is a freedom in floating on her back, weightless, thoughtless, with the water lapping over her chest and stomach every now and again as the gulls float high above her until the world drifts away and only she remains. And when she has had enough of that, she will turn onto her stomach, allow the water to splash over her face, before kicking up and putting her head under to swim to the bottom, to watch the little fish that scatter as she approaches, the sand on the bottom that is rippled by unfelt waves, the starfish bright orange against the pale background. She would like to do that now, and even toys with the idea of getting Ilias to drop her off so she can explore this little bit of coastline. The only thing that stops her is the crowd of people already on the beach and her growing need to find Christos.

The journey back seems shorter, but just as she thinks they are nearly there they stop abruptly outside a large, and rather dull, concrete building.

'The manager is very nice. He has worked here for twenty-nine years,' Ilias says as they stroll into the Hotel Atlantis. Rallou finds herself following his lead, literally walking behind him. He greets the receptionist with his lop-sided smile, and adds a boyish but seductive shyness that has all the traits of being fake. The receptionist responds and leans over the desk towards him, and hers is an encouraging smile. The manager, erect, bald and suited, comes out to talk to Rallou. Ilias is right, he is a lovely man and obviously takes pride in his role, but that does not make it any easier to explain that her husband is missing and that she is hunting him down. She tells another lie about Christos taking a break to be here but this time the imaginary aunt is ill back home and she has come to find him to relay the news. Her own lies sound hollow on her lips, and the manager says no one of Christos's description has stayed with them recently. He suggests they try another hotel, the Molto Bene. Ilias, having completed his conversation with the receptionist, overhears this part of Rallou's conversation and he looks up to see if she wants to go to this next place.

'You must have things to do other than driving me around, Ilia,' Rallou says, but Ilias glances back at the receptionist and it is clear that what he is doing suits him very well.

It turns out that he knows the receptionist at the Molto Bene as well, but this girl is less receptive to his charms. The hotel she in turn suggests has no one fitting Christos's description either, and nor does the pension next door, nor the apartments a little distance away, by the beach. Each of the owners is very kind and suggests another establishment that she might try, but it is beginning to feel like a hopeless quest. 'Enough,' Rallou says to Ilias as they climb back on the bike for what feels like the hundredth time. 'You have been very kind, Ilia, but we are just blindly following what everyone suggests. We could do a tour of every place on the island like this, when all the time he is sleeping on the beach or up in the hills.'

Ilias shrugs.

'But I do thank you, Ilia, for driving me around.'

'You are welcome,' he replies cheerily, but he has a glassy look in his eyes, as if his mind is still on one of the receptionists.

Back at Toula's house, Rallou finds all of a sudden that she is very weary, but also rather uneasy. This last emotion has something to do with spending a large part of the day following directions that were mostly delivered carelessly and with little consideration. It is an uncomfortably familiar feeling, and it also feels as if the whole world knows her business. Just the thought of this brings a flush to her face and neck and she looks away, avoiding eye contact with Bobby as they pull in. Although she is grateful for all the help that has been extended to her, what she would really like right now is somewhere she could go, to shut the world out and spend a little time coming to terms with the events of the day and the uncomfortable state it has left her in.

Ilias has pulled the bike in and parked close to the kerb, and he walks around to help her dismount as she slides from her pillion seat.

'Careful!' he shouts as she steps down, but he is too late and a burning pain sears across the back of her lower calf. She pulls at her foot but it won't move, stuck where it is between the bike and the pavement. The pain increases. Ilias and the other boy, Bobby, scramble to help.

'Ow! Move the bike!' Rallou is shouting now. She has no choice; the pain is burning into her flesh. Ilias kicks the motorbike off its stand and leans it away from Rallou, carefully rolling it forward so as not to make the situation worse. Bobby stands near her, arms out, ready to hold, or pull, or catch, whatever is needed. The moment her leg is free she turns around and sits heavily on the pavement. Bobby's hands are now supporting her, trying to take her weight.

'Oh, that hurts – oh my goodness, that hurts!' She wants to wrap her fingers around the offending part of her leg but instinct tells her to not touch.

'What have you done, lady?' Ilias asks.

'Rallou? Is that you?' Toula is hurrying down her steps, her shoes clicking on the steps' edges.

'Don't touch!' Rallou demands as she draws nearer, frightened that someone, out of concern, will go near the pain.

'What's happened?' Toula demands, shuffling quickly towards them, apron on, dishcloth in hand.

'I think the exhaust has burnt her leg,' Bobby says, concern on his young face.

Rallou turns her foot so she can see the damage. A huge blister has already swollen up and she cannot remember the last time she had such a dramatic-looking injury, but mostly she cannot get over how much it is hurting. As she watches she can see the blister is getting tighter.

'You should pop that,' Ilias says. 'Release the pressure.'

'No, leave it, get some ice, cool it down,' Bobby says.

'No, ice will burn skin even more. We should bandage it,' Ilias replies.

'I feel a bit sick,' Rallou says. The pain is making her feel a little dizzy.

'Take her to the hospital,' Toula says. 'Don't touch it, Rallou. Go to the hospital, get it treated, then come back. I will have lunch ready, and you can have a *mesimeri* sleep and by then everything will feel better.'

'I love the way you make everything sound so easy,' Rallou says and then closes her eyes and pulls a face against the pain. She does not care what she looks like.

'Okay, get back on.' Ilias is looking very worried.

'Don't be a fool,' Bobby says. 'Go borrow the car again.'

'Perhaps I'd better get a taxi,' Rallou says. The pain is growing worse and she does not want to wait for anyone to borrow anything.

Finally a taxi is called, and the boys, one on either side, propel her efficiently but respectfully towards the waiting car. Quite a crowd has gathered by now, but by this time the pain is so all-consuming that Rallou hardly cares that once again she is the centre of attention and that everyone on the island appears to know her business.

'Burnt your leg, eh? Bike exhaust?' the driver says, looking down at her ankle. The way he does this, with a sneer and no pity, makes Rallou wish she had sat in the back. 'Happens all the time! Welcome to Corfu. They are usually a lot younger than you though. Younger and stupider, and usually not Greek.' He closes the conversation.

Ordinarily she would take offence at his rude tone but right now the pain in her leg demands all her attention and renders his behaviour insignificant. She bites her lip and looks out of the window. They are by the port where she arrived and, as they pass the line of ships, Stephanos's parting words on Orino Island come to mind. 'Turn right where the boat lands you.' That is exactly where the taxi is taking her now: right at the dock!

Images of young trainee nurses flood her mind and she feels dizzy all over again.

'Here you go,' the driver says, more kindly now, as they come to a stop.

Thankfully the journey was only short, and despite feeling woozy, she insists that she get out and hobble to the hospital door unaided. The driver makes no great effort to convince her otherwise.

The hospital is big and modern. Through the automatic main door is an open area that is clean and bright, with rows of empty chairs. She hobbles to one and sits down and waits, unsure what else she should do. There are no people, no one to help, but there are noises coming from a closed door behind the reception desk, and voices from another door marked *Staff*.

What if Christos's girl is here? What if she treats the burn? But how would she know? They have never met. The pain blanks out her thoughts.

'I am Yiatros Pharmokopolous.' A man in a white coat is suddenly beside her. 'And you have a nasty burn.' He squats by Rallou's side and examines her leg critically, without touching. 'But let us not fuss. I will bandage it and give you a *depon* to ease the pain so you can be on your way. Can you walk this way all right? Yes, good, sit here.' He draws green curtains around them and, taking some gauze, he oh-so-gently bandages her leg. 'There. Now, here are two *depon*. You want water for the tablets, or …?'

Sometimes it is better to remain hard, to take control of pain and her soft side. And she has tried, tried very hard, to remain composed, but after the gentle care and concern the doctor showed her she is not sure she can stand.

'I feel a little dizzy,' Rallou says.

'Really? When did you eat breakfast?'

'I haven't – well, not yet, I–'

'So. Best you go to the cafe. Look, you see those doors? You go through there, turn left. The food is good, so eat something before you take the painkillers. If you want to change the bandages tomorrow you can come here, or do it yourself, but try not to pierce the blister. Here, let me open the door for you.' They have reached the doors he was talking about and he indicates the way she should go but there is no need, as a delicious smell drifts down the hall. With a hand on the wall, she shuffles towards it. The cafe must have large windows because the sun is streaming across the corridor. As she draws level, she sees that the windows, as she anticipated, are large – floor to ceiling – and they look out onto a grassed area with benches. Outside are three nurses sitting on one bench, all about her age, smoking.

'Rallou!' a familiar voice calls.

# Chapter 26

'Rallou! I'm glad you managed to get here so soon!'

Rallou's head spins, her eyes lose focus and she staggers. Arms are around her, a chair is pulled to the back of her legs and she is eased into it.

'Put her head down between her knees if she's dizzy,' a passing voice says.

'No, I'm fine,' Rallou manages to say. The speaker keeps walking, and she watches their feet, in white slip-on shoes. Until she understands what is happening she does not dare look up.

'Are you all right?' The arms are still around her, secure and tender.

'Dizzy. No breakfast.' Keeping it brief, she finds she is released, and now she dares to look up to watch his familiar back, the ease of his stride, his broad shoulders rocking as he walks away to the counter: all the things that excited her, attracted her, made her fall in love as a girl. He places an order and returns with coffee and cake.

'Here.' Christos smiles, but there is a crease between his eyes, a look of concern.

The cup at her lips gives her reason to stay silent. Why was he expecting her? An avalanche of thoughts jumbles in her head. Adrenaline courses through her system to help her; she reasons, filters and orders, ideas spinning into focus, receding, to be replaced by other notions. Nothing becomes clear, there is no understanding, no sense can be made of it. She cannot help herself, and looks around for the nurse who might be the girl he once knew. Everyone else in the cafe is involved in their own conversations. The only nurses in sight are outside the window, smoking, talking.

'I'm so glad you came so quickly. She is fine, just fine, but guess what?' Christos is clearly excited.

Taking a sip of the hot liquid, more thoughts come, but these are more like memories, snippets of their life together, encounters she holds tender, a collage of all the magical moments that confirm love, care, respect, but they are all one-way, from him to her. She looks him in the face. He is shining, his tanned face positively glowing. It makes the whites of his eyes appear even whiter and the browns of his irises even darker. She has not seen him look this happy, or so full of vitality, for years and years. It fills her with yearning, and she wants to see him always look that way, and for her to be the cause of such passion. She also wants to feel that animated herself. Her chest is hard-pressed to contain the joy she feels to see him so charged, looking so stimulated by life. But the joy is tainted with a bitter twinge of suspicion, or rather knowledge, that she has not been the partner he deserved. She can change that. Right now she can make up for every wrong she has ever done him, by being selfless. Whatever is making him so animated, she cannot – will not – stand in the way of it, not even if it is another woman. This may lose her her husband but at least she can win back some self-respect.

'Rallou,' he says, taking her hands, and she knows he is about to share with her why he is so fervent. 'Rallou, we are grandparents!'

The coffee covers most of the table as well as her chin. Some of the liquid goes down the wrong way and she coughs violently.

'Easy – easy, girl,' Christos says, laughing, pushing his chair back a little and grabbing paper napkins to clear up the mess she has just made.

'Natasa is fine! A little tired, of course, but just fine, and the baby, such a *koukla*! Wait till you see her. She is so beautiful, and they are taking really good care of her.'

'But …' Rallou manages and then tries to work out dates in her head, counting her fingers. 'What month are we in?' she asks. She must have her weeks confused. Maybe the cicadas are not singing early, and instead time has just slipped by her. It wouldn't be the first time.

'A little early, obviously. They would not have been here on holiday if she was due. But not very early.' Christos's grin grows even wider, his heels tapping as he fiddles with her wedding ring. He can hardly sit still in his seat, and just for a fleeting moment Rallou is back at Korifi. Her baba is sitting at the kitchen table on the porch, Christos in a chair next to him asking for her hand in marriage. She was sitting close to Christos, just like she is now, and he was fiddling with her fingers, his heels tapping. They were in an almost identical position.

'Us! Grandparents!' Christos sighs and continues to stroke her fingers, shaking his head gently as if this status is beyond his expectation. The reality of his words sinks in for a second.

She is a yiayia!

Her chest seems to feel it first: a sort of bubbling, rippling feeling. It quivers in her throat, making her giggle. The feeling surges up and out. It explodes in one syllable. 'Ha!' There is no suppressing the extraordinary feeling. She is a yiayia! How suddenly and totally it changes her perspectives. Her existence has meaning. No, not meaning – justification ... No, wrong again, it is continuity. She cannot find the word, but nor does she care. She giggles out loud now, all nervousness gone. Visions of white-haired old ladies, sitting on park benches, holding babies, spin through her mind, but they distort, they become younger, lose their grey hair, stand and skip, and the babies smile. She is on her feet, coffee forgotten.

'Where are they?' She turns one way and then the other, ready to march immediately, her bad leg forgotten. 'And why are they here?'

Christos stands in a more leisurely fashion. Taking a second to look at him, she can see that he is tired, as well as excited. His familiar face is such a welcome sight, all his faults forgotten. She releases the ridiculous ideas that he was here to meet an old love. He is here as a proud baba and even prouder papous!

'Just a holiday, then the baby decided to come.' He yawns and stretches, hands to the ceiling.

The relief comes in a wave, like water flowing across her brain, cooling, restoring. Her breathing grows deeper, easier, and the tension that she did not know she was holding in her neck untwists, the hint of a headache that she has had since leaving Orino now gone. All her fears for her future are erased. She sees herself and Christos in the future, white-haired, wrinkly-faced, still holding hands. Her Christos.

'Come.' He throws an easy arm around her shoulder and turns towards the corridor. 'Oh, you are limping, what have you done?' He stops immediately.

'Oh, it is nothing, a burn from a bike exhaust.'

'A bike exhaust? You, on a motorbike? But you don't drive?'

Rallou blinks several times and wets her lips. Hobbling back to her coffee she uses the dregs to down the painkillers.

'I think we have much to say to each other,' she says, 'but first I must see my grandchild.'

Christos first frowns and then raises his eyebrows, obviously confused. He wears his innocent, slightly lost expression.

'Just to be sure,' she asks cautiously, 'you are only here for Natasa and the baby, right?' It is ridiculous, but she just needs absolute confirmation that the whole thing has been in her head. If he has no idea what she is talking about she will brush it off, make a joke of it, deflect the conversation, but she just needs to be absolutely sure that this has all been created by her imagination.

His immediate response is to laugh. At first it is genuine, as if she has made a joke, and then less so, with an edge of confusion.

'I don't understand. You got the message, right?' There is the slightest pause. 'Of course you did! How else would you have known to come here?' There is a sudden levity to his voice, as if he has forgotten her question. 'Which did you get first?' He sounds excited now. 'I told Yanni, and I left a note on the kitchen table …' He is grinning again, supporting her more firmly than her hurt leg actually requires as he starts to lead her back to the corridor.

She stops again.

'Oh, Christo, you haven't seen the news?' she asks. There must be televisions in the hospital, and people would have talked about it. He would have heard, surely? The shock of their loss hits her all over again. The photographs of the children when they were young, instead of hanging proudly on their wall, are buried under roof tiles and wreckage, the details of their life in fragments under crumbled remains. All material evidence of their years together is destroyed.

'I have done nothing but talk to Anikitos since I arrived. The doctors were in with Natasa.' His eyes leave her face and he looks to the floor and shakes his head slowly. 'I feel I have done nothing but worry and talk, worry and talk.' He speaks dismissively of what must have been an anxious time.

Rallou knows that when he says 'worry and talk', it will have been Anikitos doing the talking. Christos will have listened – worried and listened. He needs to listen again right now, this time to her, but instead he continues, 'He was so worried for her and their baby. He was so desperately trying not to cry, and I wanted to say to him, "Cry, feel how you feel." But I felt it best to stay silent. The doctors, they did not seem too worried. So I said to Anikitos–'

'Christo, there has been a bad earthquake on the island.' She is prepared for him to stop walking but even so he halts more abruptly than she reckoned on and she almost trips over her own feet. The bandage on her bad leg scuffs against her right calf, chafing the burn underneath, making her wince.

For a moment he says nothing, and a dozen expressions flit across his face. His eyes grow dark and then become light again, his breathing quickens and then slows. He is regaining control.

'Your baba, he is all right?' The anxiety in his voice makes it slightly higher-pitched than normal.

'Yes, Korifi is fine but the town …'

'The house!' His eyes widen.

Rallou doesn't want to tell him. She pulls a face, grimacing and closing her eyes. She can feel tears coming again.

'How bad?' he asks softly.

'Gone,' she says, and waits for his reaction, his realisation that all his past efforts have gone to waste, of the future building work he will have to do, of their life together laid flat. But none of this comes. His arms are around her, he is holding her so tightly.

'My poor Rallou, you must have been so scared. Oh, my little one, and I was not there for you.' He gathers her in his arms and holds her as if he is frightened of losing her, as if she will disappear into a cloud of earthquake dust.

Rallou suddenly lets go, just lets go of absolutely everything: her crazy ideas that he is chasing a young love, worries about the house and their future, passing thoughts such as where they will sleep tonight. Every single thought is allowed to drift, melt into nothing. There is just him and her, and right now she feels the need to be very small, to be embraced completely, to hold him tightly in return and know that she is safe. She has him, they have each other. Whatever she thought was going on was inside her head. He has not gone, he does not think the marriage is over. She holds him even more tightly, her tears wetting his T-shirt. It is a blue one, faded on the shoulders, bleached by the sun. This is not a good time to remind him that this is now the only T-shirt, the only piece of clothing, he now owns.

She buries her face deeper, into the familiar warm, sensual, earthy smells of her Christos.

'So,' Christos mutters back into her hair, as if the words are his declaration of love. 'We start again. A new house.' There is a throaty chuckle to his voice that does not fit the severity of their position. He pulls her from his chest and gives her a strong, reassuring smile. 'But for now, my little Rallou, we are far away from the island.' He exhales. 'Although' – now he pauses as if to make it more dramatic – 'we are very close to where our first grandchild is sleeping!' He grins.

Their first grandchild.

Her Natasa is a mama!

The delicious feeling soaks in a little more: she is a yiayia! A new baby! Her breathing stops. Before taking another step she makes a solemn vow to herself that she will never tell Natasa what to do or how to bring up her child. This feels important, very important. A frown flits across her brow and then it is forgotten. She is a yiayia and she breathes deeply and smiles widely.

Pulling out of his arms, she tries to contain her excitement. The news of the quake will be a shock for him, and it will take time for him to absorb the impact on their lives; he won't fully realise the extent of the devastation until he stands in front of the pile of dust that was once their home. All that is to come, and must be faced – but right now she must see her granddaughter.

'Can I see them?' she asks. The need to be small has passed. Christos seems lost in some faraway thoughts and it takes him a moment to bring himself back to the present.

'Yes.Yes. Come.' But his pace is not too quick. 'Arapitsa is fine, right?' he says.

'I haven't seen her. I thought she would be with you.'

'But you know where she is? I told you in the note. I told Yanni to tell you she was with him?' He is half laughing, but there is fear in his voice.

'I wasn't in the house before the quake,' says Rallou. 'I stayed with Baba.'

'I guess if Korifi is fine, then Yanni's house on the ridge is fine. I cannot believe he forgot to tell you he had Arapitsa.' He shakes his head.

'I haven't seen Yanni. He left the island.'

Christos stops walking and laughs, throwing his head back.

'Yanni leave the island? That will be the day!'

'No, he has. He's gone to buy a donkey,' Rallou says, smiling at his response as she turns her back to the windows. They have hardly left the cafe area yet and the sun from the windows is right in her eyes. She should have told someone about Dolly.

'Really?' Christos sounds incredulous. He puts his hands in his front pocket. 'So if you did not see the note' – he looks away from her for a moment, concern in his eyes, most likely thinking about the house that no longer stands – 'and if Yanni didn't tell you, how did you know to come?' Now he looks her in the eye.

# Chapter 27

'I thought you had a girlfriend and I was stalking you.' Well, that is one answer she could give him …

'I thought you had walked out on me so I was off to explore the world.' That would be slightly less true, but not entirely false.

'I had a fantasy that you were running off with a girl you knew for a week when you were twenty-four, so, with no home left after the earthquake, I jumped on a bus, fell asleep, woke up in Patra, got given a ticket to come here as a gift from two people who just got engaged to be married, shared a cabin with a woman who knows your second cousin, and who introduced me to a boy who is less than half my age, and we drove about on a motorbike until I burnt my leg, so that brought me to the hospital to get it treated, and the long and the short of it is I met you by accident!' This last version is truthful – and completely unbelievable. Isn't it? Maybe she could pretend to be dizzy again, deflect the question. No, enough of that. Think smart.

'Oh, Christo.' She links his arms and faces down the corridor again. 'I will tell you all about it later, but' – here, she quotes the ticket seller in Patra – 'what it boils down to is that life offers you what you need when it has set a path for you. Now, let's go see our girls!'

'Very mysterious, but that is my Rallou.' He smiles and pulls her closer as he takes the lead.

They spend a few hours with Natasa and the baby, but when the darkness under Natasa's eyes grows deeper Rallou knows it is time to give both Mama and her little *moro* a break. Anitikios is already asleep in a chair. Christos, on the other hand, gives the impression that all his fatigue is forgotten.

The cafe Christos takes her to is in a building that is four storeys tall, with an impressive covered walkway along the length of the building on the ground floor, with stone arches facing the street. Chairs and tables are packed into this shaded area. Each arch has its own awning that is pulled down so the sun can only touch the shoes of those on the outermost tables. There is a dull hum of casual chatter, children laughing and white-shirted waiters deftly carrying trays over the customers' heads. She is a little taken aback by the crispness of the male customers' shirts, the cufflinks and the mother-of-pearl buttons, the tailored look of the women, with their smooth hair and painted nails. Not even the wealthier visitors to the *kafenio* she briefly worked in in Athens made as much effort. Perhaps it is the Italian influence. She looks down at her own faded clothes, the worn and bobbled threads on her skirt. Finding that every table is full, she is inclined to back away, but Christos is insistent.

'You cannot come to Corfu and not drink a coffee on Liston Square!' he whispers to her, and just at that moment a man at a nearby table folds his papers, puts some coins on his saucer and indicates that they can sit if they wish. The colour of his leather belt matches that of his shoes and he wears a gold-and-black onyx ring on his little finger.

Christos sits and Rallou pulls out her own chair and takes up the menu.

'It's a bit pricey,' she whispers, leaning forward and using the menu to hide her face from the passing waiter.

'Ah, but today we celebrate being grandparents.'

'She was so beautiful, wasn't she!' Rallou is transported back to Natasa's room. Natasa herself looked tired, and Anikitos seemed relieved. The little baby could have been Natasa herself when she was born, with her little turned-up nose and the creases between the eyes: so perfect.

A group of elderly men, wearing fine tweed jackets despite the heat, sit at the next table. In Saros they would be farmers, or shopowners. Here, who knows? One of them catches her looking and winks. Rallou grins back at him.

'Today I am a yiayia,' she says. Nothing will spoil her joy.

*'Na sas zisei,'* the man replies with a nod and she turns back to Christos, who is grinning like an idiot.

They drink their coffee and reminisce about the births of each of their own children. The youngest, so clever to be at a foreign university on a scholarship, was born at home, with only Christos there to help. He takes her hand now and kisses her knuckles. When the coffee grinds sitting at the bottom of their empty cups have gone cold, they leave and wander for a while around Corfu town. They spend twenty minutes watching a man making a portrait of a tourist who sits self-consciously, before wandering on, with no speed to their movement. As they pass a hotel, a girl asks if they have anywhere to stay. Rallou has the impression that Christos spent the night in the hospital; for tonight there is always Toula, or even Anthea if they have enough money, but right now she is not ready to think about the practicalities of life. The enthusiastic girl pushes a map of Corfu town into her hand and says that when they get lost they should remember the hotel is marked by a big cross, and that she will be happy to see them again.

Christos takes the map and his pace picks up momentum.

'Where are we going?' Rallou asks, but Christos doesn't say. They walk along the water's edge until they enter a park that follows the curve of the coast, where they can walk in the shade of the trees. When the trees end and a fairly main road begins Rallou pulls back.

'Where are we going? I am exhausted,' she pleads.

'No, we must go on, I have somewhere I want to take you!' Christos insists, and soon the main road becomes a minor road. As they walk, they talk of their courtship. He is holding her hand like they are young again. Their surroundings go unnoticed, so wrapped up is she in all they are saying, in every movement Christos makes.

'You know something, Christo?' Rallou feels a thought forming and she wants to share it, but then she realises that if she does she will have to tell him about her hunt for him on the back of Ilias's bike. But it feels important, and maybe she can tell him a half truth.

'I met a friend of yours on the boat. Well, not exactly a friend, but someone who lives in Theo's village.'

'Cousin Theo?' Christos smiles as he speaks. His pace is slowing and it feels like they have no direction. She nods.

'Well, when I got to Corfu a friend of hers offered me a roundabout lift here.' *Well, it is sort of true.* 'We went first to one place and then another and I felt like I was taken around half the island. I mean I wasn't, we were mostly in Corfu town or just on the outskirts, but – and this is the point – I think I gave away any decision-making to whoever would do it for me, or who I thought should do it for me.'

Christos is smiling down at her and he squeezes her hand.

'I am serious. I think, actually, when I think about it, I gave up the decision-making after meeting Toula.' This is also true, but the whole truth would be that she gave up her decision-making to the ticket man in Patra, or even when she got on the bus on the mainland, or perhaps even when she told the first lie to Vasillis, and Eleftheria presumed she was going to Corfu to join Christos. The point is that at some point she passed the decision-making somewhere else. She did not take control and then, as if the world was designed to please her, she expected a happy outcome. How crazy was that! Christos clears his throat.

'I think it was just easier to say yes to whatever was happening rather than actually making a decision.'

'I sort of understand. But we all say yes if it fits in with our plans, don't we?' Christos asks.

'Maybe, but I am just having a little wonder.' She is actually thinking about her hesitation over boarding the boat at Patra, dithering, whilst Christos had already made the decision and gone. 'I am wondering if, right back when we got married, I didn't just sort of – well, presume that you would make all the major decisions. You know, form our lives. And then when things didn't go as I thought they would I blamed you.' It feels hard to say.

Christos stops walking.

# Chapter 28

'And how did you think our lives would go?' Christos is not smiling now.

Rallou swallows.

'Oh, I don't know,' she stumbles. How did she think their life could have gone? More travel, maybe, but then perhaps that was never realistic with the first child coming so quickly. For all the world she would not have left the children whilst they were growing, so when exactly did she think this travelling would take place? They are still walking, towards the sea, which glistens and sparkles at the end of the lane below a cloudless sky. In the far distance is a dot that draws nearer. With it comes a hum, that becomes a rumble, and soon the lights on the wings of the plane are visible. As they reach the lane's end the aircraft appears to be heading straight for them, and the high-pitched roar changes tone as it passes low over the ground just to their left. There is no point in talking; the noise would drown out all conversation. After it has disappeared from view Rallou is left looking in the direction it went.

'That was low,' Christos says.

'You brought me here to see that?'

'No!' Christos sounds incredulous and pulls her hand. 'That!' he says, and points to a small island off the coast that can be reached by a narrow walkway. All along the causeway, fishing boats and small tourist boats in many colours are moored. On the island itself is a whitewashed monastery with a double bell tower and a tall cypress tree. She has seen many images of the place: postcards, television documentaries, pictures in magazines. She has always wanted to visit this idyllic spot, and Christos knows this.

'Oh!' Rallou exclaims. Further out is another island, one she has also seen in pictures, which is covered with lush, dark-green trees. The sea is such a light hue, almost white in places, and everywhere it glints with the sun.

They pause at the door to the church. She can hardly believe she is here.

'Before we go in,' says Christos gently, 'tell me, how did you want our lives to be?'

The question pulls her up short. She is on the spot now. She knows that what she wanted, what she had dreamed of, was not really possible with three children, but it is the only thing that, given the choice, she would change now.

'To travel more,' she says, and just the thought energises her.

'Maybe also to have our own house?' Christos sounds slightly surprised by her answer.

'To have a house at all.' The energy she so briefly felt dissipates. 'Having a house is not a dream, is it? That is one of the practicalities of life. We need somewhere to live, but what I want is to travel.' Rallou takes a deep breath, exhaling it slowly. There is so much tiring work ahead of them. She is a yiayia now and no longer young. She thought her life would be easy by this stage. The thought of her granddaughter tweaks a smile from the corners of her mouth, but the rest of her thoughts pull it back straight.

'So, we light a candle and we make a prayer, and let's see what we can do,' Christos says, both her hands in his as he leans forward to kiss her. For a moment it is just a kiss, but then Rallou, in fear of all that is to come, holds on to that kiss as if it will save her and as she does so she allows herself to slow down and actually feel. Feel his lips, feel the softness, feel the love being shown, feel the care transferred, and she is twenty again, young and free and in love, and she kisses him back with such abandon and passion she shocks herself and suddenly pulls away.

'Oh, sorry!' She looks around her, conscious of who might have seen.

'I'm not.' Christos is smiling again, and he pulls her back in and kisses her with the same passion. She almost lets go again but this time she is aware they are in a public space. He laughs gently as he pulls away, with nothing but kindness and love in his eyes.

They go into the church, which, even by the standards of someone from Orino Island, is very small. They wait for a tourist to leave, who apologises on his way out.

They are alone. Christos offers her a candle.

'One for a house,' he says, guiding her hand to light it from another that is already lit. She pushes the candle into the sand. 'And one for travel.' He takes another and lights it and passes it to Rallou, who pushes this one, next to the first, into the sand in the brass tray. There are at least twenty other candles already burning in the tray of sand.

Christos neither crosses himself nor says any sort of prayer. Rallou crosses herself but it is a reflex without any real significance. Candles have become wishes to her, but maybe wishes are prayers and prayers are wishes? Who knows where one starts and the other ends. With his hand over her shoulder, Christos leads her out and they take a short look around the monastery before making their way back across the causeway.

On the island once more, Rallou turns back the way they came, but Christos leads her into a taverna with tables so close to the sea that if they took one more step they would be swimming.

Rallou's heartbeat quickens.

'Christo,' she whispers harshly.

'What?' He mimics her tone.

'I only have enough euros for somewhere to stay tonight and to get back home. The money I had for food went on the taxi to the hospital.'

'I thought you said you came by bike?' He is laughing as if everything is a joke, and Rallou can feel a muscle by her eye begin to twitch.

'Look, all that is just details. I got the taxi because I hurt my leg, but the important thing is we cannot afford to eat here.'

'Ciao, what can I get you signora, signore?' A red-waistcoated waiter has arrived. Rallou tries to stand but Christos puts a restraining hand on her arm.

'First we have some wine, no?' he says to Rallou, ignoring the Greek waiter's forced Italian.

'No,' Rallou hisses.

'Yes,' Christos says. 'Half a kilo of red.'

The waiter does not need telling twice.

'Christo, I have taken everything from the bank account and I do not get paid till the end of the month!' Rallou can feel a panic now. 'We have only the clothes we stand up in. Not just here, but in the whole world, and we have no house to return to.' She pauses for breath. On the table between them in a vase is a bunch of small blue flowers, of the type he once gave her, but these are not wilted, and they make her want to cry.

'Christo, we cannot eat here. We do not even have enough money to stay somewhere tonight and get our tickets home.'

'But you lit a candle, didn't you, and made a wish?'

# Chapter 29

The tiny blue flowers are bent over, their heads wilting towards the tabletop. Rallou lifts a few with her fingertips, but the stems have no strength. Leaning against the vase is a photograph of her grandchild. Over a year old already. She strokes the image of the baby's little face.

'Fiorella,' she murmurs. A name acceptable in both Italy and Greece, Natasa and Anikitos told her. On the back is a print made with Fiorella's hands and feet in pink paint. Natasa has printed the date they made it followed by *Fiorella, 1 year old*.

A whole year! How can a whole year have passed since Corfu? But then again, how have they managed to achieve all they have in one year? Christos has never stopped; he has been relentless: sanding, filling and painting, and attending to all the little details. To Rallou, his talents seem without limit. Where did he, this self-confessed uneducated mountain man, learn all these skills? She asked him that very question as she watched him assemble the solar panels that would be mounted on the roof.

'Oh, here and there.' He dismissed her question in an offhand manner, but she could see the corners of his mouth trying not to twitch into a smile. 'When I work on other people's houses, I watch. If I see someone doing something I can't, I watch. It's the best way to learn.' And smiling more openly now, he continued with his task and, when he thought she wasn't looking, the smile gave way to a satisfied grin.

Rallou goes into the bedroom and looks at her half-packed suitcase again, and takes out the jumper she put in only a few minutes before. The knitwear is hung back in the wardrobe, and a waterproof coat takes its place in the suitcase. But the coat is bulky, and now the lid won't shut, so she lays it on the bed and leaves the room. On the stove, the onions are transparent and the garlic is giving off a rich, warm, homely smell, but without even tasting the tomato sauce she knows it needs oregano, which she will collect fresh from the pot outside.

The smooth wooden boards of the balcony feel like silk under her feet. Christos spent hours sanding them. The soil of the bougainvillea in its pot outside the door is slightly damp, and the plant does not need watering. Beyond this is a swinging chair, another of Christos's surprises. He made it from packing cases and used the old well chains to hang it from the stout wooden beams over the veranda.

'What did I come out for?' Rallou asks herself; unable to come up with an answer, she sits on the seat, and seconds later her legs are tucked up under her, and she relaxes to the gentle rhythm.

From this angle the hamlet is mostly hidden by trees but here and there the corner of a tiled roof can be seen, or the glimpse of a whitewashed wall, or a bright dot of colour where washing has been hung. Above the hollow, on the brow of the hill beyond, she can see her baba's house standing sure and majestic, and she can see her baba, coming around the corner of the house, picking up the apron on his way. He ties it carefully around his waist and goes down to the chicken shed. He has had quite a little trade in eggs since the earthquake. So many people moved back to Korifi whilst their houses in Orino were being repaired, and more of them than anyone would have imagined have stayed. Life up in the hills is slower, they say – less stressed, perhaps; consequently, repairs have been made to the old houses, solar panels have been installed and new furniture has been brought up.

Rallou and Christos had no choice. On their return to the island it all looked even worse than Rallou remembered.

She reaches her foot over the edge of the swing to push herself a little, following Baba's steady progress to the hut. He has so much more of a bounce in his step these days.

For some reason she had it in her mind that at least one of the walls of the Orino town house had remained standing, but on their return to the island they found it was absolutely flat. Few houses had suffered so bad a fate, but it is also true that very few had been so badly maintained.

'So much work!' she had sighed, leaning against Christos, who had gone quite pale.

'Indeed,' was all he said.

But that work was never to be done. Christos's cousins had insured the house, but the policy did not cover damage due to earthquakes and so no money was available to rebuild the house. This did nothing to stop the old arguments, however, and opinions were divided as to whether it would be better to sell the property – or, now, building plot – immediately, or to wait for a few years and hope that its value went up. It seemed that not a thought was given to Rallou and Christos or where they would live. There was nothing for it: they would have to stay with her baba, temporarily at least. Christos would have to spend the next few years doing up the family house in Korifi. It was one thing to visit her baba and be able to choose how long to stay and when to leave, but living there with Christos? At the time, she braced herself for the possible discomfort that was to come. Her main concern was that the men would not get on, that she would have to play diplomat between them.

She shakes her thoughts away and watches her baba, who has the eggs now and is walking towards the village, kicking his legs out to the side so his thighs do not hit the eggs in the pocket of the apron. When he reaches the stunted pine he stops. He sits and places the eggs in a basket in the shade there, covering them with a bit of netting and some leaves. Next to the basket is a tin for the coins that the villagers will leave when they take the eggs they need. He will not be able to see her at this distance;

his eyes are dimmed with age. But she waves anyway.

'Oregano!' She jumps up and hastens to stir the pot, to stop it burning, and then gathers handfuls of the fresh leaves. The onions have just caught but not enough to spoil the sauce. They will have pasta tonight, 'pasta Fiorella', a new speciality of Rallou's, devised with her granddaughter in mind.

With a last stir she ponders the pictures framed on the wall: new frames, new nails, in a newly painted wall. She smiles, glad they recovered what they did. How many hours did they spend sifting through the rubble of their flattened house in Orino town for trinkets and mementoes to patch their lives back together? Christos was never far from her in case she found something else that made her cry. It's true that they recovered more than she had expected to: her passport, for example. Christos did not have a passport, of course, but they found both their identity cards, which were pretty much unscathed. Also, a lot of her yiayia's bed linen was recovered, much in need of a soak and a good scrub.

'Good,' Christos said with one of his teasing smiles as she hugged them to her chest. 'Another thing we do not need to buy,' he added, as if finding them was of no emotional consequence. She threw a small piece of rubble at his feet as if he were a barking dog, and he laughed and sidestepped it before returned to his sifting, chuckling to himself. They found more than half the pictures from the walls intact, the ones of the children anyway, and the others they made little effort to find. Rallou found the kitchen drawer in one piece, still safely containing many of the children's drawings. They even found all but one of Natasa's medals.

'Enough,' Christos said finally, and she agreed. They had been lucky, and had salvaged a lot, but they agreed that they could not spend the rest of their lives scraping through the dust trying to live in the past, so they walked away. It was a strange feeling – walking away and not even knocking on Harris's door. At one time, at any other time in her life, that would have been tantamount to sacrilege. She has not spoken a word to her sister since her return and that is the way she wants to keep it, at least for a while. She has not told her baba her reasons, but he knows. She knows he knows. It is something he must have been waiting for all these years. Now, his own silence makes a lot more sense.

Turning off the bubbling sauce, she touches the wilted flowers again. The sun streaming through the window intensifies their colour. Every day, so far, he has brought the bright blue flowers home, a reminder of Corfu. He has never forgotten, whether he is working down in Orino town or up on the hills.

That time seems so long ago now. Rallou snaps a packet of spaghetti in two and lets the pasta slip into a pan, ready for later. The sauce looks amazing and smells even better. It is richer than she used to make it. She takes her time over it now, uses more tomatoes, lets them reduce down.

Once the food is ready for later, she goes out into the sunshine.

Things have been so different since Corfu. So many truths came out after they lit their candles in that church.

Her sandals are by the back door, and she slips them on.

She had her confessions to make and, it turned out, he had his.

# Chapter 30

'Here.' Christos put his hands in his front pocket and pulled out a curled and scrunched handful of euro notes. Rallou's first reaction was relief. The waiter, in his red waistcoat, returned with a jug of red wine and took their order. 'Enough to drink, eat, stay somewhere and get back home.' Christos spoke with such confidence. She didn't want to ask where he had got the money. In that moment it didn't matter, she was just grateful he had it.

She in turn pulled out her few euros and they created a little pile in the middle of the table on the blue-and-white cloth.

'Ah, you see,' said Christos, 'we also have enough to get you a new blouse.' It seemed nothing could quench his enjoyment of life. Over the years he had not changed. This was what had drawn her to him when he was in his twenties and this was how he was even now when there were hairs of grey mixed in with his dark curls.

As she sat there with the sun in her eyes, Christos against a background of blue sea, his hair lifting in the slight breeze and his muscular forearms a testament to his years of manual work, she recognised how consistent he had always been, and with the recognition came the sudden and overwhelming awareness of how capricious she was in comparison. In fact, she was guilty of more than just a whimsical fickleness; she simply didn't know who she was. She had no core, no real sense of herself.

She took a napkin from the holder, more for something to do with her hands than for any other reason, but when the paper was laid on her knee she began to shred it, tearing off little strips as her thoughts engulfed her.

Back in her early twenties, in Athens, Paris and London, she had known who she was. Even in the early years of her marriage to Christos, the question had never arisen. But shortly after that time, everything about her became a little hazy. What was all that business with Toula? She was a lovely, kind woman, to be sure, but why had Rallou just gone along with everything she said, and even allowed herself to be passed to Ilias and then from one hotel owner to another in such a passive way, as if she could not think for herself? It only took a moment's thought to realise that the island was too big for that approach to finding someone to work. But she had gone along with it instead of thinking. Even at Patra it had taken a free ticket to persuade her to get aboard a boat. What on earth had happened to her? Thirty years ago, of all her peers on the island, and not just those up at Korifi but of all of them on the island, she was the only one who had the spirit to take off to Athens and beyond.

As these thoughts percolated through her mind, it was the napkin that became the discreet evidence of her anxiety. Christos remained unaware of her turmoil, enjoying his wine as he flipped through the menu. When he tired of that, he studied the fish in the water just below where they were sitting, which fought in a writhing mass for lumps of bread thrown by the tourists at the next table.

Maybe it was the demands of having three children that had drained her of her boldness, her life's vigour, her *kefi*.

Rallou opened her mouth to try to awaken Christos to what she was going through, to ask him to help her make sense of all she was feeling, but she hesitated a moment too long. Then a man and a woman with a young child sat down at the table next to them. The mama was all smiles and their immediate appearance was that of a happy family. The mama pulled out a chair for her offspring and the girl sat down, but there seemed to be some reluctance in the child's movements. If her family had been able to afford such a luxury when she was the girl's age, Rallou thought, she would have relished such a treat. Maybe this was a spoilt and ungrateful child; she certainly wasn't smiling like the mama was. Maybe this child would drain her mama of her *kefi* to such a point that she would lose her sense of self in twenty years' time.

At that point the mama looked over, perhaps sensing Rallou staring. Rallou smiled to show she meant no harm and then gave a little shrug as if to say, 'Ha, children, what can you do?' and then smiled even more broadly to show that she too had had children and that she understood.

But the mama gave her no acknowledgement, turning back to speak to her daughter instead. She did so in a kind voice, and she leaned forward to brush some sand from the girl's skirt. 'Ah, you see,' she said, 'such a pretty dress, but it is just not in your nature to keep it clean, is it? Everything is always a little more about you than the lovely things you are given.'

She said it in such a warm, low tone that it sounded as if she was praising the girl. But the child's face crumpled.

'Ah, ah, don't start. We have brought you out for a lovely treat. Don't be ungrateful.' So softly were the words spoken, they sounded like a caress. Had she spoken harshly, her husband, Christos and no doubt anyone else nearby would have looked on in disapproval. But because of the gentle timbre of her voice it passed everyone by, except the little girl – and Rallou.

'I want to go home,' the child muttered, her voice only just audible.

'Your friends had left you anyway. They had better things to do, so we are here now,' the mama smoothly murmured, and with this she stopped brushing the sand off the child's dress and turned to her husband, who sat passively waiting for her attention. When he had it he became quite animated and the little girl was forgotten.

Rallou took the impact in her chest. The feeling was a hard sadness and it was prompted by the way the mama had spoken to her child. It spun her back into her own childhood and it took her breath way. She reached for her wine and took a swallow to steady herself, her pulse in her ears, adrenaline coursing through her solar plexus and the muscles across her chest tightening. A blast of emotional memories told her exactly how this child felt: the mortifying shame of not being good enough, the confusion of not knowing how the situation had got to this point. The child was now trying hard to sit still and be 'good', and not cry. She would grow up trying to be 'good' and do everything right. She would do all that was asked of her and more – just a bit more to gain the briefest of hugs and the smallest of praise.

Just as Rallou had done with Harris.

No wonder she had been so keen to live with Vasillis, to go to school, to work at the carpet factory so young and, eventually, not only to leave her beloved island, but also to go as far away as she dared to break the strings of need that bound her to her surrogate mama.

Rallou tried to get the attention of the child at the next table by smiling at her, to tell the girl with her eyes that she was loveable just the way she was.

But the child did not look up. She was working so hard at sitting still and being quiet.

Athens and Paris had helped to set Rallou free, but it was the events in London, the accident, her experience in that hospital bed that really made the change for her. That unexplainable event told her with full force that she was important and that she had as much right to live her life the way she wanted as every other person alive. No one was more important than her, but equally not one was less important. The love she felt when she was in that place of light lingered still, all these years later, and it gave her certain knowledge that she *had* been in that place and that the place was real. Back then – and she didn't know why she felt driven to do so – she had even compared the love she had felt in that extraordinary place to the love offered by Harris, and in comparison Harris's love seemed less important; if that place of light was where she would end up then she would go happily. So she returned to the island strong and sure and confident.

So what happened?

The first napkin was dissolved into shreds on the floor. She kicked the pieces into a small pile by the table leg and took a second.

She was fine when she first moved into Orino town with Christos. They had been excited about having their own place and swore, because of the dispute between the cousins, that it was only temporary and then …

And then what altered? Harris! Harris had moved in opposite and their relationship had picked up where it left off. She can see her now on the third day in her marital home.

'Morning, Rallou. Christos well?' Harris had called across as she cleaned her windows. Instead of shouting, Rallou had pointed to the ridge and smiled. There would be rabbit stew tonight.

'He's gone where? The hills? Again? But you have only been married two minutes! Doesn't take them long to wander, does it? Perhaps you should tempt him home with a really good dinner.' Harris had spoken so openly and so kindly; it was said with such care. 'Ah, yes, of course, maybe that is the problem. You were off studying books when I learnt to cook, weren't you? Never mind, I will come over, I can teach you. We can make dishes that he will hurry home to.'

Such comments weren't made just once. It seemed that every time they spoke she had some judgement to make, and as she had always been in the role of mama, Rallou had listened, and as she had listened the doubts had begun. Was he away longer than he needed to be?

'Of course, it is understandable, as it is not your own home,' Harris began one day as her fingers investigated the rot in one of Rallou's shutters. 'I am lucky that ours is Stephanos's family home. It feels so much more permanent to actually own your own home, and it is worth taking care of them. But I admire the effort you have put into this. Look, you have planted flowers to try and cheer the place up.' Rallou spent the rest of the week painting the shutters, planting more flowers and doing a hundred things to improve the house. Christos tried to dissuade her, pestering her to go for walks with him up in the mountains, but she was not to be deflected and so he went by himself up to the hills and in turn she felt alone.

'Gone again, has he?' Harris would shout across to her. 'Come over, we can have coffee.' And, as she contemplated the hours stretching out into the future with no one to talk to, Rallou did go across, and generally ended up going home more miserable than when she arrived, though she could never understand why. Harris told her it was the state of the house, or the lack of attention from Christos, and the cycle would begin again.

Why had she not seen all this for what it was at the time? Why was she seeing it only now?

The waiter returned and Christos ordered for them both. Beetroot with a garlic sauce, long red peppers stuffed with feta, and stuffed tomatoes.

'Will we eat all this?' Rallou asked, breaking her reverie. More to the point, how would they pay for it, she wondered. Christos smiled and told the waiter that was probably enough, and then he turned to the sea again, with a faraway look on his face that told her he was content.

After the children arrived, Harris had advice for every occasion.

'I heard her crying again just now. Does she have a temperature? Did you check? Oh, you had better check. I can't believe you didn't. These things can change so quickly if you don't remain vigilant. You see, that is where my childhood has the advantage, I have already raised you and the boys.'

And another time: 'I see Natasa has a bruise on her arm. Did she fall? Again? How does that happen so often?'

The looks that accompanied such comments would cause Rallou to wither inside. The crushing kindness Harris came out with about the children was incessant. The more she commented, the more Rallou tried harder, she could see that now. The way Harris's comments were delivered was so kind, so soft, so full of concern.

The child at the next table was trying to eat, and her mama was encouraging her, but the poor girl was having trouble swallowing. Rallou remembers that feeling too: the lump in her throat, the sluggishness of her limbs, the inability to swallow because she was so upset that she had been told off again.

'Baba, I feel I can never please Harris. Am I really so bad?' she once asked. She must have been quite small because she was nestling neatly under her baba's arm.

'My little treasure, you are perfect,' he had replied, and cuddled her tighter as they looked across the sea, which was painted orange by sun kissing the horizon in its slow descent.

'Just perfect,' he repeated to himself, and they watched as the shimmering orange disc sank lower and lower into the sea, creating a reflection of itself until the last fingernail of glow remained: going, going, gone, and then dusk was on them.

Taking another swallow of wine, Rallou sat back as the food was placed on the table. The smells of olive oil and garlic stimulated her hunger and she took up her fork. Christos paused to admire the dishes before he too tucked in, but even when he began to chew he was still smiling. He was obviously delighted to be a papous but there was something else too.

*One thing at a time.*

'Christo, do you think Harris is a nice person?' she asked, as casually as she could, pushing some *scordolia* onto her forkful of beetroot. Maybe all this negative thinking about Harris was in her head, just like all she had imagined about Christos.

He laughed, a short snorting laugh.

'You really want to know?' he said, and stabbed a forkful of the beetroot leaves. 'Do you want some *fava*?'

'Yes. And yes, I really want to know.' She knew that, whatever he said, there was probably no return so she braced herself, in her heart knowing what was to come.

'She is a competitive ...' But he didn't say the final word. Instead he put down his fork, looked into her eyes and, in a soft tone, said, 'She is in competition with you and she does everything and anything she can to make herself feel better about herself by being mean to you.'

'It has taken you twenty-nine years to tell me?' her voice asked without her permission. She felt numb.

'You love her. She was your mama and is your sister and, I am sorry to say, your poison.'

'So bad?' He was blurred through her tear-filled eyes. He didn't answer; there was no need.

She was so filled with love for him at that point that she looked away, at the vase of little blue flowers between them.

# Chapter 31

Rallou decides to wander across to see her baba. She'll make him a morning coffee, or take a little walk with him. They could go to the bees, or maybe the goats need grazing. They could do that together.

There are two ways to her baba's: in a straight line through the village, past Kyria Vetta who says that she has returned to her roots and that she is never moving again, or behind the house, along the very top of the ridge, skirting around the edge of the hamlet. Today she does not feel like seeing too many people so she will take the longer route. It will be hotter as there are no trees out of the dip, but the views of the sea will compensate.

With the people who have moved back to Korifi have come an assortment of animals. There are a few cats and one has already had kittens that have grown quite feral, and one of these now has an extended belly. Before she leaves, Rallou puts some scraps out in case any of her feline friends happen to pass by. A couple of dogs have been brought up to Korifi by their masters and they bark their daily conversations. As she reaches the top of the ridge, the dull clang of a metal bowl being dropped on concrete or stone and the sudden silence of one of the dogs signals feeding time. The mundane task of feeding animals does not inspire her today. She wants to be freer than that.

Looking beyond the village and out to the horizon, to the strip of water between the island and the mainland, Rallou can see several boats. Two water taxis are moving in opposite directions at great speed, heading towards each other in a marine version of chicken. When they pass, though, it is apparent that there is plenty of room to spare. Three small fishing boats sit unmoving and a large yacht is moored where the water is shallow enough to drop anchor. Its bright orange tender bobs alongside, a shocking dot in the field of blue.

As she walks around the perimeter of the village, Rallou looks down into the scooped-out hollow of land where the single-storey houses with their terracotta roofs are partly hidden by stunted trees and grapevines. The houses are no longer in a poor state of repair, as they had been for the last thirty years or more. Now there is evidence that people are starting to make improvements: broken windows have been glazed, and chimneys smoke from cooking fires. Washing on lines adds pinpoints of colour against white walls.

Evidence of the presence of the recent influx of inhabitants to the tiny hamlet is also carried to Rallou on the slight morning breeze, in the form of a blend of new aromas: a rich, oily smell, mixed with herbs –

something delicious cooking slowly on a stovetop – and a passing hint of laundry powder from washing hung out to dry in the sun.

She brushes past a rosemary bush, which adds to the air's perfume. The plant is another sign of the presence of people. It is not a wild bush but one that that someone has recently planted to gather from for cooking. Further up the track she passes a roughly built hut, around which is an enclosure that holds three sheep. The smell of their dung mixes with the other smells, acrid compared to the cooking but not unpleasant. One of the animals bleats a welcome as she passes. Then she is out in the scrubland and the domestic smells recede and the colours dominate: hues of bronze and browns at her feet, greys further away and the blue of sea, the navy of the mainland and the deep admiral blue of the sky. There is a haze over everything. She would like to run and take off like a bird to fly free over the beauty before her. A little further on, in the shade of some thorny scrub, grows a clump of the little blue flowers. She will take some to Baba. When she bends to pluck them they transport her back to the restaurant in Corfu once more, to the moment when she asked Christos what he thought of Harris.

Christos shared his views so gently that she was moved to tears. His hand reached out for hers but neither of them said any more about it, and of that she was glad. She needed all her thoughts to settle. They enjoyed the meal in silence and then, when it was time to leave, with tenderness, he even pulled her chair out for her and they walked back into town arm in arm. It was almost as if he had rehearsed for this day, expected it to come.

When they neared Corfu town centre, it was Rallou who spoke first.

'Toula offered me her house, for us to stay in on the way home if I found you.'

'What do you mean *if* you found me?' Christos asked, and Rallou ignored the question.

'I am going to accept her offer.' She felt determined to be herself again. 'The money I could spend on a new blouse will see us through a few days, and when we run out we can go back to Orino and stay with Vasillis, or my baba, until my payday. You and I are going to have our first proper holiday off the island.'

His mouth dropped open a little after this speech, but only for a second, and then he said, 'Welcome back.' And he was grinning.

Rallou enjoys the sense of freedom she gets in the open scrubland. If she looks to the west she can see only land and sea. In this direction there are no houses, no civilisation, just the island as it has been for thousands of years. The low-lying bushes and plants are scratchy so where these are dense she walks with her head down, but the rest of the time her chin is up and she revels in the moment.

She and Christos entered the village near Saros in the late afternoon. She didn't know what to expect but was pleasantly surprised to find it much like any Greek farming village, except perhaps smaller and slightly less cared for than most. Here the buildings had remained traditional from a lack of resources, rather than by design as was the case in Orino. The tiled roofs were a multitude of oranges and burnt umbers, lichen speckling them here and there. The whitewashed walls were peeling and the shutters, mostly blue and light grey, were flaking paint. This was a farming village, without the wealth the tourists bring to Orino. It should have felt drab but it didn't. Rather, the impression was that it was homely and lived in. They wandered up past a large church, next to which was an impressive house. A group of boys were playing football on the broad paved area in front of the church, and, as they passed, a wide ball came to Christos, who dribbled it round and past the boys for a minute, appearing to relish this reminder of youth.

A little way past the church the houses ran out, giving way to rows of orange trees on either side of the road, stretching as far as they could see into the distance, and so they turned back and took the road through the main square, past a windowless place that smelt of cheese, and beyond. Beyond the square was a row of taps mounted on the wall, evidently providing water for the locals from some stream. One of the taps dripped continually and the area was slippery with wet, and wasps hovered, circling and drinking. Rallou watched as a man pulled up in a pickup truck and filled a dozen empty water bottles from the taps, stepping carefully so as not to slip. As he returned to his truck with the full bottles, he called a greeting. A lady hosing down her front courtyard smiled and waved. Back at the central square, where the bus had dropped them when they first arrived, the woman in the kiosk, which stood under the shade of a tall palm tree, said she would be delighted to be able to help.

'Oh, welcome, welcome,' the coiffured woman called through the open glass window of her tiny emporium. Behind her, the shelves of the kiosk were filled with stacked cigarette packets, boxes of aspirin, and cartons of coffee granules, along with all manner of other essentials. On the shelf below the little window were boxes of individually wrapped sweets, a tray of lighters, another of biros, and plastic cups in cellophane wrappers labelled *Frappé – just add water and shake*.

'Ah yes, Toula's house.' The woman laughed as she spoke. 'How is she? She was here just a week or so ago. Now, her cottage, just a minute,' And with a shuffle and a squeeze she came out of her mustard-coloured box, kicking a crate out of her way, the bottles tinkling their reluctance to move. At the front of the kiosk, by the drink cabinets and the magazine racks, she stood by them companionably.

'You can go up by the church, if you have a car ...' She looked around, and seeing no car she continued, 'But on foot, I would go up there, between the pharmacy and the bakery and that's it, the main gate is directly opposite you at the top.'

They could see it from where they were standing. There had been no need for the woman to make such an effort to show them; she could simply have pointed from inside her kiosk. They thanked her and were just about to set off when she bid them wait. From one of the boxes on the shelf by her serving window she selected two wrapped sweets and pressed them into Rallou's hand.

'Now, if you need anything Marina at the corner shop has almost everything.' The kiosk lady pointed diagonally across the square and across the road. Three steps led to a small area where boxes of vegetables and more drinks cabinets jostled for room in front of an open door. 'What she doesn't have, I have, and if you do not want to cook you can go to Stella's.' Then she turned and pointed the other way, down, just out of the square, to a place with a few tables outside on the road. Here, a woman was sitting on one of the seats, legs stretched in front of her, noisily sucking through a straw the last of her drink. When she saw them looking she raised her glass in salute.

'Thanks,' Christos beamed, but his eyes were on the *kafenio*, which occupied a commanding position at the top of the square. Theo's *kafenio*, presumably.

'You want to go and see him first?' Rallou asked.

'No, no, we have time.' Christos put his arm around her waist and they walked the way the kiosk lady had pointed. He was clearly excited at the prospect of seeing his second cousin, and she was flattered that he was putting her first. She responded by letting her head drop onto his shoulder and walking in step with him to Toula's house.

The house was just as she imagined it would be: minimal and functional. However, through the back door was an unexpected delight in the form of a private little walled courtyard, with seating built in around three walls, which made sense of the deep, comfortable cushions that Rallou had found inside. While she was arranging these, Christos found and opened a folding table, placing it in the centre of the seating area. The whole space was shaded by a pale-blue plumbago canopy held up on weathered wooden supports. To Rallou's absolute delight, just outside its shadow was a circular wall, in the centre of which was a grill that was laid with firewood. She had read about these firepits in a magazine at the hairdressers, and knew they could be used for heating as well as for cooking.

Inside, Toula's larder was well stocked so Rallou made a frappé for Christos and one for herself, and settled beside him on the padded cushions in the dappled afternoon sun, and they talked nonsense to each other, rekindling the humour and silliness that years of child-rearing had eroded. That night it was as if they had just met all over again. The lifetime of knowing each other, predicting each other, dropped away and they became lost in their love.

The next day they went up to Theo's.

Christos walked straight up to the man with the frizzy halo of hair in the *kafenio* and just stood in front of him, staring. For a second, Theo frowned and looked a little afraid. His recognition came slowly, and then: '*Ella*, Christo!' Theo put down the cup he was carrying and opened his arms. His halo of frizzy hair, which was mostly grey, bobbed as he moved and Rallou immediately liked him. The similarities between him and Christos were apparent: the same litheness, the same broad shoulders, and the same lightness on their feet.

'Eh, I'm sorry I did not make the wedding.' Theo's face looked sad as he hugged Christos, but Rallou could not follow what he was talking about.

'Theo, *file*, it's been twenty-eight years since my wedding, and besides, we are seeing each other now.' Christos slapped him in a bear hug.

'Twenty-nine,' Rallou said, smiling, and Theo released Christos and took a good look at her.

'Oh my, I am so pleased to meet you,' he exclaimed, and kissed her on each cheek, then stepped back and held her at arm's length. 'Christo, you have picked well,' he teased his cousin; then he released her hand and announced, 'Now I make you coffee!' and beckoned them into the *kafenio*.

Rallou felt a little uncomfortable in the *kafenio*. Apart from when she so briefly served in one in Athens, she has always seen the *kafenio* as a man's domain. Across the road, in the shade of the palm tree, between the kiosk and a rather sad-looking dry fountain, were arranged painted wooden chairs and rusting circular three-legged metal tables, as found in *kafenios* all over Greece.

'Theo, I think we will sit outside.' Christos pre-empted her.

They sat the rest of the afternoon, talking to Theo when he wasn't busy. The two men teased each other relentlessly and Rallou loved watching them act like boys again. Theo's coffee was excellent, and he brought a second and even a third cup, and as time wound on she drank until the caffeine made her slightly dizzy. The sounds of the village were dominated by the continuous barking of dogs, and cockerels calling, much like in Orino but without the frequent sounds of donkeys. At one point, a dull clonking, which Rallou normally associated with Korifi, signalled the arrival in the square of a flock of sheep, with bells around their necks, being herded through the heart of the village. The lady from the kiosk came out to wave a rolled-up newspaper at the animals to protect her stacked boxes of crisps and racks of newspapers. The woman who was herding the sheep stopped to talk to the kiosk lady whilst her dog hurried the flock onwards.

'So, you must be hungry,' Theo came over to announce, and Rallou found that she was. By now, the sun was nudging the edge of the palm tree and would soon sink behind the hills, which were a dark purple in the distance. 'Over there is Stella's.' Theo pointed. 'You order whatever you like and tell Stella it is on me.'

Christos opened his mouth to protest.

'Ah, ah,' Theo warned, balancing a stack of dirty coffee cups on a tray. 'This is my village now, and here you are my guest. But I would suggest the chicken and lemon sauce. It is the best.'

Leaving Theo, they walked hand in hand to Stella's. There was something about having nothing – no house, no clothes, no money – that transported them both to a place of unrestrained hope, and it was a feeling she had not had since they first met.

But, although there was no tension between her and Christos – they were close, intimate –she did have just a little quiver of something that was not quite excitement in her stomach. It was a feeling that he was keeping something from her. In addition to that, she felt that all the thoughts she had been having, all the doubt and revelations about Harris, were about to accumulate into something. If she had spoken these thoughts out loud she would have thought herself crazy. This was her sister she was thinking about, the woman who had raised her like her own child. So she kept it all to herself and just walked on to the eatery.

# Chapter 32

'You want lemon sauce with that?' Stella asked, holding a plate that overflowed with chicken and chips above the counter to indicate what she was talking about. They had chosen to sit in the shade of an umbrella, at one of the tables outside, next to a stunted olive tree whose trunk had been bound with a thousand fairy lights.

'Theo says we must,' Christos answered. Rallou watched as Stella twisted off the lid with her teeth whilst still holding the plate. The action ran contrary to the slightness of her frame. Her floral print dress did nothing to reduce the impression she gave of childlikeness, but the lines around her eyes and the almost hard contours from her nose to her mouth indicated she was no younger than Rallou herself.

'So.' Stella laid down the plates in front of them. Christos ate immediately and eagerly. Rallou dipped her finger in the sauce to try it before picking up her knife and fork. 'You have been married, what? A year, two, maybe?' Stella's eyes shone in the light from the tree. Rallou smiled. What she was feeling on the inside towards Christos must have showed on the outside. She looked him over, not seeing the greying hair and weathered skin, but noticing instead his masculinity, his eyebrows dancing in delight as he savoured his food, and the twitch of a smile around his mouth that told her all was well in his world just at that moment, and she felt a strong urge to kiss him.

She mopped her mouth in case the lemon sauce had dribbled.

'Actually, we have been married twenty-eight years,' she said.

'Twenty-nine,' Christos corrected. 'This is really good,' he added, pointing to his plate with his knife. Under the table he had slipped off his shoes and his toes were tucked behind Rallou's calf. A phone rang and Stella skipped up the steps into the eatery to answer it.

The counter, and the grill behind it, were just inside the doors, so as they ate Christos and Rallou could hear the hissing and spitting of the split chickens and the sausages. Stella came out again to ask if they wanted more and if everything was fine. She was followed by a group of men, who were talking and laughing and rubbing their distended stomachs. Their rough serge trousers and rolled-up sleeves identified them as farmers. They thanked Stella kindly for her food and sauntered across the road, calling some piece of banter over their shoulders, and finally leaving the place to its silence. Once Rallou and Christos had cleaned their plates, Stella came and sat at the table next to theirs. The scent of jasmine filled the air, drifting from a cascade over the wall of the garden next door.

'So, twenty-nine years! How many children?' she asked.

'Three,' Rallou answered. The lemon sauce was amazing, quite unexpected. She wished that she wasn't so full because then she could eat it all over again.

'Ah, so lucky.' Stella sighed and lit a cigarette.

'That was good.' Christos kicked his chair back and rubbed his flat stomach.

'You want more?' Stella was ready to stand again, serve them all over again.

'I am so full,' Christos said and then he looked up towards the *kafenio*.

'Go, Christo.' Rallou said. 'You don't ever see him, so take the chance. I am tired. I will have an early night.'

'Are you sure? No, I cannot ... You wouldn't mind?' He dithered.

'Oh, go, will you? A goat is not always welcome in a sheep pen!' It was Stella who spoke, a tickle of laughter in her voice – light, fun. 'Go!' And so he went, smiling. As soon as he was on the first step up to Theo's *kafenio*, Stella was on her feet and heading inside, before returning with two glasses and a bottle of quality ouzo.

'Here you go.' Stella poured them each a drink. 'Never had any children myself.' She didn't sound sad when she said that. 'Just as well, really, because he was a – now what is a polite word? Never mind. I have a better husband now. One like yours. How lucky are we? *Yeia mas!*'

They drank, and Rallou thought she must have landed in some sort of dream. Stella was feisty and opinionated and passionate, just like she had been all those years ago. She made jokes at people's expense but never with a hurtful edge, and she spoke on subjects that Rallou did not expect. It turned out that Stella, too, had been to Paris and London, with her new husband. In talking to her, Rallou found a part of herself that had been missing: the brave, feisty side to her nature. She became herself again! Or was it the ouzo?

'Your children grown now?' Stella asked.

'Yes. We have just seen our youngest off to university.' Rallou didn't feel the usual need to brag about all her children had achieved.

'Ah, so you are free again!' Stella clinked glasses with her.

'Yes, free,' she agreed, but it did not feel like freedom, not yet.

'You hesitate.' Stella was certainly forward.

'I do,' Rallou admitted. 'You see, the thing is you get so caught up in being a parent that when you stop it takes a moment to know where you are.'

'Ah, you were a good mama.' Stella pulled a chair out in front of her to put her feet up.

Rallou didn't answer immediately.

'You know, I think I was an overbearing mama.' She said the words to see how they formed on her lips, and it was not a surprise to hear them ring with truth.

'You smoke?' Stella asked, offering a cigarette. Rallou shook her head. 'Why do you think that?'

'I think I focused so hard on my children' – Rallou didn't quite answer the question – 'that I forgot about me and Christos.'

'Ah.' Stella blew smoke out of her nose. 'The pressure to be a good mama.'

'Do you wish you had children?' Rallou asked, mostly to shift the focus elsewhere.

'I wish I had children with the man I have now, but not the one I had before. This man would have made a wonderful baba. But you know, I believe life gives you what you need and that isn't always what you want.' She smiled but it didn't quite reach her eyes.

'Someone else said to me recently … How did they put it …?' Rallou tried to recall the words Toula used. *It seems, what with free tickets and quietly departing ships, that life has plans for you.* But instead she quoted what the ticket man said: 'When life offers you something, it is because it has set a path for you.'

'Ah, how true that is.' Stella picked up the bottle again, but Rallou put her hand over her glass. 'If you try to fight life you will lose. The trick is to see what life offers you and make the best of that. It might not be the exact course you planned, but it might be the best course you are offered, so go for it with everything you've got!' Stella sounded triumphant. Rallou looked over the faded facade of the eatery and wondered how far Stella's philosophies had taken her. Stella nodded and smiled.

'This,' she said, waving her cigarette end in the direction of the eatery, 'is my fun. But' – she leaned forward across the table, and Rallou realised that now they were both a little drunk – 'I have a hotel on the beach because life offered it to me, and I have a candle factory, where we make beeswax candles that we distribute to orthodox churches worldwide. We also make Aromalite.' Stella pronounced the name in a way that made Rallou presume she should recognise it. 'They are scented candles,' Stella explained, 'that people use in some sort of therapy, very popular. So we ship worldwide. The factory is just down the road there, towards Saros. Used to be up on the hill.' She pointed above the *kafenio*. 'But it got too big. Now it is down there.' She pointed the other way, her words just slightly slurred.

Rallou raised her eyebrows at this and reassessed Stella. She didn't seem so small now; instead she had an air of authority.

'Were your parents rich?' The ouzo was making her tongue loose.

'Ha!' The one word said it all. 'I am a gypsy!' The last sentence was delivered in a proud tone.

Rallou looked her over again. Her skin was dark but nothing a good suntan could not achieve. Her hair was also dark and slightly frizzy, unruly and shoulder-length. She looked nothing like the gypsies of Athens with their long, plaited hair and flowing skirts. But then, that was a long time ago.

'Long story,' Stella said, before Rallou had a chance to ask for clarification. 'The short version is, my baba, who brought me up, was Greek, and my mama was a gypsy. But it was my baba ...' She settled back and put out her cigarette in the ashtray, then arranged the condiments neatly before finishing her sentence. 'It was my baba who first taught me to be myself, without labels. Then it was an English girl, the one I run the candle factory with. She's only young, but she has shown me the only barriers are those I make for myself. The young are so smart these days!' She tipped back the last of her drink. Her hand hesitated over the bottle for a moment, but returned to her lap. She leant her head back and looked up at the stars.

Rallou decided she liked Stella. She was honest and open and, as she said, herself.

'You know, I think I have not been myself for much of my life,' Rallou confessed, quietly. 'I have tried to be what people said I should be, pressured me to be.' She yawned without putting her hand over her mouth.

'I think the people who are just themselves are very rare,' Stella slurred as she lit another cigarette.

# Chapter 33

Rallou got back to Toula's house much later than she planned, but when she arrived, tired and a little drunk, having promised Stella that she would see her again the next day and also come back to visit the village very soon, she was not surprised to see that Christos was not back.

She tested the bed, and found it to be very comfortable. Then she decided a cup of chamomile tea under the plumbago in the garden would be the perfect thing before sleep, to dilute the ouzo a little. The evening was pleasantly cool, and Rallou gazed up at the stars. Once she could name many of the constellations, but now she only recognised Orion's belt.

'Hey, you here?' The sound of Christos clattering through the front door interrupted the peace, but Rallou didn't mind.

'Out the back,' she called, thinking that it was just as well she hadn't gone to sleep yet. Judging by the noise he was making just getting into the house, he must have drunk more with Theo than she had with Stella.

'Oh, there you are,' he said, holding on to the wall for balance and leaning towards her to steal a kiss.

'And why are we in the dark?' He flicked a switch and the stars became invisible, the table and the seats all prominent.

'Oh, please turn it off!' she said, and he was happy to comply.

'How about I light the fire?' he suggested, and lunged over to the circular wall with the grill. He took logs from a stack by the wall, and arranged them in the pit, then splashed them liberally with petrol from a can by the back door, presumably there for that very purpose.

'Sure, why not? But best, when we leave, that we clean it.'

'You are the sweetest, most thoughtful …' Christos leaned in for another kiss, lost his balance and missed. 'I'll find some matches.' He righted himself, straightened out his clothes and tried to regain his dignity. She laughed, but quietly, so he wouldn't hear. Looking again to the heavens, she wondered at her life. She now knew two people in this village, Toula and Stella, and it gave her a bigger world to think about than just the island. She would make a point of visiting as often as she could. It could be done in a day, and easily if she stayed overnight. If the confines of the island became too much, or if Harris's remarks began to get under her skin, she would recognise it now, and she could take a well-timed break to see her new friends. The thought brought her joy.

'Ta-dah!' Christos reappeared, triumphant, shaking a box of matches.

He fumbled with the first match and it broke, but the second lit and, carefully, hands around it, the flame lighting up his features, he took it to the wood and gently pushed it beneath the logs. They burst into flames, causing him to jump back.

'I think they have been doused in fuel!' he exclaimed, more to himself than to Rallou. Then he stood with his hands on his hips, admiring what he had achieved.

'Did you have a good time with Theo?'

'Yes, indeed. We must come down here, Rallou. You know, take a weekend, every now and again.'

'I was just saying to Stella, who is lovely by the way, that until now it has all been about the children. But now it is our time. I would like to come down once in a while. The two of us.'

He took a step, head forward, for another kiss. But as he did so, he staggered again, lost his balance again.

Time slowed down and Rallou saw what was about to happen before it happened. She reached to save him but the table was in her way and, as her legs pushed the table, the table pushed Christos, and he staggered, towards the now roaring fire.

Inside her head she was spinning down long-forgotten pathways to memories storied in safe and dark places.

'Pass me more flour,' Harris demanded, and Rallou wrapped both her hands around the bulging packet and cuddled it against her chest to take it from the far end of the table to where Harris was making the bread. Evgenia was watching, wrapping a strand of her hair around her little finger. 'I need water,' Harris snapped, as if little Rallou should have known and already acted upon this.

'Sorry, Evgenia,' Rallou said as she pushed past her little sister to get to the pail of water to fill a jug she had taken from the shelf.

'Can I do it?' Evgenia asked in her high-pitched tones.

'Be quiet, and don't stand so close to the fire,' Harris commanded. Rallou allowed Evgenia's little hands to cover her own and together they put the pitcher of water on the table, out of the way of Harris's kneading. Harris punched and pummelled the dough hard until the sound of the jug smashing on the flagged floor echoed in the room, making them all jump.

'What did you put it there for?' Harris shouted as the water spread dramatically across the floor, staining the pale flags dark, and Evgenia started to wail.

'Be quiet,' Harris barked, her young muscles flexing as she kneaded. She had been especially bossy since her birthday last month, which made her just nine now, to Rallou's six and little Evgenia's three.

'I will get more water,' Rallou offered and she took the pail and left the kitchen, glad to be out in the fresh winter air.

The climb to the well was steep and the bucket, even when empty, was heavy. Rallou could only manage to carry it half full. The well handle was stiff to turn but she took her time and filled the pail, testing its weight every now and again to make sure she did not fill it so much that she could not carry it. She braced her back and countered the weight with an outstretched arm. Some spilt on the return journey. As she neared the house again, Rallou could hear Evgenia wailing. She needed a cuddle. It was not unusual in those days for Harris to upset Evgenia and for Rallou to comfort her little sister. But as Rallou turned her concentration back to the bucket, from the corner of her eye she saw the table move, pushed by Harris, her hip against its edge, a sneer on her face. The other end of the table nudged tiny Evgenia and she lost her balance. After putting the water down as quickly as she could, in haste, but at the same time trying not to spill it, Rallou ran towards the house, to pick Evgenia up, to soothe her crying, check her for hurts and protect her from Harris. But as she reached the back door it opened outward, nearly hitting her in the face.

'Come,' Harris commanded. 'We'll get the eggs.' And she grabbed Rallou's arm and pulled her in the direction of the chicken coop. Neither of them had the apron on to gather the eggs.

'But Evgenia?' Rallou protested.

'Evgenia's fine.' But as Harris said this, a wail screeched from the house, so loud that Rallou turned, ready to run towards home.

'Leave her.' Harris was sharp and she held Rallou fast by her forearm. 'It will do her some good to cry for a bit. Make her realise we are not going to put up with every little tantrum.'

'But–' was as far as Rallou got. The wail continued, a horrible, blood-curdling, shrill sound.

'Evgenia is hurt!' Now she tried to pull away.

'She is being her usual dramatic self. Get the eggs.' Harris shoved her into the chicken enclosure.

'No – she is hurt.' Pushing past Harris, Rallou began to run. From the trees she saw her baba, who was also running. Harris overtook her and pushed her back, so she was the first to enter the house, the first to pull little Evgenia out of the flames. But it was Rallou who threw what was left of the water, drenching both Evgenia and Harris. Their baba crashed through the front door after them, but it was too late to alter what had happened.

The doctor said there was nothing they could do, as he opened windows to let out the smell.

Baba's eyes were red-rimmed. 'There must be something.'

He sat by her day and night. At night, Rallou's poor little sister would groan her pain, and by day she was silent in a way that could mean nothing good. Their baba sat there until little Evgenia's last breath was drawn and then he rose from where he had sat, having neither eaten nor slept, looked hard at Harris and walked out to meet the dawn. They did not see him for two days.

# Chapter 34

Of course, Christos did not need her help, and he leapt back to his feet unscathed. The fire, the initial roar of the fuel having subsided, was only just catching and the flames were easily extinguished by his size and weight.

The episode sobered him up a little though, and he tried to look nonchalant as he brushed his sleeve and shoulder and retrieved the logs that had fallen on the courtyard floor.

'Christo, I think I've just realised something,' Rallou began.

It was as if her legs suddenly could not support her weight, and she groped for the chair behind her. 'Hm?' Christos replied. He was busying himself with the fire now, trying to get it alight again.

'Christo?' said Rallou, and something in her voice must have betrayed the panic that was rising within her, because he stopped what he was doing and stood facing her.

'What is it, *moro mou*?' he asked, but Rallou could only stare up at him, and the words would not come.

In an instant he was beside her, kneeling by her chair, his arm around her.

'What is it?' he asked again, and then, when she did not answer, he held her, and his strong arms around her seemed to give her the permission she needed to feel the emotions and to remember.

They sat like that for what seemed like a long time, and finally Rallou allowed herself to voice the horror that Christos's antics with the fire had dragged from the depths of her memory.

'Harris ...' she began, and slowly, with much effort, she related the whole story to Christos.

He listened without interruption, and without taking his arms from around her.

As she spoke, her heart thumped and her vision blurred. She could feel a pulse in her temple and her tongue stuck to the roof of her mouth, her saliva thick and dry. When she reached the end she added, 'She knew why Evgenia was screaming. Baba, from the pine trees, saw she had left her. We all ran. She did it, Christo. She pushed Evgenia into the fire, and she didn't let me go to her. Harris knew Evgenia was hurt, and she made me stay away.' The dark part of her mind was in the light and it hurt more than she could ever have believed. Colours flashed in front of her eyes and there was a high-pitched whistle in her ears. The world seemed to be rocking and rotating. Christos's arms around her made no impact, the pain was too intense, too all-consuming. The memory finally made sense of her overprotective attitude to her own children. And was Harris trying to relieve her guilt, to compensate, with her constant but insincere kindnesses? Rallou's sobs came in spasms, each taking more of her breath than the last until she thought she would suffocate, and her fingers spread on the tabletop and she leaned forward.

'Breathe, my sweet, breathe.' Christos's voice penetrated her pain, made contact with the part of herself that still functioned, and she breathed.

'She killed her, Christo,' Rallou snivelled like a child, a child of five.

'Shh, my love, shh.' He rocked her.

'Baba knows.'

'It's okay, Rallou, you are safe. It's not happening now.'

'Harris knows.'

Christos kissed the top of her head, her forehead, her nose, gave her a peck on her mouth and then hugged her into himself again.

They sat like that for so long. Tears kept coming and then going, leaving her blank and spent. Then the tears came again and Christos hugged her even tighter until they subsided. She cried all the way through the dogs' evening chorus, the sounds of the shutters around the village being closed, the lights in neighbouring houses going dark, the dogs quieting down and then, finally, the village falling asleep.

A while after that, Christos asked, 'Are you all right?' and she pulled out of the safe harbour of his arms and nodded her head. They continued to sit in the quiet of the night. At one point the outline of a cat walked slowly across the top of the back wall.

'How can she live with herself?' She finally voiced the most pressing question.

She felt Christos's shoulders twitch, ready to shrug, but then they became still and she knew he was contemplating his answer.

'It explains why she behaves towards you the way she does.'

'How do you mean?' There was no haste in their talk. Somewhere in the village, outside the confinement of Toula's garden walls, an owl hooted.

'The way she puts you down – you know, sounding so concerned, when actually she is finding fault with you.'

Rallou blinked several times. She had thought the way Harris treated her was invisible to anyone but herself – maybe even that it was in her head.

'But ...' she began. Somewhere over the garden wall the owl hooted again.

'All that pressure she put on you over the children. It makes sense now. Compensating, pushing the blame somewhere else.' His arm around her shifted, tightened, and he turned his head and kissed her hair, just above her ear.

'It pushed us apart, you know.' He did not say it as an accusation or unkindly. 'When Natasa was born, I was over the moon. You remember teaching me how to change her nappy?' They chuckled quietly at the joint memory. 'We were still close then.

But then the second was born and Harris moved in and things changed. She was full of opinions of how you should do this or that for the little brood and you responded.'

She shifted uncomfortably on her cushion.

'As you would, Rallou,' he reassured her. 'She was your mama as well as your sister. You trusted her. But it squeezed me out, you wouldn't let me help.'

'I am so sorry,' she said, and the tears came silently this time.

'Don't be sorry, my little Rallou. You did what you thought was best.' He kissed her ear again.

'And then you got completely squeezed out when they started school and needed help with their homework. I was not going to let them learn only cooking and cleaning and become like Harris!' There was a harshness to her voice, and her insight over this shocked her.

'Quite right,' Christos confirmed, but there was sadness in his voice. 'You know, when I got to Natasa's bedside first in Corfu she was amazed. "Where's Mama?" she asked. I said you were following, but it was very nice being there, just me and her. After the little one was born, we talked for ages, and there was nothing missing from our relationship, Rallou, nothing.' He sounded all wistful.

'But you felt so squeezed out that you spent all your time in the hills.'

'I couldn't stand it, Rallou. The way Harris talked to you, and your love of someone so unkind.'

'Why didn't you say something?'

'What could I say? Such things must be said gently, and I did try... But she was your sister and your mama. If I had said too much it would have been me you would have turned against.'

This time it was she who hugged him tighter.

'How are you doing?' he asked, turning to look at her.

'I don't know how she can live with herself.'

The owl hoots again, a faraway dog barks twice and then all is quiet.

# Chapter 35

Rallou has just about reached her baba's house when he comes striding around the side of the building, calling out a cheery, 'Good morning!'

'Oh,' says Rallou, 'I thought you weren't up.'

'Course I'm up. I was just about to take the goats out.'

'Great.' The goats are back up the way she has come, and they walk up together, following the track round to the right, where the enclosure is tucked behind a rocky outcrop. He kicks the stone that holds the chicken-wire gate closed and the goats jostle for freedom, noisy in their excitement, jumping over one another, the bells around their neck clanging and clonking their dull resonance, a ballad Rallou knows so well. They follow the herd in silence towards the southern side of the island, along a path that has been worn smooth by the goats' hooves and her baba's feet, and the boys' when they still lived up there. The path leads only to a scrubby plateau at the island's summit.

'So, how are the olives this year?' Baba asks, his hand raised to his mouth, trying to stifle a chuckle.

'You have a lot to answer for!' Rallou retorts, pretending to be cross.

'I just can't figure out how you didn't know! You must have worked it out, suspected, something.' He no longer seems to shuffle these days. His shoulders are no longer hunched over as they were before the earthquake and his influx of neighbours.

'Don't tease!' she chides, but jokingly, as she looks at her feet, picks her way forward, Baba's worn trouser bottoms just a step in front. If she can avoid it she will not admit that she had thought Christos was just too lazy to collect the olives. On reflection, this notion had been planted by Harris anyway. A twinge of sadness passes through her.

'Didn't you miss the income?' he asks, but there is no teasing now, just concern.

'It was not a good couple of years, Baba. The children no longer children, and I was working all the hours I could for the Americans ... Christos and I had grown apart a bit. But you, Baba.' Her tone lightens and she laughs. 'You knew, and said nothing! For three years!'

'Well, no, that is not entirely true. I knew he would come up hunting and stay at his family home. I did say he could stay here, because I knew what a state time had left his place in. But he refused. So for the first year I thought nothing of it. Then when I began to hear noises I went over to investigate. He hid, you know.'

'What?'

'Yup. The first time I went to investigate, he hid when he saw me. But I saw him first so I called him out.' His laugh is relaxed. They have reached the grazing ground and he sits on a flat stone that he put there for the purpose more years ago than either of them can remember. Rallou leans against the slanting boulder, one arm across her waist and the other over her eyes for shade as she looks south to see if she can see Crete.

'But it was obvious what was going on. There were window frames in various states of repair and a pile of roof tiles outside stacked up ready to be used.'

'Yanni must have known too.'

'Of course he knew! He was delivering what was needed. Glass for the windows, a new sink for the kitchen, piping for the water. How is the water, though, in the summer – do you have it year round?'

'The well dries up in the summer,' says Rallou, 'but he has built a *sterna* now to hold the rainwater we collect from the roof. If we're careful it lasts. But I am amazed Yanni never said a word.' The goats are slowly eating their way towards them. Her baba picks up a handful of dust and throws it at the feet of the lead goat, which jolts its head up, displaying its curling horns, and runs to a safe distance. The others follow.

'Yanni is a man of few words, unless you get him on a subject that interests him. I'm glad he has found someone to share his world with though. It's not good for a man to spend years alone, which is what would have happened when his parents passed on.' There is just the slightest note of regret in his voice.

'Sophia is lovely, perfect for him. I didn't believe it when they told me he had come back from the mainland with a wife. Yanni! Choose a mainland wife and bring her home! It seemed so unlikely. But to find his childhood sweetheart and bring her back to her roots, now that fits.' She thinks for a moment and then, returning to the first subject, adds, 'But I still think he should have told me what was going on up here.'

'I can imagine your relief, one minute thinking you have no home and the next Christos telling you how he had fixed up this place.' He nods towards her house.

'Yes, that would have been a relief. But do you know what, he didn't tell me!'

'How do you mean?' He is watching a lizard that has paused in the dust by his feet. He stays very still so as not to frighten it. Its tongue darts out and then, with quick, jerky steps, it runs right over the toes of his boot. Once it is gone, he stretches out his legs.

'We came back and went to our old home, sifted through the rubble, and then came here. I thought we were coming to stay with you but he walked straight past the track and kept going to the village. I can tell you, Baba, I'm so glad I did not speak my feelings at that point.'

She was furious. It was one thing to be all close and act like they did when they first fell in love all over again, but it was quite another to think that she could go back to living rough in his derelict hovel like a teenager. She could not stand the mess and the dust again. Their house in town might have been in need of some repair, but by the time it fell down at least they had reached the point where no walls needed plastering, no floors needed digging smooth to lay tiles.

But just she was ready to speak, when she knew without a doubt that they were heading for the old house, he turned to her.

'You remember lighting the candle in that church on Corfu and making your wish?' he said, and she looked at him sceptically and then up at the house. From the outside there was something different about it, but she couldn't quite put her finger on it. 'Well ...' he continued, pushing open the gate, and she saw the newly painted window frames, with glass in every space! On the roof was a solar panel for hot water, and the yard was brushed clean. He opened the door and she squinted in the dark. 'Wait,' he said, and ran around the side of the house, out of sight, and in a minute or two she heard a rattling hum that signified a generator starting up, and the shadows inside the house burst into light.

'Oh!' She had actually squealed. The bulb in the hall was bare, but it was bright! The kitchen was all new, with new cupboards, new sink, and new drainer. It all had the touch of Christos. The corners were shaped by his hand, the tops of the cupboard doors were arched, the supports for the shelves were curved. It was all carefully and beautifully hand built. She ran from the kitchen to the small bedroom that used to be his. This was now a bathroom, and in what had been his parents' bedroom was a new bed. 'How?' was her first word, and she turned to Christos with love so strong she hardly knew what to do with it.

'Well, you know the olives you thought I hadn't picked, and the income we never made, and the days I would spend away …'

# Chapter 36

'Vasillis knew.' Her baba is chuckling. The goats are closing in on them again, and this time Rallou picks up the smallest pebble she can find and throws it at the hooves of the nearest goat, which gambol away, taking most of the others with it, their bells clonking and white tails bobbing. The sun is growing hotter, and above the scrub the air shimmers.

'And he didn't say either,' she says.

'I think when Christos started he thought it would take a much shorter time than it did. I think we all did. But the months turned to years, as they do, and at what point should we have betrayed his secret, spoilt his surprise?'

'Well, I think Vasillis should have, the night I stayed at his house after the earthquake when I thought I had no home to go to!'

'Do you? Do you really?' her baba asks, and she snorts a laugh at herself and shakes her head.

They watch the goats, and the blue of the sea, and the shadows that track the day across the barren landscape, and then they wander back down the slope; the animals follow them, stopping to eat a little more before running again, frightened to be left behind, until every last one is back in the enclosure.

'Baba, can we talk about Harris?'

He does not speak. This is the silence she has known from him for so many years, but she waits.

'What would we say?' He sighs, suddenly sounding his age. 'I mean, really, Rallou, what would we say?'

He has a point. She knows, he knows, Harris knows and, judging by the way Stephanos treats Harris, he knows too.

'We can change nothing, and Harris has suffered all her life, and will suffer for the rest of her life. It's too much punishment for a child who was out of her depth.' He speaks quietly, gently, and Rallou can hear the blame he heaps on himself. There are no more words and Rallou knows they will not mention the subject again.

'You want a coffee?' he asks, heading for the house.

'Sure, do you want me to get water?'

'No need.' He points to a line of freshly dug earth. 'Christos put some pipes in, from the well up there. Clever fellow, that husband of yours. Clever enough to catch you, at least,' he adds, and dodges into the kitchen. It's partly why she loves him. His generation was one that didn't display or talk about their feelings but, even though it goes against his instincts, he still lets her know. It makes her feel so valued.

With the coffee on the table between them, they sit and stare out across the sea. Other islands, in the distance, appear to float on a line of hazy white. Rallou traces the road on the mainland opposite, which zigzags up over the purple hills, and tries to judge whether it is the route to the village, which is now partly her village, and the thought broadens her horizons, gives her room to breathe.

'You know he didn't keep back the olive money to do up the house, don't you, Baba?' she says casually.

'If it wasn't for the house, what was it for, then?'

'Another surprise. He was just waiting till the house was finished so he could tell me at the same time. He spent maybe a year's worth of olive money on the house, out of the three he saved. We still have the rest.'

Her baba laughs. 'It doesn't surprise me. He's a cunning old fox, that one. So go on then – what is the second surprise?'

'It's for us to travel.'

'You are going to America again?' He stops looking at the view to face Rallou, the skin around his eyes all puckered and wrinkled with his smile.

'Well, the olive money allowed us to extend that stay, but that was mostly the kindness of Lori and Ted.'

'How are they, by the way?'

'Very well. You know they made up a room for me in the house in town? I couldn't have continued to work for them from up here without it.'

'It is a bit far to come and go in a day, but not as hard as it once was.' He looks down towards the chicken shed; next to it is a new hut, made of old doors from the village, with a tarpaper roof. Rallou identifies it as more of Christos's handiwork. In front of the hut is a fenced enclosure, much larger than the space that the chickens have to roam around in. A barrel, cut lengthways and supported by stones to stop it from rolling, has become a trough for water, and another line of freshly dug earth tells the tale of how it is filled.

From behind the hut a sound begins to emanate. It is a drawn-out cry, the exhalation of big lungs. The inward suck is no more than a squeak, the second, outward cry is louder, surer, and then the inward breath gains resonance as Dolly ee-aws to remind them she has not been fed.

'Apparently Yanni's mama is hassling him to buy yet another donkey,' Rallou says. 'Sophia told me.'

'Mercedes and Suzi are not enough?'

She shrugs.

'Such a kind man.' Her baba breathed out the words, to himself, not really spoken for her to hear. 'Such a kind woman.' He pats her hand. 'He knows she would not have survived without your care.'

It was a mutual decision between the three of them. After Dolly was seen at the boatyard she disappeared again and then turned up at Korifi. Baba fed and watered her and tethered her ready for Yanni's next visit. As it turned out, Yanni heard the news of Dolly's survival as soon as he returned to the island, and came straight up to find her, arriving out of breath, and kissed and stroked the animal. Her baba had ushered Rallou inside, to give the man a little privacy. After a while they had gone back out to find Yanni inspecting her wounds.

'She can't work for a while. Not like this,' he declared.

'What does she need?' Rallou asked, stroking the animal's neck. She felt she knew Dolly so well now. It was Dolly who had begun her awakening, showing her how she could get lost in the care of another being, how she had for years lost herself in the care of her children, being overly protective in a bid to ensure that no harm could possibly come to them. That had been easier than facing the memories she had suppressed for so long.

'I think she just needs rest and then a light work schedule for a while.'

And so it was decided that Dolly would stay up at Korifi. 'She will be company for me,' Rallou's baba said, and Yanni said that he would collect her when her wounds were healed sufficiently for her to make the journey along the ridge to his home.

Some months have passed since then, and Dolly accompanies Rallou into town now, which will build her muscles.

It has made her and Christos realise that they will need a donkey of their own, but until that time they have Dolly.

'Shall I feed her?' Rallou says.

'Just let her out, she'll come up here. I have her food just there.' He points to a second barrel next to the chicken feed. 'Where's Christos today? Does he have work in town?'

'Ah, no – well yes, he has popped down to see Vasillis. They will know today how much they will get for the olive oil.'

'Big day then?'

'Depends on what the prices have been like. Oh, he must have heard us – look, there he is.' Christos's figure appears far down on the track past the chicken coop, Arapitsa trotting by his side. 'I'll see you later, Baba. Come for food tonight?'

Her baba doesn't answer, just waves an acknowledging hand, and stands to greet Dolly who is approaching, neck bent, head down, ready to receive a pat and a scratch. As Rallou passes she tenderly pats Dolly's rump, but her eyes are on Christos. She meets him where her baba's track splits off the main dusty road.

'Hi,' she says, her stomach, even after all these years, turning in on itself as she studies his face. The perfect face.

'Hi, yourself.'

'So?' she asks.

'So what?' he teases.

'Oh, come on, is it a good year or a bad year?'

'Well.' He stretches the word out. 'Enough to go to see Natasa in Bari.'

'Oh.' The disappointment is evident in her voice.

'Then we can visit our son in England, or our other daughter in Australia.'

'Oh! It has been a fairly big year then?'

'Or both! Or Peru, or India, but …' He pretends to be serious now, as if to give her a warning. 'We cannot quite afford Hawaii.' He laughs

'Both! Are you serious?' But his grin tells her he is both serious and rather smug.

'So, where is it to be, my princess? Where shall we take each other?' His long arm dangles over her shoulders, pulling her in, kissing the top of her head.

They turn to pass along the ridge to take the back way to their house and she looks to the sea, first on one side of her island and then on the other, and then right to the end of the finger of land that stretches out in front of them, to the ocean that reaches all the way to Libya and Tunisia, and beyond. All there, the whole world, just waiting.

She takes his arm. He stops to turn her towards him and he kisses her.

'Or we could just go somewhere very close, but very romantic,' she suggests. He kisses her again. 'Santorini, or Monemvasia, perhaps.'

He kisses her again before saying, 'We will go. Where do you fancy the most?'

Good reviews are important to a novel's success and will help others find *Being Enough*. If you enjoyed it, please be kind and leave a review wherever you purchased the book.

I'm always delighted to receive email from readers, and I welcome new friends on Facebook.

Facebook:
> https://www.facebook.com/authorsaraalexi

Email: saraalexi@me.com


Happy reading,

*Sara Alexi*

# Also by Sara Alexi

The Illegal Gardener
Black Butterflies
The Explosive Nature of Friendship
The Gypsy's Dream
The Art of Becoming Homeless
In the Shade of the Monkey Puzzle Tree
A Handful of Pebbles
The Unquiet Mind
Watching the Wind Blow
The Reluctant Baker
The English Lesson
The Priest's Well
A Song Amongst the Orange Trees
The Stolen Book
The Rush Cutter's Legacy
Saving Septic Cyril : The Illegal Gardener Part II

PUBLISHED BY:

Oneiro Press

Being Enough
Book Seventeen of the Greek Village Collection

Copyright © 2016 by Sara Alexi

This is a work of fiction. All of the characters, organisations, and events portrayed in this novel are either products of the author's imagination or are used fictitiously.

Printed in Great Britain
by Amazon